DETROIT PUBLIC LIBRARY

P9-CCV-561

You Get What You Pray For:

Always Divas Series Book Three

CHASE BRANCH LIBRARY
17731 W. SEVEN MILE RD.
DETROIT, MI 48235
578-8002

FEB --- 2015

You Get What You Pray For:

Always Divas Series Book Three

E.N. Joy

www.urbanchristianonline.com

Urban Books, LLC
97 N18th Street
Wyandanch, NY 11798

You Get What You Pray For: Always Divas Series Book
Three Copyright © 2015 E.N. Joy

All rights reserved. No part of this book may be
reproduced in any form or by any means without prior
consent of the Publisher, excepting brief quotes used
in reviews.

ISBN 13: 978-1-60162-697-4
ISBN 10: 1-60162-697-5

First Trade Paperback Printing February 2015
Printed in the United States of America

10 9 8 7 6 5 4 3 2 1

*This is a work of fiction. Any references or similarities
to actual events, real people, living or dead, or to real
locales are intended to give the novel a sense of reality.
Any similarity in other names, characters, places, and
incidents is entirely coincidental.*

Distributed by Kensington Corp.
Submit Wholesale Orders to:
Kensington Publishing Corp.
C/O Penguin Group (USA) Inc.
Attention: Order Processing
405 Murray Hill Parkway
East Rutherford, NJ 07073-2316
Phone: 1-800-526-0275
Fax: 1-800-227-9604

You Get What You Pray For:

Always Divas Series Book Three

By

E.N. Joy

OTHER BOOKS BY E.N. JOY:

Me, Myself and Him
She Who Finds a Husband
Been There, Prayed That
Love, Honor or Stray
Trying to Stay Saved
I Can Do Better All By Myself
And You Call Yourself a Christian
The Perfect Christian
The Sunday Only Christian
Ordained by the Streets
"A Woman's Revenge" (Anthology: *Best Served Cold*)
I Ain't Me No More
More Than I Can Bear
Behind Every Good Woman (eBook only)
First Lady Conference Part I: She's No Angel (eBook series)
Flower in My Hair
Even Sinners Have Souls (Edited by E.N. Joy)
Even Sinners Have Souls Too (Edited by E.N. Joy)
Even Sinners Still Have Souls (Edited by E.N. Joy)
The Secret Olivia Told Me (N. Joy)
Operation Get Rid of Mom's New Boyfriend (N. Joy)
Sabella and the Castle Belonging to the Troll (N. Joy)

Dedication

Since this particular story is about a mother and her relationship with her oldest child, how could I not dedicate this book to my oldest child? I love you, Ran-Ran.

Acknowledgments

I wish to express my deepest thanks to my husband, Nicholas Ross. Just as Lorain, the main character in this story, has a good man named Nicholas, to God be the glory, I do too!

Thank God for Facebook! I get to chat with my sisters all over the world at the same time. You guys teach me, minister to me, and enlighten me on so many situations and subject matters. We had one conversation that was so deep that I actually copied and pasted it from my Facebook status post into this manuscript. And thank you all for agreeing to allow me to use your real names. Your free copy of this book is in the mail!

Chapter 1

"I wouldn't change this million-dollar lifestyle for two million," Lorain said as she stood in the middle of her great room, admiring the soft yellow vaulted ceiling and the custom-designed crystal chandelier. Her home in Malvonia, Ohio was more than she'd ever imagined herself living in.

Sitting on the sand-colored couch with yellow accent pillows always made Lorain feel as though she were sitting on one of the beaches of Saint Martin. Although she, her husband, and their twin daughters had lived in their built-from-the-ground-up house for almost a year, every day that she woke up in her home was still like a dream come true. For the first couple of weeks after moving in, she would wake up, run downstairs, go stand in the middle of the great room, and not only admire it but also spin around in awe, kind of like Belle when the Beast introduced her to the library in his castle.

She had been introduced to something, all right—the good life. And just thinking about how good her life was at that very moment, she felt the urge rise up inside of her to take a good ole spin. So there she went, doing her fairy-tale, *Gone with the Wind*, "I'm so fabulous, and so is life" spin. As her spinning came to a slow, winding halt, she asked herself, *How does a wretch like me go from the hood life to the good life?*

Dressed in a silky-satin white blouse with short sleeves, puffy shoulders, and ruffles down the front, a red pencil skirt, and crystal-studded, strappy four-inch heels—all by designers whose names she couldn't pronounce without practicing several times out loud—Lorain felt like a queen. And no one could tell her she didn't reside in a palace. The six-thousand-square-foot home, which featured five bedrooms, four and a half baths, a finished basement with a grand wine cellar, a stainless-steel gourmet kitchen, an exquisite dining room, and a to-die-for great room, was everything she had prayed for . . . and then some. The lower-level mini theater, which could seat a little over a half dozen people, and the modest indoor pool were the "then some." The gray-, black-, and white-marble Jacuzzi in her master suite, which could fit four adults, was heaven. The custom-made walk-in closet was the size of her bedroom when she was a little girl. As a matter of fact, Lorain had subconsciously had it painted the same teal green color of her childhood sleeping quarters.

Growing up, Lorain had never been poor. The house she was raised in, though, was on the imaginary line dividing the good side of town and the bad side. When her father left the home when she was ten years old, he stayed current on child support and Lorain's mother kept a full-time job, so Lorain was never forced to do without. So even though she might not have grown up having and getting everything she wanted, she'd always had enough. Now she had more than enough. And there were often times when she felt she didn't deserve it, but God had blessed her with it all, so obviously, He felt she did deserve it. And who was she to argue with God?

It seemed like yesterday that Lorain was thirteen years old, hiding a pregnancy, then giving birth to a baby on the nasty, hard cement bathroom floor of her middle school and, with squirming infant in arms, taking the longest trek ever to the Dumpster to dispose of the new life. When she walked away from that Dumpster, she never looked back, even though the horrible stench followed behind her. Still, Lorain kept moving on in life, heading down a path of destruction. Every act she committed from that point on had been suicidal, only she never died. To God be the glory!

God had shown her mercy by not punishing her with a deadly sexually transmitted disease after years of jumping from one man's bed to the next. Purposely having unprotected sex with men whose last names she didn't even know was suicidal. Sleeping with a married man in the bed he and his wife shared, knowing the wife could come home at any minute and blow both their brains out, was suicidal. That was all her younger years had consisted of, until an HIV scare had her life flashing before her eyes. It was then that she realized that she really did want life over death.

While she waited for the results of the HIV test, she promised God that if He spared her life, she'd give it to Him. She had actually kept that promise. After she received the negative results of her HIV test, there were no more one-night stands or sex with other women's men. Now on the other side of forty, Lorain didn't have to settle for sloppy seconds. She was finally somebody's wife herself, and a doctor's wife, to boot.

"Hot dang! Won't God do it?" she said aloud. She clapped her hands and got a little Holy Ghost dance on in her stilettos. Her thousand-dollar pair of shoes did a two-step on the carpet, which was a shade darker than the couch. From the outside, it might have looked as though Lorain was giving God some praise. On the inside, though, she was plain old dancing for joy, glad that the hand she'd been dealt had turned out to be a full house. She had it going on!

After getting her shout on, Lorain, with her size twelve, voluptuous figure, stood with her legs spread and her hands on her hips. She looked so much like a model, trendy and chic. She'd always had a short, edgy haircut that complemented her long, thin face. Her golden-honey hair enhanced her mocha-brown skin. Her nails, decorated by the personal manicurist who came to her home once a week, tapped her size ten waistline. . . . Well, at least the Spanx made it look like she had a size ten waist. The corners of her mouth were turned upward in an expression of pride. Surprisingly, she didn't get a chill from the air she had about herself.

She admired her custom-made designer furniture, which consisted of the sand-colored couch, a light yellow love seat, two oversized chairs, one chair the color of the couch and the other the color of the love seat, handmade solid oak tables, and antique lamps dripping with crystals that matched the chandelier. The gleaming, thirty-five-hundred-dollar vase that was the centerpiece of the awkwardly, yet uniquely shaped coffee table seemed to wink at her. Her eyes couldn't help but roll over the sunset-yellow and orange Italian rug that the designer in Italy had personally shipped her. One of the doctors' wives had passed the designer's information on to her after Lorain had made such a fuss over the rug she'd seen in the parlor at a doctors' wives' meeting a few months ago. That thought reminded Lorain that the clock was ticking. This month's meeting was at her house. The wives would be arriving shortly, and she hadn't done a final check-in with the staff.

Although it was no easy feat to host the doctors' wives monthly meeting, Lorain nonetheless experienced an adrenaline rush whenever it was her turn. The women always spent months preparing to host the meeting, as it involved coming up with unique, outrageous, and over-the-top ideas to show off their husband's money and resources. The pressure was really on if a holiday fell in the hosting month, which was the case for Lorain, as it just so happened to be February. So of course, she had to incorporate the whole Valentine's Day love theme into the meeting. Her husband, Nicholas, whom everyone called Nick, had urged her to make her theme Black History Month instead. She wasn't convinced that this would go over well with the three non–African American wives. She didn't want there to be confusion or negative chatter because some of the wives lacked an understanding of her culture.

"That's all the more reason to highlight it," Nicholas had told her. "School them on the history of our culture so that they will have a better understanding."

"Maybe next year, when I have more time to prepare," Lorain had replied. "Besides, I've already made purchases for the Valentine's theme."

"So I noticed when I was paying bills and balancing the checkbook," he'd told her in a tone that let her know she might have gone overboard with her spending. His single raised eyebrow only confirmed his dismay.

Lorain's meeting had been only three months out at the time Nicholas suggested the Black History Month theme, and by then she'd already invested a couple grand in the affair.

"Well, the next time it's your turn to host, you can do it," Nicholas had told her. "Every month of the year should be Black History Month, anyway."

Lorain would consider it, but for now she had to focus on this month's meeting. And as she did a final walk-through of the areas of her home where the women would be entertained, she was quite pleased to have stuck to her decision about the Valentine's theme. The house had been transformed into a love shack. It looked as if Cupid himself had shot an arrow into her home, releasing red dye and hearts everywhere, but the decorating was tasteful and on point. She was sure her meeting would be the talk of the women for at least a week.

It would definitely stay on their minds until the March meeting, for which St. Paddy's Day would more than likely be the theme. Irish or not, Lorain was certain the host would go with the whole four-leaf clover, beer, and leprechaun theme. She only hoped that whoever was assigned March this year would eliminate the green eggs and ham. That had been done two times too many. It had lost its novelty, and besides, all the wives had agreed that green eggs and ham should be reserved for Dr. Seuss's birthday month.

Of course, the whole heart and love theme of Valentine's Day had been done a million times over, but this time around, Lorain had done something none of the other women had thought to do thus far. The water in the round fountain, made of various stones, that sat in the middle of the foyer had been dyed red and rose petals were floating on it. The fountain's installation had been completed just last week, and in the nick of time. The women almost expected to be shown something new each time they visited one another's home. Lorain was certain the fountain would be a showstopper. The sound of the water in the fountain pouring down the mini mountain of rocks was so serene. If you closed your eyes, the smell of the fresh water would have you thinking you were standing in a Costa Rican rain forest.

But if the fountain didn't do the trick, Lorain knew what would. Each wife who entered her home would have a rose boutonniere pinned on her by a hunk of chocolate. Not the edible kind that was an integral part of Valentine's Day, but a shirtless hunk of a chocolate man who, besides the bow tie, wore only the bottom portion of his tux, cummerbund included.

She'd rented a red carpet, and adorned with red rose petals, it led from the front door to the dining room, where, of course, a triple punch fountain rained a specially prepared red beverage. The origami pink, white, and red hearts hanging from the dining room ceiling were almost like little butterflies flying about the room. The cupcake display on the side table that was created by the one and only Chocolates and Stilettos was to die for. The cupcakes had icing that was the same color as the floating hearts, and there were way more than the six women could possibly devour, even if half of them weren't on diets or didn't have a Lap-Band. But at least three dozen cupcakes had been needed to form the huge heart-shaped cupcake tower Lorain had envisioned.

The chefs had done a wonderful job overall with the food coloring, making the red and pink delicacies look delicious. They'd even given the Scotch eggs a little shot from Cupid. The whites of the eggs were now pink, and those pink egg whites looked so dainty in between the yellow yolks and the browned crumbled sausage. Lorain had wanted the yolks dyed too, but the head chef, Omar, had wasted at least two dozen eggs in an attempt to do so. "I think this would go over better with deviled eggs, ma'am," he had told her. Lorain had agreed with a nod, even though her inner voice had pleaded with Omar to give it one more try with the Scotch eggs. If he could have pulled that off, Lorain knew the women would have been highly impressed. Besides, deviled eggs were reserved for the summer meetings, so Lorain didn't dare opt for that.

"Madame, I believe your guests are starting to arrive," announced the hired hunk as he entered the dining room, his bare feet padding on the light blue carpeted floor. The carpet was about two shades darker than the ocean-blue painted walls. He was carrying with one hand the sterling silver tray that held the boutonnieres.

"Oh, my. I didn't even hear the doorbell, and I haven't done my final check with the staff." Lorain was in a fix. Did she run to the kitchen and let the incredible hunk answer the door, and thus miss the expression on the ladies' faces as they were greeted? Or did she go make sure everything was perfect, since she was paying an obscene amount of money for it to be?

The doorbell rang again.

"We don't want to keep them waiting," the chocolate hunk said.

Lorain looked him up and down. *Gosh, he is so much better than a chocolate heart or that stupid, big, fake walking chocolate bunny that weirded everybody out at last April's meeting.* Knowing the women would lose their minds over this man, Lorain wouldn't miss their reactions for the world.

"You're right. No, we don't want to keep them waiting. Come, come." Lorain whisked past him and made her way to the door. He was right on her heels. She looked through the glass blocks around the double doors and could make out at least three figures. Excitedly, she smoothed out her clothing and then stood to the side. "Okay, let them in," she ordered the hunk.

He nodded, then walked over to the door, holding the tray above his shoulder. He held the tray with his one hand while he opened the door with the other.

Fine and adept at multitasking, Lorain thought to herself.

One of the women started fussing as she dashed through the door after ringing the doorbell twice before being let in. "It's February, Lorain. It's cold out there."

Standing off to the side after having opened the door for the women to enter, the hunk greeted the guests. "Good afternoon, ladies."

All eyes immediately landed on him. Lorain hadn't thought about the fact that he would steal the fountain's glory.

"But it's hot in here!" the fussed woman exclaimed.

And just like that, the complaints were nipped in the bud by the chocolate stud.

"Welcome to the Wright residence." He lifted a boutonniere. "May I put it on you?" he asked one of the women in a sexy tone, with raised eyebrows.

"Child, like Tamar Braxton's song says, 'put it *all* on me!'" Carrie shouted.

Leave it to Carrie, the newlywed, married and inducted into the doctors' wives' clique only two months ago, to be all loud and ghetto. Thing was, no one was ever embarrassed by her brash antics and unfiltered tongue. Most of the time the women found her quite amusing and entertaining.

"You can say that again for me," Mary said, cutting in front of Carrie to have her boutonniere pinned on her first.

Mary was Asian. Her birth name was Meizhen, which meant "beautiful pearl," but she had changed her name ten years ago, when she became a U.S. citizen. She'd informed the wives that changing their names once they became U.S. citizens was something many Asian women did. She said it made them seem more Americanized and enabled them to fit into American culture and society better. She'd also told them that the name Mary looked better on her résumé and job applications. Her birth name was a dead giveaway that she was foreign born, and therefore, it could potentially hinder her from getting a job due to someone's personal hang-ups or ignorance.

Mary, the daughter of two doctors, had been educated at Ivy League schools, and so she looked good enough on paper to get a first interview. By the time she wowed the interviewer with her genuine brilliance and charm, it didn't matter if she was an alien from Mars. The girl was bad in every sense of the word. She was brains and beauty wrapped up in sushi, an egg roll, spring roll, or whatever. Her husband, Dr. Gerald Haroll, thought so as well.

As luck would have it, Gerald was the doctor who had interviewed Mary for her internship during medical school. She'd graduated from med school with honors, but instead of following in both her parents' footsteps, she'd followed in only her mother's . . . at least in one of her footsteps, anyway. Mary became the wife of a doctor. And not just of any doctor. Dr. Gerald Haroll was one of the best pediatricians in the state of Ohio. Lorain even took her girls to him.

"Some American men can be intimidated by a woman who is equally as smart and as wealthy as they are," Mary had said to the women. "So imagine how my dear husband would feel if he realized I am much smarter than he'll ever be." She placed her index finger on her lips as the women laughed. "And I was wealthier when I was only eighteen than he is now," she had confessed. "But he needn't know about the trust fund my grand-parents and parents set up for me, which I never touch." She'd winked. "We live off of his money, and his money alone."

"Mary, you sneaky little devil, you," Lorain had said, tsk-tsking and shaking her head.

"Hmm, you American women taught me well. But the heck with just a secret bank account on the side. I've got a whole trust fund."

Of course, at the time Lorain had had no concept of
the notion of trying to provide for every contingency,
but eventually, she'd kick herself for not learning a thing
or two from Mary about having a plan B. But perhaps
if Lorain had stuck with God's plan, she wouldn't have
ever found herself in the position of needing a plan B
in the first place.

Chapter 2

"Next time you'll have to use my guy," Tabby said, sitting down at the dining room table holding the Scotch egg in her hand and observing it. "Clifton could have done something with this yolk besides leaving it yellow." She bit the egg. "Umm, but it is tasty." She smiled.

Lorain shot Tabby a fake smile, all the while really wanting to show her the saliva dripping from her fangs. That dang Tabby. If Lorain wasn't such a lady, she'd snatch those thousand-dollar extensions off Tabby's head, soak them in the fountain, and send her out of her house coordinated with the whole Valentine's theme. But that wasn't who Lorain was anymore, thank God. And thank God that He'd forgiven her for the times in her past when she had gotten out of line and resorted to getting physical. He'd even forgiven Lorain for the ultimate no-no of putting her hands on her own mother.

At one point, having such an estranged and nasty relationship with her mother, Lorain had resorted to laying her hands on her, and not in the spiritual sense, either. It wasn't until after being tried time and time again by her mother that Lorain lost control of herself. It was still no excuse for Lorain to black out like that. But when her mother accused her of perhaps having a sexual relationship with her own biological father, Lorain snapped. So hanging Tabby's snooty, stuck-up tail out to dry wouldn't have been a problem for Lorain. Sure, God would forgive her, as He had forgiven her for the incident with her mother and had even restored their relationship. But how many days of her life had been shortened by dishonoring her mother? Only God knew. And Lorain wasn't about to make her days—her days of freedom, at least—any shorter by going at Tabby.

Besides, that was the old Lorain: the angry, bitter Lorain, who deep down inside had blamed her mother for not protecting her from her molester, who had impregnated her at thirteen. It was an act that Lorain had never told her mother about as a young girl. Years later she'd only wished she had, since, adding salt to the wound, her mother brought the molester into her home, not knowing what he'd done to Lorain all those years ago. On top of that, Lorain's mother ran off and eloped with the man. The old, unforgiving Lorain had felt her mother definitely deserved to have hands laid on her for that one.

According to Lorain, if a woman married the man who raped her daughter when her daughter was a child, then the daughter had every right to be mad . . . at the whole darn world! And for quite some time, Lorain had been mad at the world, especially the male species. Men became nothing more than pawns in Lorain's miserable world. She became numb to anything they had to offer. They were toys in her game of life, and they had to pay to play. That was until she met the one and only Dr. Nicholas Wright. He changed her life, in more ways than one. Were it not for him, she wouldn't be entertaining these wives of doctors in her house right now. She'd be off somewhere with their husbands, while these women ate cupcakes.

"I'll make sure to get your guy's number for the next time Scotch eggs are on the menu," Lorain lied to Tabby.

"Pink, white, yellow, or green," Mary said, finishing off an egg of her own, "these babies are to die for."

"Well, thank you kindly, Mary." This time Lorain offered a genuine smile, one that came from inside her.

"So, how's Nicholas and Tom's new private practice coming along?" one of the women asked Lorain.

Lorain lit up at the opportunity to boast about her husband's year-old private practice. "It couldn't be better. He couldn't have partnered with a better physician." Lorain smiled at Angel, Tom's wife, who stood over at the punch fountain.

"The feeling is mutual." Angel held up her crystal cup full of punch.

"I can't believe it's been a year already," Lorain continued. "Nicholas is so much happier, it seems, now that he's his own boss."

"Doesn't he still do work in the ER?" another one of the wives asked, chiming in.

"Yes, as community service one weekend a month," Lorain answered. "He says it keeps him grounded."

"You know what they say. Charity is the best gift." Mary smiled.

"I thought the saying was 'Charity starts at home,'" Tabby noted and then turned her nose up as she looked around the room.

She allowed her eyes to gaze briefly at the long glass dining table, which sat ten people, four on each side and one at each end. She felt that the table's stone base, which was akin to a white mountain, was cheap looking. The high-back chairs, smothered in custom-fitted chair skirts, were eye-catching. But the chair skirts were a shade darker than the table's stone base, and Tabby felt that anything custom made should match the stone base to the T. The chair skirts threw it all off. That was something only Tabby would notice . . . and be bothered by. As she swept the room with her eyes, a stern expression on her face, she silently insulted Lorain's taste in decor. Since she did a little wedding planning on the side, Tabby felt she was always one up on everybody else when it came to decor. She claimed to have been in charge of the decor for million-dollar weddings.

"You would know about charity needing to start at home, wouldn't you?" Lorain retorted, then chuckled.

"Ladies." Isabella joined the women at the table after grabbing a red frosted chocolate cupcake. "I sense a hint of sarcasm on both ends, and we all know the rules." Isabella was the oldest wife in the group and, clearly, the voice of reason and the peacemaker. She was always there to break up a fight before the first punch was ever even thrown.

Lorain rolled her eyes as the women, herself included, chanted their mantra. "We're doctors' wives living fabulous lives, taking giant strides to avoid the not so wise, and as we come together, joining as one, we're friends, not enemies, six strong but all one."

A couple of the ladies clapped and cheered, as the air was now clear. No *shade* was being thrown whatsoever.

For the remaining two hours of fellowshipping, the women did their regular routine: they bragged about new pieces of jewelry their husbands had gifted them; about exotic vacations they had taken or planned to take; about parties, events, and affairs; and about their children's stellar progress in school. Then there was talk of suspicious, sexy receptionists or nurses accused of having designs on one of the husbands.

"Tom's a good man, a good doctor, and a good husband," Lorain assured Angel after she voiced her concerns about the receptionist at their husbands' joint private practice.

"I know," Angel said. "But I have my reasons to be worried. That Helen reeks of sex."

"Oh, stop it," Lorain said. "Helen goes to the church I used to attend. Remember, I'm the one who told her about the position. I would never bring trouble to our doorstep."

"I know you wouldn't," Angel said. "Not on purpose, anyway, but in this case you didn't know any better." The women urged Angel to explain herself by staring her down. "See, Tom cheated on his last wife with his receptionist."

A couple of the women gasped in disbelief.

"It's true," Angel assured them.

"No way. Not Tom." Lorain refused to believe that Tom even had such tendencies. He had always seemed like such a nice, respectful man. "How do you know?"

"Honey, I was his last receptionist," Angel revealed.

The women couldn't help but burst out laughing.

"And I thought *I* was a hot mess," Carrie said. "Girl-friend, you do the most." She stood. "And on that note, I'm 'bout to run my tail home, get buck naked, and wait for my husband in bed. I'll be wearing nothing but my white-red bottoms and a stethoscope around my neck." Carrie ran her hands down her hips. "Gotta let him know he got his own dirty little nurse at home to play with. Muah!" She blew the women a kiss.

The women began to whistle and give catcalls as Carrie swished away. Carrie suddenly stopped and turned around to face Lorain.

"Girl, let me borrow some of these rose petals," Carrie said. "He likes how they stick to me after some sweaty, stinky—"

"Girl, please. They are all yours!" Lorain said, holding her hand up to signal that she did not need to hear any more details of Carrie and her husband's sexual rendezvous.

"You are just nasty." Tabby placed her hand on her chest in disbelief and stood as well. "And on *that* note, *I'm* going to call it a day as well." She leaned into Lorain and in a loud whisper said, "And can I have some rose petals too?"

There was more laughter and some side eyes from the women.

"What?" Tabby raised her hands, in question mode. "Carrie is a newlywed. I think she may be on to something here about keeping the relationship fresh."

Carrie inhaled. "Uh-huh, nothing like the smell of fresh roses on top of the smell of some hot, stinky sex!"

"Oh, now, stop it." Isabella blushed and stood.

Carrie snapped her neck back. "Don't you even act like you and Dr. Sam ain't freaks," Carrie teased Isabella. She then looked at the other women. "Don't let her gray hair fool ya." She pointed at Isabella. "I bet I know where some other gray hairs are that Dr. Sam likes."

"Child, silence your tongue." Isabella wagged her hand at Carrie as she turned beet red.

The ladies bent over laughing at the sight of Isabella in all her discomfort and at the entire exchange itself.

"Okay, ladies," Lorain said after she was able to calm down from laughing so hard. She stood up. "Let me escort you all out before Carrie turns our monthly meetings into something we'll have to host at a strip club or an adult toy store."

"Hmm." Carrie put her index finger on her chin, in thought. "That gives me an idea for my theme for the month I host."

"Oh, God, Lorain. See what you've done?" Isabella said. "You've given the girl ideas that could get us all into trouble with our husbands."

"Get your girdle out of a bunch, Mama." Carrie slapped Isabella on the butt. "I know what you and Dr. Sam keep in that antique chest y'all have in the den."

Now it wasn't only Isabella's cheeks that turned redder than the water in the fountain in the foyer. Her neck and arms even reddened, as she was so flustered.

"Uh-huh," Carrie continued. "Y'all probably nick-named the room the Lion's Den, like that adult toy store over there on—"

"Enough, Carrie," Tabby said, shaking her head. "You're going to make poor Isabella here hyperventilate." She turned to Lorain. "Lorain, darling, outstanding. Everything was lovely and delicious." She kissed Lorain on each cheek as she grabbed her purse.

"Yes, just lovely," the other women agreed in unison, collecting their belongings and then allowing themselves to be escorted to the front door. If the women hadn't remained on the red carpet as they went, the sounds of their heels tapping on the maple floor in the foyer would have been heard.

Carrie opened her Chanel bag and scooped rose petals into it on her way out.

"Really, Carrie?" Lorain stood with her hands on her hips.

"Oh, you thought I was just playing?" Carrie said, snapping her neck back. "Child, my mama wouldn't even send me to preschool, because I don't play."

"Lord, help her." Lorain looked up to the heavens and laughed.

After smiles, good-byes, and kisses on each cheek, Lorain closed the door to her last guest. She walked into her great room, went over to the couch, and flopped down. Her body was like a limp noodle. She took off her shoes, which had been killing her feet. She kept herself from cussing out loud at her throbbing little toes as she flung the shoes across the room and closed her eyes.

"Whoa. I'm glad to see you too."

Her eyes opened, and she looked up, taking note of the medium height, the dark skin, the mini Afro, and the soft brown eyes of the chocolate hunk of a man, who was standing there, her sparkling stilettos at his feet. He stepped over them and began walking toward Lorain.

"What a sight for sore eyes." Lorain smiled and then squirmed in a sexy manner on the couch. She was tired and worn-out to the hilt, but no way would she pass up this opportunity for sex on her proverbial beach. "You are exactly what I need right about now."

"Leon is always right on time," he said, speaking in the third person.

"Leon, huh?"

"Yeah, baby." He began to unbutton the top two buttons on his shirt while looking around the room. "Where is everybody?"

"The staff is in the kitchen, cleaning up."

"Your mother and the girls?" he questioned.

"Next door, at her place." Lorain nodded in the direction of her mother's house.

The detached in-law suite, which was only twenty feet away from the main house, had been the deal closer for Nick and Lorain. They couldn't close on the house soon enough after becoming aware of that amenity, one that they hadn't been searching for initially. Being a doctor's wife who did charity work in the community and having two kids wasn't easy. Keepin' up with the Joneses, that is, the other doctors' wives, was a job in itself as well. From day one Lorain's mother had been her right-hand gal, keeping the girls whenever Lorain needed someone to care for them. They'd had to purchase two of almost everything because the girls spent so much time in both houses. Now having her mother right next door to help her with the girls was a blessing from God. It was really going to pay off now that she had Leon all to herself.

"Then it sounds like Leon can take you in his arms. . . ." He walked over to Lorain and scooped her up. "Take you upstairs." He kissed her on the lips. "And do all kinds of nasty things to you that Nick could never dream of doing to you."

"Oh, Nick can dream," Lorain said, wrapping her arms around her knight in shining armor's neck. "But what Leon does to me is every woman's fantasy come true."

"Then why are we wasting time standing here, talking, when we should be upstairs in that big bed, doing what grown folks do?"

"Then put your money where your mouth is, and put your mouth—"

"Are all them stuck-up hussies gone?"

At the sound of Eleanor's voice booming from the dining room, Lorain quickly found herself back down on the couch, right where she had been mere seconds ago.

"Looks like Leon will have to take a rain check," Nicholas said, putting away his alter ego, for now, anyway.

Lorain poked her lips out in disappointment. She loved it when her husband role-played as Leon. Leon was actually his middle name. Lorain always teased him and told him the name sounded like it belonged to some young black gigolo whom married women hired to keep them company while their husbands were away on business trips. Nicholas had taken it and run with it, becoming her imaginary sidekick. They both had to admit that it kept their four-year marriage fresh. Leave it to Eleanor to spoil the moment.

"Hello, Mother," Lorain said as Eleanor entered the great room. She looked behind her mother, certain she would have seen two mini figures trailing behind her, but she didn't. "Where are the girls?"

"In there eating up all that pink- and red-sugar stuff, of course," Eleanor replied.

Lorain sat up straight. "Mom, you can't let them eat all that sweet stuff. They get one sweet treat a week. You know darn well diabetes runs on my father's side of the family."

"It ain't running that fast," Eleanor said, "seeing that it ain't caught up with him and killed him yet."

"Mom, please. Besides that, we've invested too much money in the girls' dance and ballet classes. Ballerinas are not chubby, and sweets lead to chubbiness." The more Lorain thought about it, the more upset she got. She stood up. "And they know better. They have a competition next weekend. Let me go get them. . . ." Lorain started walking away, but Eleanor stopped her in her tracks.

"Child, they ain't but five years old." She looked Lorain up and down. "And I don't see you depriving your size fourteen self of any cupcakes."

"Twelve," Lorain said, correcting her.

"Your clothes might be a twelve. That little black thing you wear up under them that cuts off your breathing and blood circulation might make you look like a ten, but them hips and that tummy pouch scream fourteen."

Lorain was highly offended. "Well, I never."

"You never what? Been black before? Because that's sure how you acting." Eleanor shook her hand at Lorain. "We black folks . . . that's what we do . . . eat."

"And we get high blood pressure and sugar diabetes," Lorain argued. "I don't want my girls having to stick a needle in their stomach and prick their fingers all the time."

"Heck, you married a doctor." Eleanor rolled her eyes. "Let him do it. He knows what he's doing." She shooed Lorain. "You worry too much. Let them kids be kids." Eleanor pushed Lorain out of the way as she headed for the couch. "Now, move on out my way before you make me cuss." She sat down in a huff. "And I ain't like none of them ole fake Christians, talking about the cussword slipped out. When I cuss, I cuss on purpose, and you know I know how to string my words together to cut you up so tough, it'll make ya heart bleed." She looked up, for the first time acknowledging her son-in-

law. "Hey, Nick. How you doing, sweet baby?" Her tone
was now laced with nothing but sugary gumdrops and
cotton candy.

"I'm good, Ma. I'm good." Nicholas smiled and shook
his head as he walked over and kissed his dear mother-
in-law on the forehead.

"I don't know how you stay good." She pointed at Lorain. "With that one over there acting like Diahann Carroll, a black woman trapped in a white woman's body."

"That is not who Diahann Carroll is," Lorain said, dis-
puting her mother's claim. "That's just a role she plays."

"My point exactly. You been pretending to be somebody you're not ever since you got involved with all that
doctors' wives business." She shook her head at Nicholas, as if he'd fibbed. "And you good. Tell me anything."
She looked back at her daughter and wagged her finger
at her. "But I know you good . . . good at pretending. I
watched how you were around them women at that last
party thing y'all had here at the house. Made me sick to
my stomach. That's why I couldn't be around 'em today
or have my grandbabies around them, either. Fake, fake,
fake, the all of you. Fake as a two-dollar bill."

"Two-dollar bills are real," Lorain said, correcting her
mother for the second time in their conversation.

"Then it looks like a two-dollar bill has got one up on
you," Eleanor snapped back.

Nicholas couldn't hold it in any longer. He let a
chuckle slip out. No matter how many times he witnessed the back-and-forth banter between mother and
daughter, he couldn't get used to how comical it was.

Lorain snapped her neck toward Nicholas and gave
him the evil eye.

"See? Even your own husband knows you're fake," Eleanor said, rolling her eyes.

"Nick, really?" Lorain said. "You're really going to let
her stand here and talk to your wife like that?"

Nicholas snapped his own neck back and gave Lorain a crazy look. "She's yo' mama. Besides, if I don't take her side, she might not make me any of her famous neck bones, black-eyed peas, and corn bread." He kissed Eleanor on the forehead and then his wife on her pouty lips.

"Hmm," Lorain said to her husband. "You need to be worried about what you might not get from me."

"Child, you are forty plus. He ain't studdin' none of that vintage vagina," Eleanor said. "Besides, he's a good-looking man with 'Ph.D.' behind his name. He can get pu—"

"Ahem." Nicholas cleared his throat loudly to interrupt Eleanor's rant.

"From anywhere," Eleanor said, finishing her statement.

Nicholas shook his head. "I'm going to leave you two alone and go check on my two beautiful daughters. You two ladies finish up your conversation without me." He gave Lorain another kiss and then headed off.

"Coward," Lorrain shot at him under her breath, then folded her arms. She then looked at her mother. "I can't believe you even waste your time getting up on Sunday mornings to go to church and use that mouth to praise the Lord when all week long, nothing but junk comes out of it. Just sickening."

"Well, ain't the church like a hospital? Ain't it for sick people to go and get better?"

Lorain threw her hands up. "Why do I bother? I can't beat you."

"And I thought by now you would have stopped trying. But I ain't mad that you haven't. Keeps my mind sharp."

"You mean your tongue?" Lorain flopped down to rest her tired body. This time she landed on the oversize yellow chair across from the couch. She laid her head back and closed her eyes.

"Mommy's baby worn out?" Eleanor asked, back to her sweet, buttery tone.

"Indeed." Lorain exhaled.

"I'm sure it is draining pretending to be something you're not."

Lorain opened her eyes and lifted her head. "You know what? I'm not sure how much more of you calling me fake and phony I'm going to endure. I'm the same person I was yesterday and will be tomorrow."

"But you ain't the same person you were before you got involved in that little clique." Eleanor thought for a minute. "As a matter of fact, you really ain't the same person you were when Unique left for West Virginia."

Lorain tried to hide the uneasiness that swept over her at the mention of her firstborn's name. Unique was the baby Lorain had thrown away in the trash and had left for dead. When the baby was found alive in the garbage and placed in the foster-care system, Lorain had been none the wiser. For years Lorain had been under the impression that the baby had died and had been carried off to a hole in the earth by a garbage truck. When Lorain met a young, fresh-mouthed, single welfare mother of three boys with three different fathers, she had had no idea that she'd come to learn that this young woman was her biological daughter. She'd been clueless about the fact that her daughter was even walking the earth. Lorain always joked that in hindsight, she should have easily been able to put the family connection together, given Unique's mouth and Eleanor's mouth. Unique had gotten her fresh tongue from her grandmother for sure.

Eleanor snapped her fingers. "That's it, ain't it? You miss your baby girl, so now you're trying to forget all about that life with her, or the life you didn't have with her. You're doing it by having this new life with Victoria and Heaven. I should have figured it all out before now."

Eleanor began to show a sympathetic side. "Why didn't you just tell Mama? I would have understood and saved my digs for somebody who really deserved them."

"Mom!" Lorain said, agitated. "That's nonsense. Why would I try to cover up an old life with a new one?" She let out a nervous chuckle. Her insides jittered due to her fear of being found out and called on the carpet by her mother. She had received a rug burn or two thanks to her mother and knew how painful they could be. But then again, the truth had a tendency to be painful. "That doesn't make any sense at all. Besides, it's impossible."

"Not really. Covering up your old life with a new one . . . Ain't that part of being born again?"

"Yes, when the Lord does it," Lorain said. "He washes away people's old life for a new one all the time." Her mother was right. Lorain couldn't argue with that.

"But then again," Eleanor said, "I guess it works only when He does it. When we try to run from our old life or cover it up with plastic, I guess, just like with plastic, eventually, folks are going to see through to the real you, anyway."

Eleanor's theory sent chills down Lorain's spine. As crazy as some of the stuff that came out of her mother's mouth was, it always tended to be right on point. Lorain had been desperately trying to cover up her old life. There was entirely too much guilt and shame to bear in acknowledging it. So, yes, at first she had felt that burying her past was for all the right reasons. She'd hated the person she was growing up and the promiscuous life she once lived. Once she gave her life to Christ, though, she didn't have to cover it up anymore. It was washed away. She had admitted it, quit it, and been forgiven for it. Who she used to be no longer haunted her or taunted her.

God began to give her opportunities to atone for her past. He opened the door for her to be able to release the secrets and the lies, for them to become a testimony. But it was almost as if once the door opened, all the skeletons fell out of the closet right on top of Lorain and began to suffocate her. There were too many truths she'd have to tell to make things right, and all of her truths were falling upon her at once. There was Unique being back in her life. There was having her molester back in her life. Then the twins came along. In the midst of all that, she was juggling her relationship with Nicholas. Everything was connected.

Lorain got lost in the shuffle. She didn't know what to share, how much to share, who to share it with, and when. Too many secrets and too many lies to protect made it difficult for Lorain to be the honest Christian woman she had set out to be. The more secrets she kept and the more lies she told in order to keep the secrets a secret, the further she felt she was drifting away from God. And it was her own doing. But she kept promising herself that as soon as she got things under control, she'd get right with God.

Time was all Lorain felt she needed. She needed enough time to pass so that she felt comfortable enough to be real . . . with everybody. But time needed to hurry along. If not, one of two things was going to happen as far as Lorain was concerned. One, everyone was going to eventually see right through her phony, plastic self, just as her mother had said. Or two, she was going to suffocate underneath it all.

Chapter 3

Wearing green and black plaid pajamas, Nicholas didn't looked up from the medical journal he was reading in order to speak to his wife. "Did you finally get the twins to bed?" he asked Lorain as she entered their master suite and closed the door behind her.

He lay in their California king bed, which was decorated in burgundy and silver. The three fringed decorative pillows had been thrown to the foot of the bed. The draperies were cream and had burgundy tassels. Lorain had gone with lighter draperies because dark curtains in addition to dark bedding were too depressing, in Lorain's opinion, but she couldn't do without the comforter set. It was the decorator's idea to go with the cream draperies instead of the ones that matched the comforter.

"Yes, one bedtime story, two books read, and three prayers later, Victoria and Heaven are sound asleep," Lorain said as she walked over to her wooden antique vanity table and sat down. She'd lucked out and snagged it at an estate sale at a Victorian home in a neighboring suburb. Every time she sat down at it, she felt like Joan Crawford at the height of her career. Lorain had already showered and changed into her nightclothes. The only thing she needed to do before calling it a night was to wrap her hair.

"I'm so sorry they wore you out." Nicholas placed the journal on the nightstand so that he could give all his attention to his wife. After all, this was their sacred time together. During the day their lives were so busy that they'd agreed that at night, when alone in their bedroom, they would have their special time together. Whether they were enjoying one of those reality shows Lorain forced him to watch; talking about their lives, other people's lives, the future, or the kids; simply holding one another in their arms; or getting their married grown man and grown woman on; they refused to take that time for granted. They referred to it as their mini vacation, even though they never even left the house. Their bed was an island.

"No need for you to apologize. That mother-in-law of yours is the one to blame, letting the girls eat all those cupcakes. They were on a sugar high." Lorain looked into the oval-shaped, unframed mirror and began wrapping her hair with her hairbrush.

Nicholas laughed.

Lorain briskly turned on the stool, its original upholstery burgundy mixed with dark blue and tan, to face her husband. "Oh, you still think she's funny, huh?"

"Come on. Your mother is a character, and you know it. Surely, you don't take her serious and let her get to you. She's harmless." He shrugged.

"No, she's just from the old school, where older people get a pass for speaking their mind. She clearly takes advantage of that."

"Well, isn't that what the new school considers 'keeping it real'? Same difference."

"Yeah, and I don't like either one, not when speaking your mind or keeping it real means hurting someone's feelings." Lorain faced the mirror and continued wrapping her hair.

"Life's too short. Brush it off. You have only one mother."

The last thing Nicholas had said made Lorain pause. She quickly regrouped, swiped her hand around her wrapped hair, then reached for her silk scarf. She proceeded to wrap the scarf around her head in a stylish manner. Nicholas's words still echoed in her ear.

You have only one mother.

She had only one mother; that was true. But that wasn't the case with Unique. Let Korica, the woman who had raised Unique, tell it, and Lorain was only some woman who had popped back in the picture. So what that she happened to be the woman who had given birth to Unique. And Korica made it her business to remind Lorain that she wasn't the woman who had raised Unique. She was not the woman whom Unique called Mommy. Unique called Lorain Mom—short and sweet, to represent the time she'd been present in her life.

It was true enough that Unique had a special bond with Korica, and for good reason. That had been evident the day Lorain went to the jail to visit Unique. Unique had been arrested and charged not only with some sort of drug trafficking, but also with the death of her three sons. Lorain could only imagine how Unique had felt all alone in that jail cell, just wanting somebody, anybody, to be there for her. Lorain had wanted to make sure she was there for her, but she hadn't been the only one. Korica had been there waiting to visit Unique as well.

When the guard called for Unique Gray's mother to come back to visit, both women had stood. That was their first time ever meeting one another. It was quite awkward for Lorain, to say the least. The guard thought it was a joke that both women insisted they were Unique's mother. Eventually, it was determined that they'd let the alleged daughter decide which woman she wanted to come back first.

Lorain thought the wind had been knocked out of her when the guard returned, only to tell them that Unique wanted to see Korica before she visited with Lorain. Lorain would never forget the look of victory Korica gave her before the guard escorted her back to spend time with Unique. That was the beginning of the battle of the moms . . . and Korica had fired the first shot, shooting Lorain right in the gut. And she had many more bullets where that one had come from, taking aim at Lorain every chance she got. That was not to say that Lorain didn't carry her own ammunition.

Once Lorain discovered that Unique was her baby girl, alive and well, she tried to connect with Unique and be the mother she hadn't been to her all those years. Once Unique was in the battle of her life, fighting for her freedom, Lorain was determined to be there for every round. Korica didn't like that at all. It brought out the green-eyed monster in Korica. She saw it as Lorain coming into the picture to replace her.

"You might be the woman who spit her out from between your legs, but I'm her real mother," Korica had said to Lorain. "I'm the one who, all those years ago, sacrificed being able to take care of my own flesh and blood so that I could take care of yours. I'll be darned if I sit back and watch you take over the reins after all I've done to raise Unique."

Now sitting at her vanity table, which was covered with the finest oils and perfumes, and hearing Korica's words play back in her head made Lorain's blood boil all over again. "I should have beaten her—"

"Did you say something, honey?"

Lorain hadn't realized she was muttering the words out loud through her teeth. "Oh, nothing." She took a deep breath, counted to ten, and continued fiddling with the scarf.

"Come on to bed and quit letting your mother's words get to you," Nicholas said. He patted the empty spot next to him on the bed, where his lovely wife usually lay.

It wasn't just Eleanor's words that Lorain had allowed to get her all riled up. Somehow Korica's words—even though she hadn't heard a peep out of that woman in years—had managed to resurface and agitate her as well. Lorain had worked too hard to fit into the mold of a doctor's wife, and she wasn't going to let the witch of Christian past, Korica, or the witch of Christian present, her mother, make it all for naught and ruin her future. All she wanted to do was live happily ever after as the wife of Dr. Nicholas Wright and the mother of Heaven and Victoria Wright and the *mom* of Unique.

Nicholas was right. Life was too short to be worried about nonsense, and so was the night. Lorain had a handsome husband waiting for her in a warm bed. Thinking of all the naughty things they could fit into the last hours of the night, Lorain quickly used a technique she'd seen on YouTube to finish tying the scarf fashionably around her head. Searching the Internet for fashionable ways to wrap her hair with a scarf was something her mother had urged her to do.

"Can't you do nothing better with that scarf around your head?" Eleanor had fussed. "I mean, does your husband really think that's sexy? You coming to bed, looking like Aunt Jemima?"

Well, as fine as Lorain was looking, she was sure that Nicholas was glad Lorain *ain't hismima*. She stood, shed the gown-like robe to the matching short nightie underneath, and sashayed over to the bed. "You are right," Lorain cooed to Nicholas as she climbed into the bed. "Life is short, and perhaps so is the night. But I know something that's not so short." She made googly eyes at him, then peeked underneath the covers.

"My, my, my." Nicholas licked his lips. "When no other words will do, like my man Johnny Gill said, my, my my!" He took Lorain in his arms, and then he took over her body, kissing and being attentive to every nook and cranny before he shot her off into a world of ecstasy.

Lorain and Nicholas were proof that married Christian couples could enjoy one another as freely as the next couple. Sex was not taboo for them at all, and they didn't walk around acting all offended at the idea of sex. Christians had sex, even some who weren't married, God bless 'em. No, the latter scenario didn't line up with God's Word, but it was a fact of life.

As far as Lorain was concerned, she had to minister to the saints on the streets, but she couldn't allow that to take away from ministering to her husband between the sheets. The same way she didn't always feel like doing community work, going to church, or doing Bible study after a long day, especially with having to chase two twin girls around, she didn't always feel like ministering to her husband in bed. But she recalled Pastor Margie of New Day Temple of Faith once telling her that if a person didn't answer the phone when God called on them for ministry, he or she should not worry, because He would find somebody else to do it. Well, Lorain didn't mind if God found somebody else to pass out tracts on the street corner, but she'd be darned if someone else ministered to her husband in bed.

Lorain pulled a few tricks of her own out of her bag of magic and used them on her husband. Moments ago Nicholas might have been quoting Johnny Gill, but in Lorain's mind, it was nothing but Michael Jackson all the way. *The way you make me feel . . .*

Nicholas always had a way of making Lorain feel brand new inside, and it had nothing to do with the fact that literally every week she had something new. What

Nicholas provided Lorain went beyond material things. This man did what a person was supposed to do with their mate—bring out the best in them.

From her very first relationship with a man—starting with her father, who divorced Lorain right along with her mother—Lorain had experienced only negativity. She'd never seen a man as anything other than a money bag or a living dildo. Because of the pain she had endured in the past when dealing with the male species, Lorain had become numb inside when it came to men. So Nicholas was either the first real man she'd ever met in her entire life or the kryptonite that was able to break her down to exactly who she was, a woman. Not the woman who for years had been guided and controlled by the hurt little girl inside of her. No, Nicholas had brought the grown woman out in her, trampling on and sending to the pits of hell the spirit of the little girl whose mission had been to have Lorain live a life of fornication until the day she burned in hell, playing men like chess pieces along the way.

With all she'd endured in her past, Lorain felt as if she'd personally been to hell and back. "Going to hell and back" was nothing more than a cliché, an expression. Because if it was actually possible for someone to go to hell and back, then that meant there was a possibility that the hurt and bitter little girl, the one whom Lorain had exiled, could soon return from hell . . . and bring a couple of little imps along with her.

Chapter 4

Lorain sat with the other dance moms behind the glass partition that separated them from the interior of dance studio three. It was three-tiered bench seating, which allowed all the parents to observe their children. The only time parents were allowed in the actual dance studio while the children were performing was when the instructor requested their presence. That was usually to show them up close what their child was doing wrong technically. Lorain preferred this seating arrangement versus being inside the dance studio, inhaling all that sweat and malodor. Did all dance classrooms smell like basketball practice had been going on all week and feel like a massive heat wave on top of that? The ends of Lorain's hair frizzed up after she was in the dance classroom for only five minutes. She hated to think about what she'd look and smell like if she had to endure being in there for the entire dance session.

Lorain watched as the dance teacher took a moment during the group dance to make sure Heaven and Victoria were on point with their choreography, as they were both playing lead roles in this weekend's group competition number. When Lorain got the girls involved in dance, she had no idea how much of her time it would involve.

Her other tasks as a mom took up a great deal of her time as well. It was a blessing that she'd been able to quit her nine-to-five job once she married Nicholas. He was old school and didn't believe in doing that fifty-fifty thing, where the man paid half of the mortgage and the bills and the woman paid the other half. In his family the men were providers, period. His mother had once told him that if the man wasn't going to do half the laundry, cook half the food, clean half the house, dress and feed half the kids, then why should the woman have to pay half the bills? "The man is the head of the family, but the woman is the head of the home. We run it like a business," his mother had said many times.

If Lorain wanted to work, Nicholas had no qualms about that. He wasn't a caveman to the point where he felt a woman shouldn't work and instead should stay in the kitchen, barefoot and pregnant. But his wife's money was no good with him, meaning it was useless for her to try to even give him any toward bills.

Since Lorain had had a job that she could take or leave—and not a career that she loved—at the time that she and Nicholas got married, she had had no problem putting in her two weeks' notice. Nicholas didn't have her on an allowance, or any craziness like that, either. They had a joint account for savings, a joint account for living expenses, a college fund for the twins, and a joint mad money account for discretionary spending. A certain amount of money was placed into the mad money account monthly for both their use, though Lorain always spent the majority of. Once it was gone, it was gone. Lorain wasn't too crazy with money, so after she ran through the mad money, she never tried to dip into any of the other accounts when, for instance, a handbag she had been eyeballing was on sale. But whenever that mad money account ran dry, she was not happy. Sometimes it felt as if she'd run out of food stamps in the middle of the month.

But Nicholas always made sure that she had whatever she wanted, and the girls definitely always had what they wanted as well. And thank God, because this whole dance thing was not cheap. Some of these mothers had gone bankrupt and had lost husbands because they were so vested in dance. It seemed to be their entire life. A prime example was Ivy, who, if you let her tell it, knew she was going to give birth to a dance star from the moment she conceived.

"Your girls are so lucky," Ivy said, slinging her long blond hair over her shoulder. "It's Black History Month, so your girls were a shoo-in for the leading roles in this one. I mean, what would my blue-eyed, blond, pale-skinned Gabrielle look like dancing the role of Rosa Parks?" She let out a chuckle and gave Lorain's knee a playful slap.

If Lorain hadn't been texting when she entered the viewing room and sat down, she would have realized she had sat down next to her worst nightmare—a certified grade A dance mom. Tolerating Ivy was no easy feat for Lorain . . . or for any of the other moms, for that matter.

Lorain had mastered fitting in with the elite Malvonia socialites just fine since becoming a doctor's wife. She'd mastered smiling when she really wanted to snatch somebody's weave off, and she'd mastered taking the time to think before she spoke or reacted when somebody had pissed her off real good. *I'm a doctor's wife,* she would tell herself. *This isn't just about me. It's about my husband and his reputation.* And Ivy should pray to the gods that Lorain always took those five seconds to remind herself of that. This time around, during Lorain's five-second pause, Jacquelyn, another one of the dance moms, stepped in to throw water on the flames before they turned into a wildfire.

"And we all know your dear Gabby is the most talented dancer on the competition dance team," Jacquelyn told Ivy.

"Thanks, Jacks. I'm glad someone recognizes that." Ivy put her nose up in the air, too stuck on herself to realize that Jacquelyn was being sarcastic. "Some of these other moms don't get that my Gabby is special . . . all by herself." Ivy turned her attention back to the girls, who were still practicing.

Jacquelyn, who was sitting on the other side of Ivy, on the burnt orange–colored bench, which matched the burnt orange walls, simply looked at Lorain and rolled her eyes.

"But, Lorain, I hate to admit that your girls have great potential." Ivy added, starting up again. "Outside of the whole twin thing, which can take away from a real dancer's true talent, your girls have wonderful posture and those long legs. . . ." Ivy looked Lorain up and down. "Funny, neither you nor your husband are above average in height. They must get it from somewhere else in the family tree." She shrugged, almost knowingly. Or maybe it just appeared that way to Lorain.

Lorain tensed up. This Ivy chick was really trying her holy nerves, sitting over there with that snooty look on her face, acting like she knew things about Lorain's family. *But what can she possibly know?* Lorain asked herself. *Nothing. How can she?* Lorain was friendly with the dance moms, but she wasn't close enough to any of them to hang out and tell them her business. Upon coming to that conclusion, Lorain relaxed her shoulders a bit. Ivy might try to get under Lorain's skin, but Lorain was going to fight tooth and nail not to let her. Lately, she'd been doing so well at keeping her cool and staying in control of her emotions. Now along came a spider . . . named Ivy.

It was as if God had seen how well Lorain had been doing in dealing with folks and their wicked ways, and now He wanted to test her by siccing Ivy on her. God had to be behind this. How else would Ivy know that the very buttons she did not want to push were the ones that had something to do with her daughters?

Heaven and Victoria were Lorain's pride and joy. They were her life. Her second chance at motherhood. And only a handful of people knew that biologically, they were her granddaughters and not her daughters.

When Unique first shared with Lorain the fact that she was pregnant with the twins, who were her fourth and fifth children as an unwed mother, she was set on giving the babies up for adoption. At the time she'd already had three sons by three different men, and on top of that, she was living in her sister's basement with the boys. Unique wasn't even making ends meet in her current living situation, so adding two more mouths to feed could possibly land her on the streets. Besides, she was a babe in Christ and was teetering the fence, backsliding, or whatever church folks wanted to call it, every now and then. The last thing she needed was for them church hens to be pecking at her and challenging her Christianity. A single mother of three with all them baby daddies, she'd already given them enough to talk about.

At least when she was pregnant with the twins, she didn't have to deal with a fourth baby daddy, as Unique's pregnancy was the result of a drunken one-night stand she'd had with her oldest son's father. But he hadn't even been half taking care of the son she already had with him. He'd been too busy trying to make a dollar out of fifteen cents by selling dope. To this day, Unique had never even bothered to tell him that he was the father of the twins. He'd never asked.

Lorain expressed her disappointment that Unique was hell-bent on adoption. Knowing that Unique was her biological daughter, she couldn't imagine sitting by while Unique handed her grandbabies, her flesh and blood, over to some strangers. But then a light bulb went off in Lorain's head. Not only did she decide to support Unique's decision to choose the route of adoption, but she also had the perfect suggestion when it came to the person to whom Unique should give the babies. Namely, herself.

Initially, Lorain and Unique decided they would tell everyone that Unique was acting as a surrogate for Lorain. At that point no one but the two of them knew that Unique was actually Lorain's biological daughter. Sharing this fact involved too much explaining, and Lorain wasn't quite prepared to share her story.

All would have gone well had Eleanor not begun to put two and two together. Eleanor was clueless about the fact that her thirteen-year-old daughter had been pregnant and had given birth. So when she figured out the whole situation regarding Lorain and Unique, she about lost her mind, putting the situation on blast in the church sanctuary. It was a mess. It was something Lorain had not wanted the members of New Day Temple of Faith to be privy to. Thanks to Eleanor, though, that wasn't how it turned out. But by then Lorain was living a whole new life, in a whole new world. She rarely ever had to see the folks up at New Day.

She attended Nicholas's family church at least one Sunday out of the month so that when someone asked her what church she went to, she could avoid the embarrassment of not having a home church to rattle off. But the last thing she needed was to have church folk all up in her business. She didn't mind all church folk, but all it took was one busybody to set things off. Besides, she didn't need to be up in church all the time to prove that she was a Christian and loved the Lord. God knew her heart. On top of that, a socialite such as herself didn't have a lot of time for church, for participating in this

committee and that committee. And being a mommy
to her adopted girls also took up a lot of time.

Originally, Lorain wasn't going to adopt the girls legally; she intended to serve as their guardian. This was
because she figured that once Unique was in a better
position financially and emotionally, she might want to
take the girls back and raise them herself. So instead of
pursuing a full adoption, Lorain basically took temporary custody of the twins. She was their legal guardian,
and she was responsible for them financially. She didn't
want that burden to be placed on Unique, otherwise
it would defeat the very purpose of Lorain raising the
twins. This left the door open for Lorain and Unique to
do a multitude of things when it came to raising the girls
and shifting custody.

After the death of the boys, and during her battle to
be found innocent of the drug trafficking charge and
the charges related to her sons' deaths, Unique felt she
didn't have it in her to be a mommy. She didn't feel
that it was part of her calling, her destiny. Although her
church family tried to tell her it wasn't so, after the boys
died, she felt as though she was no longer a mother. She
felt stripped of that title in every way and didn't even
want to get back into the ring to try to earn her title back.

Although she had never voiced it, Lorain begged to
differ. She'd seen how Unique was with her boys. Lorain
was engrossed by the relationship Unique had with her
sons. She'd watched them interact, in awe, wondering
whether she would have had the same type of bond with
Unique when she was a child if things had turned out
differently. Unique's bond with her children, their connection with each other and their love for each other,
showed in each of their eyes. Without question, Unique
had been a great mother to those boys. Some women
were born with that motherly instinct, and it did not

falter, no matter the circumstance they themselves had been born into. Unique was one of those women. She definitely had it in her to be a great mother to the twins.

By the time Unique made it known that she had no intention of taking the twins back, Lorain had formed a bond of her own with Heaven and Victoria, one that paralleled the bond Unique had had with the boys. She didn't want to risk losing them. So when Unique came to her house not too long after she was released from jail, and asked Lorain to consider assuming full custody of the girls, Lorain acted selfishly instead of selflessly. She didn't tell Unique what was really on her heart, which was that mothering the girls would be the best form of healing for Unique. She simply agreed with Unique's decision and buried her thoughts and feelings on the matter.

By then Nicholas and Lorain were no longer just dating. They were husband and wife. His arm did not have to be twisted when it came to the girls. Within a few months Nicholas and Lorain had legally adopted Heaven and Victoria. Even before the legal adoption, many members at New Day Temple of Faith still thought Lorain was the twins' biological mother, in spite of rumors that were circulating.

So Lorain wasn't upset when she had to leave the church in order to worship at Nicholas's family church. She'd married him. They were now one. He was the head of their family, so where he worshipped, she worshipped. Under different circumstances Lorain might have put up a fight about having to leave her home church, but she was more relieved than anything. She could now go to a church where no one knew anything about her or any of her business. And just like that, the mess was swept under the church rug, and Lorain moved on. It was safe to say that Ivy had kicked up a little dust, though.

The twins had been at the dance school ever since they were two years old. They'd been in a many of the showcases, and they were now of age to start performing in competitions. Ivy's eleven-year old-daughter, Gabrielle, on the other hand, had been on the competition team for the past six years. And for those six years, she'd pretty much been the star, getting the leads and a solo at almost every competition.

Lorain had been warned by some of the other mothers that Ivy was a handful, out for herself instead of the team, and that Ivy was always trying to make sure that no one else on the team attempted to outshine her daughter. The fact that Heaven and Victoria were adorable twins who could easily steal the spotlight immediately made the hairs on Ivy's neck rise the moment they were placed on the team by the studio owner only five months ago. It was an unspoken thing that the twins were unique and stood out. All eyes in the room went to the twins, so the fact that there was a chance that Gabrielle would lose all the attention she'd been getting during the past six years didn't sit well with Ivy at all. Ivy was a full-figured mother who was living vicariously through her size zero daughter. A win for Gabrielle was a win for herself in Ivy's eyes. The same went for a loss. Ivy was not the kind of mother who would sit back and allow her daughter to take a loss . . . or to be cheat out of a win by another, for that matter.

"My girls pretty much have the perfect dancer's body, don't they?" Lorain was just as smug as she could be, having decided to view Ivy's words as a compliment instead of the dig the hussy was throwing her way. "Thank you, Ivy. That's mighty big of you." Lorain looked her up and down. "And speaking of big, have you lost weight?"

Okay, one point for God and two points for the devil. Obviously, Lorain was still a work in progress.

Chapter 5

"Where have you been? We've been waiting forever, and your cell is off. My calls kept going straight to voice mail," Nicholas said to Lorain as she walked through the front door with two Neiman Marcus bags in tow. He looked down at the bags. "Well, I guess I don't have to ask where you've been." He kissed her on the forehead. "Put those bags down and come into the kitchen." Nicholas removed the bags from Lorain's hands and sat them on the foyer floor, by the fountain.

"What are you doing home?" Lorain was so surprised that Nicholas was greeting her at the door when she walked in.

Usually, the tables were turned, and she was the one doing the greeting. No matter how many errands were on Lorain's to-do list, up until now she had always managed to beat Nicholas home. There was always one last patient to see, one last file to look over, or one last patient admitted to the hospital whom he needed to check in on. With such a hectic schedule, Nicholas was never afforded the pleasure of arriving home before seven o'clock, even though his office closed at five.

Lorain looked down at her watch. Her mouth dropped. "It's after seven?" As it turned out, Nicholas was right on his usual schedule. Lorain was the one who had let time get away from her. "Gosh. I lost track of time," she admitted. "They were doing the final clearance of all the Christmas leftovers and returns. You know me. One man's junk is another man's treasure."

It didn't matter how much money was in Lorain's bank account. A great deal was a great deal. And not only did the wives enjoy bragging about their expensive items, but they also loved bragging about a good bargain at the same time. It was never a good thing for one wife to have something identical to the next wife, *unless* she could rub it in her face that she'd gotten it way below retail. Oh, there was pleasure in making the next wife feel as though she'd been ripped off by paying double for something. Fashionistas and bargainistas had the same ranking in their clique.

"I'm so sorry I'm late." Lorain kissed her husband on the cheek. "I have a nice, healthy light dinner planned for us that calls for chicken breasts. I need to marinade the chicken, though, so it will take a minute to prepare." She looked at her watch again. "But since it's so late, I guess I'll have to whip something else up."

It was at times like this when Lorain wished she had a kitchen staff on hand full-time. She hired a kitchen staff only when she was planning an event or wanted a special, intimate meal with Nicholas and didn't have time to review an instructional culinary video on YouTube.

"No worries," Nicholas told her. "I've already got something special for you waiting in the kitchen."

"Oh, lovey-dovey, how sweet." Lorain kissed him on the lips this time. She then pulled away, raising an eyebrow. "Wait a minute. Am I having dinner with you . . . ?" She wiggled both brows. "Or with Leon? And does this 'something special' involve chocolate syrup and whipped cream?" She grabbed him by his collar and looked over her shoulders. "Are the girls with my mom?" She lifted her leg and wrapped it around Nicholas's waist.

"Woman, cut it out," he said, spanking her on the behind.

"Ooh, so it is Leon." She offered her husband a mischievous grin.

He shook his head, pushed Lorain's leg down, and grabbed her by the hand. "Is that all you ever think about? Come on, gutter mind." Nicholas led his wife through the dining room and into the kitchen.

Even before they entered the gourmet kitchen, one that every professional chef Lorain had invited to cook in salivated at, the smell of an all too familiar meal teased Lorain's nose. She immediately knew that the "something special" waiting for her in the kitchen was not the doing of her husband.

"Just as I thought," Lorain said when she followed Nicholas through the kitchen door and saw her mother at the six-burner, stainless-steel stove, stirring something in a pot. She made a beeline over to her mother. "Your famous neck bones, black-eyed peas, and corn bread." She put her arm around her mother's shoulders. "Ordinarily, I wouldn't want such a high-sodium meal this late in the day and in the middle of the week." The weekends were usually when Lorain was more lenient with meals and snacks. "But you are an absolute lifesaver, Mom." She kissed Eleanor on her head of dark brown hair. It was her natural color, not dyed. Lorain always joked that Eleanor caused everyone else to have gray hair but didn't have a single one on her own head. "Thank you. Sorry I'm late."

"No problem," Eleanor said. "I got the girls off the bus and did their little homework with them." Putting the girls on the bus and getting them off the bus was something Eleanor did every day, so that was nothing new. She insisted on earning her keep in any way she could and devoted herself to caring for the girls, especially since Nicholas and Lorain refused to accept any rent money from her. When Eleanor sold her home to move in with them, she had tried to bless the couple with a few grand at least, but they wouldn't hear of it. Eleanor hadn't pressed the issue. That meant more bingo nights for her.

While Eleanor talked, Lorain stole a sliver of corn bread and stuffed it in her mouth. She could taste the hint of sugar and the real butter that had melted on the top and seeped into the sweet, cake-like delicacy.

"Where are the girls at now?" she asked with her mouth full.

A little smirk appeared on Eleanor's face. She nodded over her shoulder. "Right there."

Lorain turned around.

"Surprise!"

Lorain swallowed a hunk of corn bread practically whole and began choking. She tried to cough it up, but it was stuck in her throat. She hunched over in a ball, with her hands gripping her neck, like she was trying to squeeze the bread out of her throat. She couldn't breathe.

"Oh, dear God!" she heard her mother cry out. "I'll call nine-one-one!"

Lorain didn't know how much time had passed, but it felt like forever and a day. The very air she breathed had been ripped from her in a matter of seconds. Just as she felt she was going to black out, she sensed a presence behind her. Then she felt arms around her. She felt fists gripping her under her breasts. Next, she felt the pressure on her chest from repeated pumping. The corn bread came back up, and she spit it out onto the floor. She felt the arms release her.

"Are you okay?" Nicholas asked after releasing Lorain.

"Yes, Mom, are you okay?" Unique asked as she ran over to Lorain. She had come into town unannounced.

Lorain was speechless. She hadn't seen Unique in months. The few times that Unique had been in town since moving to West Virginia, she had tried to connect with Lorain, but Lorain had never seemed to have any openings in her schedule.

"Honey, talk to me. Are you all right?" Nicholas said, worried.

"She just better be," Eleanor spat. "Because we can't be having a repeat of the last time she choked, fell over, bumped her head, and didn't remember a thang." Eleanor reminded everybody in the room of an incident a few years ago, when Lorain had gotten a grape stuck in her throat. After choking, falling, and bumping her head, she woke up in the hospital, suffering from selective memory loss. Slowly but surely, her full memory returned and she was able to put the pieces of her life back together. But now it looked as though everything could possibly fall apart again.

"You gave us quite a scare back in the kitchen, honey," Nicholas said to Lorain as he dug the meat out of a neck bone with his fork. They were all sitting at the dining table, eating dinner.

"It was like déjà vu," Eleanor said, sucking the meat off of a bone. She looked at Lorain. "Unique yelled, 'Surprise!' and you lost your breath."

"I'm okay." Lorain smiled. "I was just . . . well . . . surprised." She batted her eyes. She turned to Heaven, who was sitting next to her, and started brushing invisible crumbs from Heaven's dress.

"I didn't mean to cause all that drama," Unique said. "I tried to call you once I got into town, but you didn't answer, so after I finished handling my business, I decided to head over here on my way back out of town."

Lorain's phone had died during her shopping spree. No telling how many calls she'd missed.

"And when I saw my oldest grandbaby was in town," Eleanor said, jumping in, "I wasn't about to send her on her way without one of my home-cooked meals. No, sir. So I convinced her to stay for dinner."

"And I appreciate it." Unique smiled.

"West Virginia is a long drive," Lorain said to Eleanor. "You shouldn't have kept her from hitting the road, especially not for a meal. She's a caterer, or have you forgotten? She's always cooking and, I'm sure, eating." Lorain looked over at Unique's small frame. "Although it looks as though she's not eating much. Still, I'm sure getting a meal is the least of her worries."

"Yeah, but she has to follow the recipes of that Tamarra girl she works for. Ain't nothing like her grandmother's cooking. Ain't that right, baby?" Eleanor turned to Unique, who sat next to her, for support.

"Indeed," Unique confirmed. "And it feels good to have somebody else do the cooking for once." She rested her hand on Eleanor's and said softly, "Thank you, Great-grandmama Eleanor." It melted Eleanor's heart when Unique called her what her three grandsons used to call her before they passed.

Lorain cleared her throat. "So, uh, what brought you into town, anyway?"

"Actually, 'that Tamarra girl' needed to talk with me," Unique said, mimicking Eleanor.

"Is everything good? Is everything okay with the catering contract with that nursing home in West Virginia?" Lorain quizzed.

"Yes, everything is good in West Virginia, but it looks like Tamarra might need me back here to run things."

"That would be wonderful," Nicholas said. He turned to his wife. "Wouldn't it, honey?"

It took Lorain a moment to reply. "Yes, absolutely." Lorain's mouth said one thing, but her brain thought the total opposite. She looked at Unique. "But if you come back here to run things, then who will handle things in West Virginia?"

"You know that was only supposed to be a three-month contract, until the nursing home found a local company and signed a permanent local contract," Unique reminded Lorain.

"It was a blessing that they found Tamarra's company on the Internet and reached out to her, even though she wasn't local," Nicholas said.

"Yeah. Didn't the nursing home have to get rid of the other company that was handling the kitchen because they found that the company was purchasing items on their dime and using the products for other gigs?" Lorain asked.

"Yes," Unique confirmed.

Eleanor tsk-tsked. "Just ratchet."

Unique and the twins chuckled at Eleanor's use of slang.

"They thought that within three months they'd surely have another company, which is why I kept my place in Malvonia," Unique said.

"So have they finally found someone?" Lorain asked. "Are they cutting you guys loose just like that? Seems kind of inconsiderate, considering that when they couldn't find someone permanent after the initial three months, you guys didn't pull out and instead agreed to extend the contract for . . . what? Has it been . . . six more months?"

"Just about," Nicholas said, jumping into the conversation. He looked at Unique. "Because you've been down there now for what? Nine months or so?" he asked.

Unique nodded. "Just about."

"I can't imagine living in an extended-stay hotel and being in a city with no one to hang out with for that long." He shook his head.

"Well, uh, you get used to it," Unique said, losing eye contact, shoveling food into her mouth and then swallowing hard. She washed her food down with continuous gulps of lemonade. It appeared as though she was purposely trying to keep her mouth full. But all eyes were still on her as everyone waited to hear more, forcing her to continue. "But, uh, yeah, you know how before I ever temporarily relocated to West Virginia, I went down there those couple of weekends and interviewed staff?"

"Uh-huh," Lorain said.

"I still work with that original staff," Unique said. "Everyone worked out fine. My assistant, Patsy, knows the ropes. She can easily manage things without me when I come back to Malvonia. Tamarra will probably bump Patsy up to my position and hire Patsy as an assistant."

"When?" Lorain said.

"I'm not sure. We'd have to set up interviews, of course, Unique said.

"But you said *when* you come back to Malvonia, not *if*," Lorain said, trying not to sound so anxious. "So it's a sure thing?"

"Um, pretty much, I think." Unique nodded.

"Thank you, Jesus," Eleanor said, lifting holy hands.

"Wow, I didn't know you missed me so much," Unique said to her grandmother.

"Things have been weird with your mama since you left," Eleanor said. Then she put her hand to her mouth and whispered, "Although she won't admit it."

"I've been fine," Lorain said, begging to differ.

"You're worshipping Satan right about now with that lying tongue," Eleanor scolded. She turned and looked at Unique. "You know, for a minute there, you and Lorain was tight like two greased-up pigtails in hair ballies. The ones that gave you Chinese eyes when you was little. You know what I'm talking about."

Unique laughed. "Yes, Gran, I know what you're talking about."

"Well, a little after you left town, and after Dr. McHottie here started his own practice, your mama got to hanging around with all these bourgeois doctors' wives and stuff. Now she act all funny and stuff." Eleanor shook her hand. "At least with you back in town, things can go back to normal. She'll have you to hang with, and she won't have to use those mannequins to fill the void."

"Mom, "I'm not using those women," Lorain insisted. "They are my friends. I enjoy our monthly get-togethers."

"Monthly get-togethers? Is that what y'all call it?" Eleanor sucked her teeth. "It's more like a bunch of men standing around the urinal and dropping they drawers to see who got the biggest d—"

"Dessert!" Nicholas shouted to interrupt Eleanor. "Would you girls like dessert now?" Nicholas asked the twins, figuring he best get the little ones out of the room before Eleanor got started.

"Yay! Yes!" the twins yelled in unison.

"The rice pudding is in the oven, settling," Eleanor told her son-in-law.

Nicholas rose from the table. "Come on, girls. Let's go get some of Gran's rice pudding."

The girls jumped up from the table.

"Oh, you sit down and finish your food, Nick," Unique said. "I'll take them." She stood.

"Oh, no. He's finished," Lorain quickly interrupted. "He can take them."

Nick stood over his plate, which still had several bites on it. He definitely wouldn't mind finishing off his meal. He looked down at his plate and then at his wife. He then repeated the act, hoping Lorain would get the hint.

"Let sissy Nique get it," Heaven said. "She gives us the most bigger scoops than you, Daddy."

"*Bigger* scoops," Victoria said, correcting her sister. "She gives us bigger scoops. You can even say she gives us the biggest scoops, but 'most bigger' is not how you say it."

Heaven heeded her sister's advice. "Sissy Nique gives us the biggest scoops. Can she do it, please?" She put her hands together in a begging manner, and Victoria followed suit.

A smile spread across Unique's lips as she watched the girls interact. Victoria reminded her of her oldest boy, who had always corrected his younger siblings' vocabulary. Even though Victoria was technically the youngest twin, born three minutes after Heaven, she was wise beyond her years, like Unique's older son had been. Victoria was so mature and quiet, while Heaven could talk someone's head off if given the chance. But both were nice, respectful, well-mannered little ladies. Typically, they spoke only when spoken to . . . which was totally the opposite of the women in their family tree.

"You heard Heaven," Nicholas said, sitting back down. "Sissy Nique gives the most bigger scoops, so I'll let her do it."

"Here. I'll come help." Lorain went to get up.

Nicholas signaled her to remain sitting. "I'm sure with Unique being a caterer and all—and cooking and eating all the time—she knows how to scoop up rice pudding all by herself."

"Come on, girls." Unique took the girls by the hand and led them into the kitchen.

"Humph, guess he told you," Eleanor said under her breath before eating a bite of corn bread.

Lorain slowly sat back down. Nicholas had gone back to finishing his meal, so he didn't see the evil eye his wife was giving him. The three finished their meals in silence.

"Ma, that was delicious," Nicholas said to Eleanor and then wiped his mouth with his napkin. "Now, if you ladies will excuse me, I think I'm going to go head into the kitchen and grab me a little bit of dessert myself." He stood and went to join Unique and the girls in the kitchen.

Lorain wiped her mouth with her napkin. Feeling a set of eyes burning a hole through her, she looked up. "What?" she said to Eleanor, who was staring her down.

"I didn't see you 'bout ready to do a somersault over the table to go fix your husband's dessert, and he's the main one whose plate you ought to be fixing."

"Well, I—"

"Remember," Eleanor said in a warning tone, pointing at her eyes with her index finger and middle finger and then at Lorain's, "plastic . . . I can see right through it."

Chapter 6

"I'm glad I talked you into staying in town for the night," Eleanor said to Unique as the younger woman helped her load the dishwasher.

"Yeah, you had a point when I tried to put up a fight," Unique said, placing a glass on the top rack in the dishwasher.

"Well, you had said it yourself. That assistant knows the ropes and can run things on a permanent basis, so surely, she can run things for one day, tomorrow, while you spend some time with your family tonight." Eleanor handed Unique the last dish to place in the dishwasher. While Unique repositioned a few dishes, Eleanor began to wipe down the black-and-white granite countertops. They complemented the kitchen appliances, which were stainless steel with black trimming.

"Where do you guys keep the broom?" Unique asked, looking around the kitchen.

"Right over thataway." Eleanor nodded in the direction of the closet pantry, where they kept canned goods and cleaning supplies.

Unique went into the closet and grabbed the broom and dustpan. She began to sweep the white tiled floor. The flooring brightened up the entire kitchen, which was otherwise decorated with dark colors.

"Child, I can get that," Eleanor told her. "You done drove all morning, handled business all afternoon, sat up with us and clowned all evening, and you have to get right back on the road in the morning."

"That's okay, Gran. I got it," Unique assured her.

"Uh-huh." Eleanor took the broom from her. "You go on and sit down. I got this."

Unique sat down at the square white wooden table in the kitchen. It seated six. This was where the Wrights usually enjoyed dinner together when it was just them . . . no guests. Eleanor proceeded to sweep.

"Next time your mama wanna keep up with the Joneses and buy a great big ole house like this," Eleanor said, "she better think twice about how much work is going to have to go into keeping it clean."

"I said I'd do it, Gran." Unique rose up from her seat.

"No, no. You sit on back down," Eleanor told her. "I'm just doing my regular fussing."

Unique smiled. She fondled the fresh flower arrangement that stood in the vase in the center of the table.

"So, how do you feel about coming back to Malvonia?" Eleanor asked her.

Unique stared off into the distance for a moment. "You know, I really don't know," she admitted. "After the boys' . . ." She couldn't even bring her lips to say the word *death*. Visions of her three boys down on the backseat floor of that car on that hot summer day had haunted her since the moment she learned of their fate.

Unique had planned on leaving the boys in the car for only a couple minutes. She had wanted to go to the dope house out of which her oldest son's father slung drugs to try to get some child-support money from him. He had been avoiding her calls and had not been returning her text messages.

Initially, she left the windows of the car cracked, but when some young thug came over, trying to sell her drugs, and then got belligerent when she didn't want to cop any, she didn't want him to have access to her car with her babies in it. She was well aware that she

was practically in a drug-infested war zone, and so she
didn't want to take the boys to the dope house, either.
She had a tough decision to make.

"Y'all stay here. I'm not going to be but a second," she
told her boys.

It was nothing but the worst luck in the world when
Unique went into that drug house moments before it
was raided by the police.

Unique remembered hearing the shouts. "Police!"
She'd looked over her shoulder to see a swarm of men
dressed in black, with caps and masks and bullet shields,
storming the place. Since she was right there in front
of the door, she received the wrath of what felt like a
human tidal wave. The rushing bodies pushed her to
the floor, and her head slammed on the edge of a table
on the way down. That was pretty much all that Unique
remembered before she found herself sitting in an interrogation room, being questioned by police officers,
accused of dealing drugs. She was dazed, confused, and
completely overwhelmed after being questioned for
hours, partly due to the hard blow she'd taken to her
head. By the time she remembered where her children
were, which was in the backseat of the car, with the windows rolled up, on the hottest day of the year, it was too
late. The boys were found dead.

Initially, Unique was charged with their deaths,
and even forbidden to attend their funeral. But once
all the facts came out, she was cleared of all charges.
Even though the state hadn't found her negligent in the
death of her sons, that didn't mean guilt didn't haunt
her. So when Tamarra gave Unique the opportunity to
go to West Virginia, she hopped on it. Malvonia had too
many memories, too many reminders of her boys that
she couldn't seem to escape. It didn't matter how many
years had gone by; she couldn't let it go. She prayed that
a little bit of time away would help.

Truth be told, Unique was happy when the contract at the nursing home got extended. When she moved away, she felt like she was able to breathe for the first time in years. It gave her time to try to come to terms with things without any interference. She had been thrust into this new life as a single woman and was no longer a single mother. But now Tamarra needed her, and she was faced with the inevitable, returning to Malvonia. She had no idea if she was strong enough yet to face her demons that dwelled in this city.

"I know it's hard for you," Eleanor said to her granddaughter, placing the broom up against the counter and going to sit down next to Unique. "But you'll get through it. I know the past few years have been stranger than fiction for you, something out of a bestselling novel, but it's real. As real as it gets. You can do that 'fake it until you make it' stuff all you want . . . you and your mama both. But I'm telling you, the weight of it all is going to come crashing down in the worst way if you don't deal with it. You know?"

"Yes, Gran, I know." Unique sighed, looking down at the black- and white-checkered place mat that sat in front of her. She agreed with her grandmother, but it was easier said than done. And unless a person had lost not one child, not two children, but three on the same day, he or she could never know what she was dealing with. And she didn't want to deal with it. "Mom should have the girls bathed and stuff by now. I want to go make sure I kiss them good night before she tucks them in for bed."

"Oh, you're a tad bit late," Lorain said, entering the kitchen. "I read them a book, and they were out like a light bulb before I even got halfway through it." Lorain felt immediate guilt from the little white lie she'd just told. Of course, in her book, every lie was a mere white one, instead of a bright, spicy red one.

"Awww." Unique was disappointed.

"Don't worry," Eleanor told her. "You can help me get them on the bus in the morning. I'm sure they'd like that." Eleanor looked at Lorain. "Don't you think?"

"Uh, yes, of course. I'm sure they'd love to have their big sister put them on the bus," Lorain said. It wasn't clear whether it was subconscious or a conscious choice on the part of Lorain to remind Unique of her place in the girls' lives.

"Okay, fine, then," Unique said, not bothered at all by Lorain's reference to her as the girls' sister. That was the role she'd been playing for all their lives. "I guess I'll head to my place and make sure I stop by in the morning on my way back to West Virginia." She looked at Eleanor. "What time do you put the girls on the bus?"

"Nine-fifteen." Eleanor announced.

"Perfect. That should get me back to West Virginia right on time for lunch service," Unique said, clearly still concerned about not putting in a full day's work.

"You sure you don't want to stay the night here, in the guest room? Your mom has got it set up all nice. Got it wallpapered with these navy blue and silver squiggly designs. She got rid of the full-size bed and replaced it with a queen," Eleanor offered. "I got a guest room at my place too. It only has a full-size bed, but it's comfortable as all get-out. Or you can sleep with me in my big ole bed. We can have a slumber party."

"Oh, no. I have been in these clothes all day." Unique looked down at her black skinny jeans and red sequined top. "Plus, it will be nice to sleep in my own bed."

"You sure you don't want to stay?" Lorain asked, absolutely certain of what Unique's answer would be.

"No, but thank you so much," Unique replied. She then stood up. "I'm going to head on out."

"Let us walk you out," Lorain said, leading the way to the foyer.

Unique stopped off in the great room and grabbed her purse and then met up with Lorain and Eleanor by the front door.

"Thanks again for dinner, Gran," Unique said, kissing Eleanor on the cheek.

"Anything for Grandma's baby." Eleanor hugged Unique.

"So good seeing you, Mom," Unique said to Lorain, hugging her.

Eleanor watched observantly as the two women embraced.

Lorain released Unique and then went and opened the door. "See you in the morning."

"Okay. Have a good night." Unique exited the house, and Lorain closed the door behind her.

Lorain briskly turned around, intent on heading to the shower and then to bed, then abruptly stopped in her tracks. Eleanor was standing in her path with her hands on her hips.

"It's a shame when mother and daughter embrace and it's as awkward as the wife having tea with the mistress," Eleanor said.

"Oh, for Pete's sake, what are you rambling on about now?" Lorain said.

"You mean to tell me you didn't see that? Feel that? The two of you act like you don't even know how to be around each other anymore. It's like you both are walking on eggshells. I don't know who created that distance between you two, but somebody needs to tell me what's really going on. It's like you both got something on the tip of your tongue and it's stuck there. Do I need to knock somebody upside the back of they head until it comes flying out?"

Lorain listened to her mother and then exhaled. She breathed for what felt like the first time since she'd turned around that evening and caught sight of Unique sitting at the kitchen table with the twins. Lorain opened her mouth, but no words came out. She wanted to talk. She'd been wanting to talk . . . to her mother . . . to anybody. But instead she'd kept it all bottled up. Well, her mother was continuously shaking up that bottle, and now Lorain was doing all she could not to pop the cap on her emotions and have them explode everywhere. But all the strength she thought she possessed—all the strength she'd used to keep all her emotions in the closet by pressing both hands against the closet door—had vanished. The door had flung open, and now here she went, crashing to the floor.

"Oh, Mommy." Tears spilled out of Lorain's eyes like milk in a full glass turned upside down on purpose. She ran into Eleanor's arms and cried over the spilled milk.

"Baby girl, what in the world?"

Eleanor was caught off guard by her daughter's sudden emotional outburst. She hadn't seen her so torn up since the boys' funeral. Since then, Lorain had done an excellent job of walking around with her head held high and a smile on her face, like nothing could bring her down. Even though Eleanor had sensed that it was all a front and that one day Lorain would break, she hadn't expected it to happen at this moment, and so abruptly. But the one thing she had always known, though, was that she would be there for her daughter whenever the dam did break.

"Mommy's here." Eleanor wrapped her arms around her daughter and allowed her to weep.

Lorain sniffled. She would have been drunk from the tears on her tongue if the salt from the liquid was an intoxicant. She cried a nice size dam.

"There, there now," Eleanor said, patting her on the back. "Let's go sit down and tell Mommy all about it." Eleanor had to practically peel Lorain's arms from around her. Lorain was holding on to her like a prayer she refused to let go of until God answered it.

"Come on now, baby." Eleanor coaxed Lorain over to the couch, and the two sat down. "Let me get you a tissue." Eleanor reached over to the end table and grabbed a tissue from the Kleenex box that was encased in a crystal holder. "Here you go." She handed the tissue to Lorain, and Lorain blew into it like an elephant. "Lord Jesus. I knew you were full of it, but—"

"Mom, really? You can't show a little empathy even now?" Lorain huffed.

"Oh, baby, I'm sorry." Eleanor pulled Lorain into her arms. "Go on. Get it all out. Whatever it is on your mind . . . and all that snot too."

"Forget it." Lorain went to get up, but Eleanor pulled her back down.

"Okay, okay, I'm sorry. I'm all ears."

"I need you to be more than all ears right now," Lorain told her mother. "I need you to be all heart. Because after I finish telling you all that has been heavy on my own heart, I'm going to need for you to still have love in your heart for me."

"Let me tell you something, baby," Eleanor said sternly. "I don't give a dern what you do, think, or say. You are my baby girl. I'm going to be here for you always. Right or wrong, I've got your back."

Lorain knew that to be true, so despite the shame she felt, she went on to tell her mother about her selfishness when it came to keeping Unique from the twins, dating all the way back to the aftermath of the boys' death. Lorain shared how back when both she and Unique were still attending New Day Temple of Faith, she would go

out of her way to avoid Unique when she was with the
girls. She feared that Unique would share a moment
with the twins and something in her would be triggered,
that her connection with the girls would make her want
to raise them herself, to be a Mommy again.

Lorain didn't want Unique to feel as though she
needed to replace her lost boys with the girls. Every day
Lorain repented for this, but the next day she would
wake up thinking about it and go to bed thinking about
how to keep Unique from bonding with Victoria and
Heaven. As manipulative as she thought Korica was,
deep down inside, Lorain figured that she wasn't any
better. That was something she'd have to live with, and
she justified it by her love for the twins.

It pained Lorain to share with her mother that she
was relieved the day Unique moved to West Virginia. It
had given her some breathing space and time to breathe,
period. She had always felt she was waiting with bated
breath for Unique to decide to tell the girls the truth
about who their biological mother was. Even though
Unique's move to West Virginia wasn't permanent, it
put both a physical and a mental distance between
Unique and the girls. Yes, it meant there was a distance
between mother and daughter, as well, but it was a sacrifice Lorain was willing to make.

"I felt like I was throwing Unique away all over again,"
Lorain confessed to Eleanor. "I'm the devil."

"Oh, girl, hush on up with that nonsense. I'm already
at the pity party, and you don't have to entice me to stay
by pulling out the top-shelf liquor."

"But even today you saw me. I couldn't get Unique
out of here soon enough. The girls begged me to read
them another book—I usually give in to their pleas for
more—but I knew Unique would want to tell them good
night, so I cut the reading short. I couldn't risk having

her tuck her kids into bed, a moment a mother relishes. I couldn't." Lorain shook her head and began to weep again. "I'm going to hell." Lorain waited for Eleanor to say something positive and encouraging, to disagree with her and tell her she would spend eternal life in heaven with all the rest of the saints.

Eleanor sat there with her lips poked out, twiddling her thumbs and scanning the room as if she was looking for something.

"Really, Ma?" Lorain spat. "Did you not hear what I said? I said I'm going to hell."

Eleanor remained in the same position.

"I knew it. You think I'm going to hell too. You hate me."

"Stop it. I don't hate you. You hate yourself. Well, at least you hate the way you've acted," Eleanor said. "It was wrong. It was bad. I'd feel awful, too, if the shoe was on the other foot. A mother is supposed to—"

Lorain couldn't sit there any longer and listen to her mother tell her what a bad person she was. "I shouldn't have said anything. You said right or wrong, you would still have my back," Lorain said and then stood up. "You're beating me up like I've been beating myself up all these years."

Eleanor rose and stood next to her. "And I do have your back, right or wrong. But if you're wrong, it's my job to help you get it right."

"By beating me up with your words?"

"I spotted a good switch out back the other day, when I was walking up to the house. I'm old school, so you know I'd rather use that to beat your behind with, anyway. But I'm getting old, and you're getting bigger by the bite, so I ain't got time for that. My words is all I got left to beat you with. But like a good mama, I'ma beat ya, and then I'm going to tend to the wounds. Now come on here." Eleanor took Lorain in her arms again. "I love you, and we're going to get through this. We're going to make things right between the women in this family."

"Thank you, Mom," Lorain said, truly believing it was possible. She released her mother and then straightened herself out. "Let me get myself on upstairs. I have to face the music tomorrow. Aka Unique."

Chapter 7

Lorain watched out her bedroom window as Unique and Eleanor put the twins on the bus. Lorain's mornings usually consisted of getting up, then heading to the kitchen to get Nicholas's and the girls' breakfast cooked. While they ate, she packed their lunches. After they finished eating, she would see Nicholas off to work, then make sure the twins washed up, brushed their teeth, and got dressed. Next, she would do their hair: one ponytail for Heaven and two pigtails for Victoria. This was a request the girls' teachers had made in order to tell the identical twins apart. After that Eleanor always took over, getting the girls safely on the bus, which stopped at the foot of their driveway to pick them up. By then Lorain was usually getting her own self dressed and prepared for the day. But today she hadn't even started to get herself together and stood in her robe and watched a scene fit for a movie on the ABC Family network.

While they'd waited for the bus, Unique had managed to play patty-cake with the girls, pick them up and swing them around, and make a fuss over their lunch, which was healthier than it was delicious. Whatever Unique had said had put a smile on the girls' faces. Heaven and Victoria had squeezed her tightly, eyes closed, before climbing on the bus. Now, as the bus drove off, Lorain watched them wave at Unique through the bus window, the biggest smiles she'd ever seen on their little faces.

She closed the curtain and went and sat down on the bed. She replayed times spent with the girls over and over in her head. Had she ever seen them smile that big at her? How had Unique gotten them excited about fat free cheese sandwiches on wheat bread, with Wheat Thins and cucumber slices as a snack, along with flavored vitamin water for their drink? They'd frowned and complained just an hour ago, as they watched Lorain pack their lunches.

"Becka's mom gives her Lunchables that got Oreo cookies in 'em," Heaven had fussed.

"That *have* Oreo cookies in them," Victoria had said, correcting her.

"Well, I'm not Becka's mom," had been Lorain's comeback.

What had Unique said to the girls about their lunches that made them smile after she sealed their lunch bags back up tightly? That was when it hit Lorain. Unique had probably told them what a mother, a real mother, would say to her children. After all, that was who Unique was: their real mother. Lorain shook that thought right out of her head and went into the bathroom to shower.

She pulled the frosted-glass shower door open, reached her hand inside the roomy stone shower stall, and then turned on the shower spigot. While the water warmed, she walked over to the his-and-her double sinks and rubbed Noxzema on her face. "*I* am their real mother," she said to herself as she looked in the mirror, which took up the entire wall where the sinks were stationed and went all the way up to the ceiling. "*I'm* the one raising them. *I'm* the one taking care of them every day, making sure they are clothed and well fed." The more she talked, the harder she rubbed in the skin cleanser. "It doesn't matter that I didn't go nine months with them in my womb. It takes more than that to be a mother. . . ." Lorain's words trailed off, because for a moment there, she couldn't decide whether or not she was talking or replaying words Korica had said to her.

A twinge of guilt flowed through Lorain. She rinsed her hands, disrobed, and got into the shower. She did a quick wash-up, got out of the shower, dried off, and unwrapped her hair. Less than fifteen minutes later, she was dressed and fingering her hair out while heading downstairs. Eleanor and Unique were waiting in the living room so that Unique could say her good-byes.

"Ah, there you are," Eleanor said when she saw Lorain coming down the staircase. "I was about to call for you."

"I know. It took me a minute. Sorry," Lorain said, apologizing. "Did the girls get off to school okay?" she asked, knowing darn well they had, because she'd witnessed them doing so.

"They sure did," Eleanor said excitedly. "Unique here even made the girls feel like that manna and honey water you packed them was like pizza and Coke."

Eleanor and Unique laughed. Lorain remained straight-faced.

"Is that so?" Lorain managed to force a smile. "Well, I have to keep them nice and healthy. Can't weigh them down with a bunch of junk. Besides, they have a dance competition this weekend."

"Awww, I'd love to see them perform," Unique said.

"Well, hopefully, when you move back," Eleanor said, "you can see them perform all the time."

"Their competitions are on Saturdays," Lorain said, jumping in. "You know that's typically when Unique has her biggest gigs . . . parties, weddings, and all."

Eleanor shot Lorain a look that said, "You're doing it again."

Getting the hint, Lorain took Unique by the arm. "Come sit down. Let's talk." Lorain guided Unique toward the living room.

"Well, yeah, for just a minute, though. Mommy is waiting on me. I promised her I would meet her for a quick breakfast on my way out of town."

"Oh." Lorain paused. Inside, she was feeling jealous, disappointed, and cheated, cheated out of the time she'd pumped herself up to spend with Unique before she got back on the road. Time in which she was going to express to Unique how she'd been feeling since taking in the girls.

Opening up to her mother last night had taken a load off of Lorain. She had thought about it all night and knew that she needed to have the same conversation with Unique. She needed to apologize to her firstborn, repent, and start fresh. She'd planned on doing so today, but with all that needed to be said, she knew that if Unique had to run off to meet with Korica, there wouldn't be sufficient time. She didn't want Unique to make an exit after hearing only half of what she had to say. She didn't want her to come to any conclusions or judge her based on partial information. This was serious, and Unique deserved to be able to process it all at once, and not in bits and pieces.

In addition to that, there was no telling how Unique was going to feel after hearing what Lorain had to say. The last thing she wanted her to do was run off into the arms of the woman who had raised her. Lorain was well aware of the powerful bond the two shared. All it would take was for Korica to get into Unique's ear at a vulnerable time, and Lorain could lose Unique forever. Lord knows, Korica would love nothing more than for that to happen.

"Just give me Unique. You can have the twins," Korica had pleaded with Lorain years ago. Those very words were part of what had motivated Lorain to put a distance between herself and Unique. That Korica was the devil, as far as Lorain was concerned, and there was no telling how she'd use her evil devices to make good on her underlying threat disguised as a plead.

Lorain was torn, though, because she didn't want just Unique and she didn't want just the girls. She wanted them all. She wanted to be Unique's only mother. She wanted to be Heaven and Victoria's only mother. But Korica had made her feel as if she had to choose. And now, if Lorain didn't play her cards right, she could end up being nobody's mother. Eventually, Lorain would have to sacrifice something. There was no such thing as having it all, anyway. If that were the case, then what would be left for the rest of the world? Lorain couldn't have her cake and eat it too. She'd settle for a slice . . . as long as it was the biggest.

She shook off her same old selfish thoughts, which were creeping back. She had to get it right this time. Unfortunately, the right time was not now.

"Okay, well, maybe the next time you're in town, we can have lunch or something," Lorain told Unique. "Just me and you." Lorain looked down.

"Is everything okay, Mom?"

Lorain looked up at Unique. *Mom.* Lorain was Mom. Korica was called Mommy, the more endearing term.

"No, it's not," Eleanor answered on Lorain's behalf. She took both Unique and Lorain by the elbow. "You two need to talk. Sit yourselves on down somewhere and have a long talk. I believe that Lorain wanted to have a talk with you today, before you left town." Eleanor looked at Lorain for confirmation.

"Uh, yes. But you go on and meet with your . . . with Korica," Lorain said. "We'll talk another time, when you're not rushed."

"Are you sure?" Unique asked with concern. "I can cancel breakfast."

"Oh, no, no." The last thing Lorain wanted was for Unique to set off the woman she called Mommy by telling her she was canceling breakfast with her to spend time with her mom. Lorain was not trying to give Korica any reason to retaliate. It wasn't as if she feared the woman. She feared her own actions as a result of dealing with Korica.

"Are you fine? Are the girls fine?" Unique asked Lorain, worry now etched on her face.

"Well, heck, I'm the one getting up there in years," Eleanor said. "Ain't you wondering if I'm fine?"

"Oh, Gran." Unique smiled and laid her head against Eleanor. "I know you're fine. Your feisty self is going to outlive us all."

"Oh, no. Y'all ain't dying first on me. Black folks ain't never got no insurance, and I ain't pawning my good jewelry to bury nobody!"

Unique laughed, while Lorain shook her head, cracking a smile.

"Anyway," Lorain said, pulling Unique away from trouble, "please let me know ahead of time when you come back to town. Everybody is fine. I just want to share some things with you that have been heavy on my spirit, is all."

"All right. Well, the next time I come back, it might be for good, so we can take all the time you'd like for our talk," Unique said. "But let me get to going. I'll talk to you guys later."

Unique gave each woman a kiss. They said their good-byes, and then Unique left.

"Well, you can't say I didn't try," Lorain told Eleanor after closing the front door.

"I know, baby," Eleanor said as she and Lorain stood next to the fountain in the foyer. "But you and that child needs to talk and talk fast. 'Cause you ain't the only one acting phony. That girl is hiding something too, and we ain't never going to get to the bottom of it unless you two quit treating plastic like it's a fashion statement." She put her hands on her hips and struck a model's pose. "Plastic, it's the new black."

"Oh, Mother, stop it," Lorain said.

"All right. I'm done messing with you for the day. I'm gonna head back over to my place and whip me up something to eat."

"You can eat here. I've got some leftovers from this morning's breakfast."

Eleanor huffed. "Child, please. Hay is for horses. And in your case, I really mean that." Eleanor moseyed on into the kitchen so that she could exit through the side door and head straight over to her own dwelling. "I'll see you this afternoon, after I get the girls off the bus," she called from the kitchen.

"All right, Ma. I love you," Lorain said and then headed to her home office.

Lorain sat down at her DMI Rue de Lyon Right Executive L Desk, which was crafted from maple solids and other select hardwoods. It wasn't handmade, nor had it been shipped in from Italy. But she had got free delivery from Staples. She opened her desk calendar to make sure she didn't have anything scheduled that she had forgotten about. After confirming that she didn't, she logged on to her computer to check her e-mails. That was where the latest gossip from the wives would be. There was always far too much drama taking place to text it all.

Lorain clicked on a couple of e-mails, but she couldn't really focus. She found herself wondering what Unique and Korica were talking about. After the last couple of conversations Lorain had had with Korica, there was no telling. Lorain remembered one comment in particular.

"Will you listen?" Korica had said in an almost normal tone, which was unusual for her loud and obnoxious self. "Look, you've already got the twins. You're attached to them. They know you as their mommy. Leave me Unique. She's mine. She's been mine. I don't care if she is a grown woman. She's mine. So I'll tell you what. You fade out, and I'll help Unique get over her loss of the boys, you know, so she won't try to fill the empty void with something like, you know, wanting Heaven and Victoria back."

It had been clear to Lorain at the time that Korica was issuing a veiled threat. At the time, though, Lorain didn't let on that she felt threatened by her. She simply walked away and left Korica standing there, looking and feeling stupid for even daring to threaten her. However, all the while Korica's words had penetrated Lorain like a bee's stinger.

"All right," Korica had yelled at Lorain's back. "Have it your way, but the day you're packing up Heaven and Victoria's things and handing them over to Unique, don't say I didn't warn you."

For the rest of the day Lorain couldn't help but wonder if Korica ever planned to make good on her threat.

Chapter 8

"Oh, my baby!" Korica said as soon as she saw Unique walk into Captain Souls Restaurant.

Even though it was a run-down, truck stop–looking hole-in-the-wall, it had character. Not only that, but it had great food. A person with an OCD issue might not be able to break bread there, but Captain Souls was Unique's favorite place for some good old-fashioned soul-food cooking. Like Eleanor's old-school soul-food meals, the food at Captain Souls hit the spot for Unique. All morning Unique had had her mouth set on some fried catfish and cheese grits for breakfast.

"Mommy, it's so good to see you. I've missed you," Unique said, embracing the woman she called Mommy, the woman who had raised her after her foster parents abandoned her.

Korica had been the couple's next-door neighbor. She'd initially taken Unique in as part of a scam she and the couple were running on the system. But then the couple ran off to start a new life. They didn't want their new life to include Unique, but they also didn't want to give up the monthly check the county provided them for being foster parents to Unique. That was where Korica came in. Korica agreed to care for the child in their absence for a fifty-fifty cut of the monthly stipend. Korica had to do a lot of finagling in order not to get busted, but everything seemed to work out in her favor.

Unique's caseworkers seemed to change every other
month. Given all the shifting of paperwork and files
and the different computer systems, poor little Unique
fell through the cracks. The system basically forgot all
about her existence and stopped doing home visits and
sending checks. By then Korica and her children had
already taken to Unique and considered her part of the
family. Her birth mama had dumped her. Her foster
parents had dumped her. The system had dumped her.
Korica refused to add her name to the list of dumpers.
So she kept the child. She'd been struggling to take care
of her blood children. What was one more added to the
brood? And that bond that Korica had formed with
young Unique was sacred, and she wasn't going to let
anyone come between them, not even Lorain, the birth
mother, who had the nerve to pop up years later.

Korica and Unique broke their embrace and took a
seat in a red wooden booth with a view of the parking lot. Korica struck up a conversation as they flipped
through the menu, waiting for their waitress to come
take their order.

"So tell me more about you moving back here to your
place soon," Korica said. Her long acrylic nails with gold
glitter nail polish tapped the menu while she looked it
over. Her clear fair skin glistened with excitement.

"Yeah, Tamarra needs me back here to kind of take
over things," Unique said.

"She can't be running you back and forth like she's a
puppet master." Korica flipped her straight, thirty-two-
inch Raggedy Ann–red weave over her shoulder.

"She's not running me. Trust me, Tamarra is awesome. I'm so grateful that after letting me go when I
was pregnant with the twins and was going through all
that drama, she let me start working with her again after I got out of jail." Unique spoke without taking her

eyes away from the menu. Although she pretty much knew exactly what she wanted, she skimmed the menu, anyway, to see if something else grabbed her attention. "Tamarra went to the doctor, and I guess, in short, he told her she needs to slow down. She was talking about retiring from the business altogether and turning over the reins to me." Unique wagged her hand. "But she's only talking smack, I'm sure. She's invested so much time and money into building her catering business. As soon as she gets to feeling like her normal self, she'll go right back to being the control freak that she is."

"So how long are we talking before you move back?" Korica asked, closing her menu. Her mind was set on a six-ounce sirloin, medium rare and smothered in onions, with some scrambled cheese eggs on the side and a country biscuit.

"Two weeks." Unique closed her menu. She was going to stick with what her mouth had been watering for.

Korica clapped. "Yay. You can come back home, get settled, and maybe even, you know, start getting the girls."

There was an awkward moment of silence before Unique shot her mother a look.

"What?" Korica shrugged. "You know that ole stuck-up wench won't let me see my grandbabies. I gotta go through you to get to them."

"Mommy, please." Unique exhaled. "We've been through this already. The girls are not your grandbabies. They are my sisters through my biological mother. So technically—"

Korica pointed and wagged an acrylic finger as close to Unique's face as she could from across the table. "I wish you would." She glared at Unique. "I done told you once and I done told you a thousand times, you and that woman can do whatever y'all want to do . . . file whatever paperwork y'all want to, but those are my grandbabies. Period!" Korica crossed her arms, and her bottom lip began to tremble.

"Mommy, I know this is hard for you, but it's been five years."

"And in five more years, if I don't get to have a relationship with my grandbabies, we still gon' be having this same conversation."

"That's why I can't trust having them around you," Unique said.

"Come again." Korica was visibly appalled. Her long, fake eyelashes capped with mascara fluttered like butterflies. They dang near beat the sky-blue and silver eye shadow off her eyelids. Why wouldn't she allow Unique to teach her how to apply her makeup properly, without overdoing it? Less was more, even when it came to beating a face.

"I can't risk you saying the wrong thing to the girls. Mentally, they aren't ready to deal with all that right now."

"Uh-huh. Then we can table the conversation for now. But like I said, we still gon' end up having this same discussion."

"Well, I'm not," Unique said, trying to be as empathetic as possible. "Lorain and Nick are Heaven and Victoria's parents. That is never, ever going to change. Yeah, maybe one day, when the girls are older, we'll explain everything to them, but for now . . . for the next five years . . . the way I see it, things aren't going to change."

Korica leaned in and, almost with a hint of venom, said, "You carried those babies in your womb. You are their birth mother, their biological mother. You are my daughter, which makes them my grandbabies. And that, Miss Thang, is what's not ever going to change." Korica leaned back hard in her seat.

"I understand, Mommy. I know how hard this is for you."

"You'd think it would be hard for you, considering." Korica rolled her eyes.

"Considering what?" Unique couldn't help but ask. "On second thought, don't answer that. I want to enjoy breakfast with my mommy, and I see that this convo is about to go left of center and crash, resulting in fatalities."

Korica folded her arms and turned her face from Unique.

Unique smiled and play kicked Korica under the table. "Come on. You know you missed me. You know you love me. Go ahead and say it. I'm your favorite. Don't worry. I won't tell the others." Unique play kicked her again.

Korica tried hard not to crack a smile, but to no avail. "Ooh, I can't stand you, girl. So dang stubborn."

"I take after you, so I got it honest."

Korica looked into Unique's eyes. "Yeah, you did, didn't you?"

"Absolutely. Now, where the heck is that waitress? I've been dreaming about Captain Souls."

Korica and Unique looked around and made eye contact with the waitress, who got the hint and hurried over and took their orders. The two women spent the next hour eating and catching up. Korica bit her tongue and didn't bring up the twins again. She had hoped that Unique would cooperate so that she didn't have to resort to other tactics in order to get what she wanted. But now it looked like she didn't have a choice.

Immediately after finishing breakfast with Korica, Unique hit the road, driving straight to West Virginia without stopping. It took her only about three hours to get there. After eating that soul-food breakfast, she had had the itis and had wanted to go back to her place in Malvonia and go to bed. But she'd caught a second wind upon getting behind the wheel and turning on her Mary Mary CD. But it was Tamar Braxton's *Love and War* CD that had taken her into the homestretch.

Once upon a time, a person wouldn't have found anything but Tupac, Jay-Z, DMX, or Biggie blaring from Unique's speakers. In her Christianity walk, she'd weaned herself from that genre of music. It wasn't because she felt hip-hop or rap music was the devil's music with coded messages. She'd simply outgrown it. When she was living in the world, clubbing it and whatnot, what the artists were singing about was pretty much the life she was living, or the one she dreamed of living if she could snag the right baller or be a side chick or whatever. But she wasn't that person anymore. And on top of that, she was far more mature now. At some point a person had to be too old to have songs about nothing but bling, alcohol, and sex bouncing around in their head. Yeah, some of the R & B Unique listened to was a little on the ratchet side . . . but she believed in baby steps.

Speaking of baby steps, Unique felt like a toddler as she walked up the path to the nursing home's back door, which led to the kitchen and served as the delivery entrance. Her legs were tired and a little numb from being in the same position for almost three hours straight. One leg even felt like it was about to go to sleep. Unique could have easily waited it out in the car or walked it off in the parking lot, but being the workaholic that she was, five minutes was five minutes too many to waste. So she wobbled on into the kitchen of the nursing home.

"Hey, Miss Unique," one of the dishwashers greeted as Unique entered the kitchen. His hands were busy scrubbing a pot.

"How you doing, Charlie?" Unique replied with a wave.

"I can't complain. Well, I can, but I won't. When you work at a place like this, you learn better."

"I heard that," Unique agreed.

There were people in this place who weren't entirely in their right mind. There were others who were but who couldn't even go to the bathroom without help. Some couldn't communicate in any manner or walk. So if they weren't complaining, nobody else had a right to.

"Is Patsy around?" Unique asked, scanning the kitchen for her assistant.

"I think she's doing rounds, talking to the patients to make sure everyone is satisfied."

A proud smile came across Unique's face. Talking to the residents was something Unique made sure she did after every meal served, if time permitted. At first Unique had thought she was there just to help prepare and serve the food and then check in with a patient here and there to make sure the food was to their liking. This particular job had turned out to be far more than just a gig. She had had no idea that spiritual food would end up on the menu as well. It was really a ministry in disguise, as Unique took extra minutes to listen to the patients, pray with them, and sometimes read with them. And not only from the Bible. Unique was surprised at how many of those older folks loved them some Zane and P. R. Hawkins novels.

Unique had never been big on reading prior to coming to West Virginia. But this job had certainly turned her on to reading. Black Expressions Book Club now automatically sent her books every month. Nice hardbacks, which she found herself cuddling up with at night. She wasn't a techie and didn't know a whole lot about those eBook thingamajigs, but she could cuddle up in bed with a good hardback any night of the week, especially since she didn't have anything else that was hard lying next to her in bed, not that she didn't desire a nice, hard body next to her every now and then. But after that one-night stand with her oldest son's father, she'd vowed not to give her body to anybody who wasn't her husband.

Not only that, but sex had been the last thing on Unique's mind of late. Sex had led to her giving birth to five kids by three different men, and not one of them had made an honest woman out of her. But then the Lord had spoken to her and had let her know that she could sit around all she wanted, waiting for some man to make an honest woman out of her, but that true self-respect came when a woman made an honest woman out of herself. For Unique, when it came to her legs, there was no spreadin' without a weddin'.

Unique had rarely been in the company of only herself before moving to West Virginia. She was living at home when she became a teenage mother. After that, she always had her kids in tow and always seemed to end up living with someone. Even after the boys passed away and she got her own place, she was there alone only when it was time for bed. She kept herself busy with helping Tamarra with catering jobs. On top of that, she worked as a Mary Kay consultant and spent a good deal of time either hosting parties, doing facials, or teaching skin-care classes at her house, other people's houses, and churches, you name it. Even now in West Virginia, it seemed like she was alone only when it was bedtime. She was constantly with patients and had even managed to build a nice little Mary Kay clientele.

Come to think of it, even at bedtime she wasn't alone, as she usually prayed, talked to God, and listened to Him until she fell off to sleep. Lately, though, she'd found herself thinking about maybe, just maybe, starting over . . . doing things right. Allowing a man to earn her womanhood and then starting a family. A real family that started with wedding vows. Having those thoughts didn't concern Unique. It was the person to whom her spirit was drawing her, the person with whom she perhaps would begin this new life, that had her apprehensive.

Chapter 9

"I feel like I'm in the Emerald City," Lorain said as she sat in the parlor of Tabby's house.

The average person would call it a sitting room, but Tabby looked at her home more like a manor, estate, or plantation. Considering that she had a full-time staff of mainly African Americans, some might refer to her place as a plantation. But, not to get it twisted, she was not running any type of underground slavery. The folks who worked for Tabby and her husband did not work for free. They were getting paid . . . and paid well.

"What good is a blessing that causes overflow if you don't share it?" Tabby had once asked the wives.

Tabby and her husband shared so much, it was rumored that her husband was doing more than treating patients, that he had his own little business on the side, one that might involve some illegal prescription writing. It was simply a rumor. No one had ever had any concrete proof, nothing more than some she said, he said. If the whole illegal prescription thing wasn't true, Tabby's husband's patients sure were paying him well, because the couple was always giving to this charity or that charity. And certainly a little wedding planning on the side here and there wasn't bringing in the big bucks. Tabby had once claimed that a man whose life her husband had saved had left him over five million dollars in his will when he died.

The wives couldn't believe it the time the couple purchased a new car for every single person on their staff, right down to the landscapers, who were the only employees who weren't of African American decent. And not one of the landscapers in this three-man outfit spoke a word of clear English. They were Mexicans who had fled their country, had struggled to become legal U.S. citizens, and then had started their own landscaping company. Tabby and her husband wrote each vehicle off as a gift, a work expense, or something of that nature.

Tabby was, indeed, the queen of bragging and boasting. Although Tabby had an air of superiority about her, as if she felt she was better than all the other women, it was undeniable that she was a giver from the heart, or at least it appeared that way.

"Since it's March, I wanted to go with the whole St. Patrick's Day green theme," Tabby said to Lorain. "But I wanted to avoid the whole leprechaun and shamrock leitmotif everyone would be expecting. So I went with the whole *Wizard of Oz*–Emerald City theme." Tabby's eye's widened with glee as she looked proudly around the room.

The green bulbs she'd placed in all the crystal lamps with dangling crystal teardrops gave the room such a fairy-tale feel. She had placed mirrors about the room, and the green lighting reflected in them made the women feel as if they were actually in another world. Given all the time and money Tabby had put into the decorations, it was obvious that her desire was to make the women green with envy.

"Oh, you did a great job with your Emerald City–*Wizard of Oz* thing, all right," Carrie said as she walked by, popping a green grape in her mouth that she'd gotten from the fresh fruit platter.

The platter had only green fruits on it, such as green grapes, kiwi slices, green apple and pear slices, lime slices, and honeydew melon chunks, and a green yogurt dip adorned the center. It sat opposite the vegetable platter, which featured broccoli florets, celery stalks, cucumber slices, snap peas, and green bell pepper slices, with a dill dip in the center. Between the two platters was a huge bowl of a signature green alcoholic beverage. Tabby hadn't yet shared the recipe, but it was evident that the drink contained mint leaves, as they were floating atop the liquid and really enhanced the flavor.

Carrie stopped suddenly, turned, and faced Tabby. "You even have the wicked witch and all," she said and then kept it moving.

Tabby looked up. "Lord, I repent."

"For what?" Lorain asked, confused.

"For just praying that she chokes on that grape."

A couple of the other wives who were in earshot giggled.

Lorain shook her head. She probably would have laughed herself if she hadn't actually choked on a grape herself before. It was nothing nice.

"I heard that," Carrie said as she sat down on the white couch, which, due to the lighting, looked light mint green.

"You were supposed to," Tabby said in a singsong voice as she walked through the archway leading into the dining room. She observed the table as her staff brought the hot food out. Then she called out to the wives. "Ladies, I think we are about set now. You guys can come on in here, and we can chow down."

The women had been nibbling on rabbit food for about an hour, so they practically charged into the dining room like bulls.

"Wow. Everything looks delectable," Mary said.

"I concur," added Lorain as she admired the spread.

"What are those?" Angel pointed to a platter with little, round, crispy things on it.

"Green cherry tomatoes, fried," Tabby said.

"Oh, bite-size fried green tomatoes. How cute." Lorain scooted into one of the high-back, wrought-iron chair.

There was also a platter with bite-size spinach quiche.

"That green-bean casserole looks yummy," Carrie said, licking her lips. "What's that meat in it?"

"Ground chuck. It's my mother-in-law's recipe." Tabby looked so proud.

"Yours and Big Mama's on Twenty-Fifth, over in the Linden area," Carrie said. She was referencing the neighborhood mother that almost every kid in the hood had grown up with. Most of them were nicknamed either Big Mama or Mama Dukes.

"What?" Tabby had a huge question mark on her face.

"I'm sure it's delicious," Isabella interrupted.

Also on the table was sushi wrapped in seaweed, along with some other items. The meal was random and not really cohesive at all, but it was obviously tasty, because the women dived in. A half hour later the servers brought out some hot green tea.

"By the way, Tabby . . . ," Lorain began. "Did you and the family end up flying out for your niece's wedding a couple weeks ago?"

Tabby, who had popped her last bite of sushi in her mouth, mumbled, "Absolutely not." She shook her head to reiterate. Once she had swallowed her food, she wiped her mouth and said, "She was marrying another woman, for Pete's sake. I can't even believe my sister-in-law had the nerve to get invitations drawn up and to spend money on such a sinful affair. I should have known something was funny about that girl when they started calling her Sam, instead of her given name, Samantha." She harrumphed. "My poor brother-in-law and sister-sister-in-law spent so much time thinking that it was her son who was gay, God rest his soul, that they didn't even notice that it was her daughter who was going to live in eternal hell."

"Oh, stop it, Tabby," Isabella said. "You are being so harsh. No one here has a heaven or a hell to place anyone in."

"I'm so disappointed in my husband's brother and his wife. We moved to Ohio only because they were here. My husband and I weren't raised in the church or anything like that, but we did find Christ eventually. And with my sister-in-law calling herself a Christian, I can't believe she not only supported the idea but also paid for practically the entire family to go on that cruise to attend that . . . that . . . Oh, I can't even fix my lips to say it." Tabby took a sip of her tea, hoping it would calm her nerves.

"Wait a minute," Carrie said, pointing her finger at Tabby. There was something about her tone that suggested craziness might fall from her lips next. "How you gon' say you wouldn't go to your gay niece's wedding when just last month you were bragging about the extravagant baby shower you threw for your unwed daughter who is pregnant by her cousin's husband?" Carrie said to Tabby.

As Tabby practically choked on her tea, she made a mental note to be careful what she prayed for. A little while ago she'd prayed that Carrie would choke on a grape, and here she was, barely able to catch her breath.

Isabella, who was sitting next to Tabby, stood and patted her back. "Are you okay?"

Tabby coughed a few times before replying. "Yes, I'm fine."

"Well, good," Carrie said, starting back in. "Now that you are fine, you can answer my question."

With flushed cheeks, Tabby replied, "My niece's and my daughter's situations . . . well, they're different."

"Oh, so you can support a ho but not a homo. Makes perfect sense to me," Carrie said, throwing her hands in the air.

"Now, you wait one dang on second." Tabby jumped out of her seat. "Are you calling my daughter a ho?" Isabella grabbed hold of Tabby's arms as Tabby took a step toward Carrie.

"Oh, I see. Since there is a green theme going on up in this piece, homegirl wanna get froggy. Homegirl wanna jump. Oh, okay." Carrie had this smug grin on her face. She kept right on eating her food, as if she wasn't even fazed by the host.

"What?" Tabby said, scrunching her face in puzzlement. "Will you speak proper English for once so that someone besides hoodlums and thugs will know what the heck you are saying?"

"Hoodlum? Thug? You're the one jumping all bad, yet calling somebody else a hoodlum and a thug?" Now Carrie stood, which caused Lorain to stand as well, because she knew Isabella might be able to handle Tabby, but gaining control of Carrie would be out of the question for her. Lorain knew Carrie's kind. She was Unique before she got saved . . . well, and a couple years after that too.

"That's only because you called my daughter a . . . a . . . a garden tool," Tabby countered.

The room went dead silent, and everyone looked at Tabby.

"It's a shame you're too snooty to even say 'ho.'" Carrie shook her head and wagged her hand at Tabby. "Child, I ain't fooling with you. I ain't got time to be catching no case." She looked Tabby up and down. "And you are not worth a second strike."

Now all eyes shot directly to Carrie.

"Don't judge me," Carrie said, then sat back down and finished off a quiche.

"Oh, no, you don't, missy," Tabby said. She was so angry, she was shaking. "How dare you talk about my family and then think you're going to sit down and eat my food without even apologizing!"

"Oh, girl, I'm sorry," Carrie said with a stuffed mouth. "You're daughter ain't no more of a ho than Lorain's daughter, with her three baby daddies."

Nothing but gasps filled the room.

There was a long moment of silence while Lorain let Carrie's words sink in. "What did you say?" Lorain glared at Carrie. Had she really heard what she thought she had?

"What?" Carrie looked at a couple of the women, dumbfounded. Her eyes landed on Tabby. "Was this supposed to be a secret or something? Tabby, you're the one who told me she had all them kids with different fathers," Carrie said, as if she should be held innocent. "You said you Googled an article or something about an incident . . . jail or something."

Tabby turned her head in embarrassment and began to scratch her scalp, which wasn't itching.

"Tabby," Mary said, shocked.

Everyone was staring at Tabby like she was the Antichrist.

After feeling a sense of uneasiness for a moment too long, Tabby finally spoke. "Oh, please. Don't act like you all weren't two- and three-waying each other on the phone to spread the news when I found out. All it took was me confiding in one person before the whole bunch of you found out."

Lorain was speechless, a tornado of emotions running through her. How much information about her did these women have? Had they been smiling in her face yet pointing fingers and judging her behind her back? Exactly which articles about her and her family had they found on the Internet? Nobody's business and information were safe anymore with today's technology.

Lorain had told the wives that her oldest daughter had lost her three sons in a freak accident, but she'd never given the details and they'd never picked her for any. She definitely hadn't told them about Unique giving birth to the twins and her adopting them.

Here all this time Lorain had thought these women were too busy with their own lives to concern themselves with hers, or at best, they were respecting her privacy, waiting for her to talk when she felt like opening up to them . . . which probably would have been never. She'd come to find out that these nosy broads had taken it upon themselves to go dig up all they could on her and then gossip to one another about it.

She had no words for these women, whom she'd called her like-minded friends. On second thought, she had words for them, but they were words she didn't even think God would forgive her for spewing. So instead of even trying to speak, Lorain grabbed her short-strapped red designer handbag, which matched her crisscross-strapped red pumps, and headed for the door.

"Lorain, I'm so sorry," Tabby said, following behind her. "I didn't mean any harm. The ladies and I just—"

Lorain turned around sharply, stopping Tabby in her tracks. She shot Tabby the look of death, silently warning her that it was in her best interest not to say another word to her. When Tabby didn't move and didn't speak, Lorain knew she'd gotten the message. She turned back around and allowed her heels to click on the hardwood floor as she walked to the front door. She let herself out, slamming the door so hard that all the chandeliers played a soft melody.

Tabby gathered her composure and walked back into the dining room. The tension was so thick, it would be a challenge for a samurai's sword to slice through it. She looked at each woman to see if anyone had anything to say, considering they'd all had a part in the Nancy Drew detective work gone wrong.

"Well, do any of you have anything to say for your-selves, considering you threw me under the bus and let it roll right on over me without lifting a finger to save me?"

The women looked from one to the other before Isabella grabbed a platter on the table and said, "Fried green tomatoes, anyone?"

When everyone simply shot her the evil eye, Isabella popped one in her mouth. She was careful to chew at least thirty-two times, like "they" said you should. Because she was almost certain one of these women was praying she'd choke on that little tomato.

Chapter 10

Unique was busy unpacking her suitcases. She was finally back in Malvonia, Ohio, for good. She really didn't know how to feel about it, either. Since she hadn't been 100 percent gung ho about packing up and going to West Virginia ten months ago, she had had no idea it would be this hard to leave the state behind. She loved her job at the nursing home there, as well as the people she worked with on the staff and, definitely, the patients. Then there was that unexpected person whom she had never dreamed she'd miss. As a matter of fact, the first time she met this person she wanted to do bodily harm to him.

"Lord, you surely work in mysterious ways," Unique said as she hung in her bedroom closet the three church dresses she'd taken to West Virginia and alternated wearing whenever she could make it to a Sunday service there.

Now that she was back in her home, sweet home, she couldn't wait to get back to her home church, New Day Temple of Faith. She'd missed the congregation, her pastor, and despite all its shenanigans, she had missed the singles' ministry too.

"Singles' ministry," she said under her breath, pulling a pair of slacks out of the suitcase that lay on her bed. She flopped down on the bed, and the slacks landed on her lap. Did she even want to get back into the singles' ministry? Who knew? In the past few years it had shut down, then started back up again, and it had changed leadership so much, it might not even be a functioning ministry anymore.

Sure, Unique knew that when Mother Doreen initially received the vision from God to form the ministry and reported that vision to Pastor Margie, who ultimately approved the ministry's creation, its purpose was to support single members of the church. But most of the women who joined the ministry didn't want support in being single. They wanted help in finding a man. Unique felt that it was pretty safe to say that she no longer needed help in finding a man.

She removed her hands from atop the slacks and began to fondle the diamond heart necklace she wore around her neck. A smile crept across her face as she thought back to the moment she received the gift. It had been in a little box, tucked down inside a vase of red roses that sat in the middle of the table at which they dined. Their table for two was on the patio of a nice little quaint restaurant they'd driven forty-five minutes to get to. It was their fifth official date.

They had talked on the phone, had had lunch together, and had watched a couple movies together with some of the patients in the activity room at the nursing home. Had Unique's suitor not had been several years older than her and had they attended high school together, they probably would have been voted the most unlikely couple. True, the moment they met, fireworks went off, but not in a good way. Having two hotheads in one room was bound to cause an explosion. But once they both put their guard down and managed to tame their sharp tongue, they began to connect like Legos, which was exactly what Unique called the two of them.

"I don't want to be that far away from you," Unique had said after telling her newfound love she'd be heading back to Malvonia for good. "We're like Legos, you and I. We may snap, but we snap together. We were made to be together. As corny and as cliché as that sounds, it's true. At least it feels that way to me."

"I feel the same way." His charming smile and his hand brushing against Unique's cheek had made her melt. "Legos are meant to be together. After all, how much fun can you have with just one Lego?"

She smiled, grateful that he had the sensitivity and the understanding to grasp the comparison she was making. "Yeah, I mean at first, when we met, we snapped at each other . But then we started to build something beautiful, like one does with Legos. But . . ." Unique put her head down. "But when you're playing with Legos and you build something so tall and beautiful, it eventually falls down, and it seems like that's what is happening to us."

"Malvonia is only three hours away, Unique. Some people live on opposite coasts and have relationships over the Internet. We can make this work."

Unique sighed. "I've changed in recent years . . . a lot."

And, boy, oh boy, was that the truth. Being in jail, losing the boys, giving up custody of her daughters— these were grown-up situations that had forced Unique to mature and act like she had good sense. This whole change that had taken place within her was ironic to Unique. Seemed like all that bad stuff would have made her angrier, bitter, and over the top, but instead it had calmed her, had made her pay attention to and appreciate life. She figured that was what had made it so easy to give her love interest a chance. She'd changed. After all, over three years had passed between their first meeting and their second. She wasn't that same feisty ball of fire she'd been back then, and she based her decision to give love a shot strictly on that fact. It was possible they both had changed. Besides, she felt it would be nice to do a little dating while in West Virginia, especially with no busybody church hens or two mothers there to have to spill the tea to.

That was the reason why Unique hadn't mentioned her relationship to anyone back at home. She didn't want input from anybody but God. In the past she had tried doing things her own way and had failed miserably each time. Yes, God had been there to catch her when she fell, but she had vowed that the next time He picked her up, she would allow Him to carry her wherever He wanted her to be. Taking her own route had led her only to a dead end, to this feeling that she had to start the journey of life all over again. Maybe she did. She would look at that as a good thing.

God had taken her to West Virginia. At first her flesh had been hesitant, but her soul had said yes. That chapter in her life had, in fact, turned out to be a good thing. Was God now asking her to let that good thing go? Was this romance supposed to be temporary bliss, since her stay in West Virginia hadn't been permanent to begin with? When the nursing home contract was extended, Unique knew it was God's way of keeping them together. Could they still have the same type of bond if they were three hours away from one another? Would distance make their hearts grow much fonder?

It had been a pleasant surprise, indeed, for Unique, finding love. The fact that the two of them, of all people, had formed a relationship was the biggest surprise of all. No one would believe it, which was another reason why Unique never mentioned it to anyone—that and the fact that she really didn't know how serious things would ultimately get between the two of them.

But now, with all this distance between them, when all was said and done, would she even have a man, or would she become a lifetime member of the New Day Temple of Faith Singles' Ministry?

***

"Thanks for coming over, Mommy, but I told you I didn't need any help," Unique said after closing the door behind Korica. "It's not like I'm relocating from West Virginia to here. I lived in an extended-stay hotel there, and all I had was my clothes. I did not need three men and a truck to help me move a boatload of boxes to West Virginia, and therefore, I don't need you to help me unpack any."

"Sheesh. Well, shoot me and cook me up for Sunday supper," Korica said with her fists on her hips. "Can't a mother just want to come by and see her child who's been living in another state for months?"

Unique put her hand on her head. "I'm sorry, Mommy," she said, apologizing. "It's been such a long day. Driving here, putting all my clothes away. Saying good-bye to Patsy and all my staff, saying good-bye to all the patients, and saying good-bye to—" Unique caught herself before she uttered that name. Now was definitely not the time to mention the relationship she'd been having in West Virginia.

"Oh, baby. I understand." Korica walked Unique over to her black leather sofa in the modest two-bedroom, twelve-hundred-square-foot apartment. They sat down, and she put her arm around Unique. "I know it was much more than a job you were doing back at the nursing home. It was part of your calling. But what's that you Christian folks are always saying about the world being big enough for stuff like that."

"God making room for our gifts and talents?" Unique said.

"Yeah, that mess." Korica waved her hand as if she was shooing a fly, which was basically what church talk was to her, anyway. Something that just bugged the crap out of her. She felt as if there was some book that people received immediately after joining a church that listed all the church sayings. In order to go to heaven people had to memorize at least half of them.

"It's not a mess, Mommy. It's scripture," Unique said, exasperated. "But I know what you're trying to say, and I believe God's Word, so I'm sure He'll find something just as fulfilling for me here in Malvonia." Unique prayed that this was true in more ways than one.

Chapter 11

"I can't believe you're making me go to this party alone," Nicholas said as he looked at himself in the mirror while straightening his bow tie.

"And I can't believe you're going at all," Lorain retorted, pouting and crossing her arms as she sat on the edge of the bed and watched Nicholas get dressed.

"But it's a black-tie affair. You love those," Nicholas said, trying to reason with her.

"Yeah, but if I'm within two feet of Tabby, it might turn into a black-eye affair."

"Listen . . ." Nicholas sounded exasperated. "Lance and Tabby invited us to this event long before you and Tabby had your little falling-out."

"Little falling-out." Lorain stood up in a huff. "That woman is spreading lies about your family, and you think it's nothing. You wanna go over there and break bread with her?"

"What lies? If she got information from the Internet, then it must be the truth. You and I both know everything on the Internet is true." Nicholas cracked a smile at Lorain through the mirror.

"Nicholas Leon Wright, I'm being serious. This is no time for jokes. Your family's reputation is at stake here."

"Look, honey." Nicholas walked over to Lorain and placed his hands on her shoulders. "I'm a man, and I don't get in the middle of what goes on with you wives. Lance agrees. I'm sorry. Men aren't built that way."

"Peter is," Lorain huffed. "Peter says he doesn't care why his wife doesn't like somebody. If she don't like them, then he doesn't, either. Now, that's what I call a man supporting his wife."

"And that's what I call a man who just wants to get some from his wife." Nicholas laughed at his comment.

"And he laughs, still thinking this is a joke." Lorain raised her arms and then allowed them to flop back down at her sides. She sat back down on the bed.

"Honey, lighten up, would you? Come on. What you are saying sounds like the antics of a high school clique of teenage girls." Nicholas sat down next to his wife. "Who is this Peter, anyway?"

"He's Cynthia's husband."

Nicholas was puzzled. "Cynthia?" He thought for a moment, saying the name over and over in his head, trying to recall where they knew a Cynthia from.

"Yeah, from *Real Housewives of Atlanta*."

Nicholas stared at Lorain momentarily to see if she was being serious. Her stone face indicated that she was dead serious. Nicholas shook it off, then stood. "Us doctors are an elite circle here. Women are women, and we can't—we won't—let what goes on with you guys interfere with the support and bonds we have with one another. It's not that we are betraying our wives or siding with the enemy. I wish you could understand." Nicholas walked back over to the mirror to give himself a final once-over before he headed out to the party.

One of the doctors at the medical group that Lance and Tom had partnered with had received recognition from the Ohio Medical Board for outstanding service to the medical community. Lance was throwing tonight's shindig in celebration of this accomplishment. Nicholas was right; Lorain loved a black-tie affair, as well as any other opportunity to be the trophy on Nicholas's arm.

But she had vowed not to step foot on Tabby's *plantation* ever again.

"I wish you could understand what it means to put me first and support me."

Lorain's words made Nicholas stop what he was doing momentarily. Then he straightened his tie one last time and turned to walk out of the room. "Sweetheart, you have no idea how I've put you first, how I've supported you in everything you've wanted to do. Just like when it came to our *wedding*." He shot her a knowing look.

Lorain was taken aback. Nicholas seemed to turn icy for a few seconds, and then, suddenly, the chill was gone and he was his usual warm self again.

He walked over and kissed her on the forehead, then headed for the bedroom door. "I'll tell Tabby and Lance that you said hello and that you are sorry you couldn't make it." Nicholas exited the room, closing the door behind him.

Lorain sat on the bed, feeling uneasy. What had just happened with her and Nicholas? Why had he suddenly turned so cold, then gone back to his usual self, like nothing had happened? And why had he mentioned their wedding? It was as if he had some underlying disdain for her.

Lorain stood and began to pace. She had a funny feeling, but she couldn't put her finger on it. Every time Nicholas mentioned anything about their wedding, he always seemed to freeze up, like if he didn't freeze his thoughts, they would boil over and burn her. Lorain couldn't understand why. After all, he was the one who had agreed to elope, skipping the big wedding their parents wanted them to have in a church and opting for a chapel in Las Vegas. She hadn't forced him to. Sure, she'd been pretty aggressive in convincing him that a big church wedding didn't make sense, that marriage was something they should do sooner rather than later, but she hadn't twisted his arm.

The question of whether or not Nicholas resented her for robbing him of the holy matrimony he had envisioned for himself was now gnawing at Lorain. To make matters even worse, Lorain had promised Nicholas that they would have a huge reception after they married, something that she'd allow their mothers to plan, but that, too, had never happened. Lorain had got too caught up in taking care of the twins. Then Nicholas had started his own practice. The time had never seemed right.

Could it really be that Nicholas had been holding this against Lorain for all these years? Maybe so, but something deep within Lorain told her that there was much more to it. But what else could there be?

Lorain went and checked on the girls. She peeked into the white and pink room they shared, each girl with her own full-size bed decorated Hello Kitty style. She made sure they were tucked nicely in bed and sleeping soundly. She then returned to her own bedroom. She lay down on the bed and tried to sleep, but thoughts of Nicholas and the whole wedding business kept her up thinking.

She wasn't quite sure what was broken. Something was, though, and by the time she closed her eyes, she had an idea how to fix it.

"A surprise wedding? Child, you done lost your mind," Eleanor said as she and Lorain sat in the kitchen nook over at Eleanor's place. Eleanor's house wasn't nearly as large as the main house, nor did she have a gourmet kitchen. But her kitchen was big enough for her to burn on that stove. And it was big enough to hold the residue of the bomb Lorain had just dropped. "But you're already married."

"I know that, Mother, but Nick and I never had a real wedding, or the reception I promised him we'd have to make up for not having a real wedding." Lorain was full of excitement as the wheels turned in her head as she contemplated how to make this the best wedding her husband could ever imagine.

"Oh, I get it now. No real wedding and no real reception means you didn't get no real gifts, either," Eleanor mused. "Folks kill me with that. Especially the ones who want a wedding to be all small and intimate but then want to turn around and invite everybody and they mama to their big ole reception so they can rake in all the gifts they signed up for on their registry." Eleanor let out a harrumph. "If I ain't good enough to come to the wedding, then I ain't good enough to come to no reception, bearing gifts, either."

"You know me better than that. It's not about the gifts." Lorain immediately shot down Eleanor's theory. "I can go out and buy whatever I need, that is, if we didn't already have everything we need."

"Be careful with your words. Having everything you want is completely different from having everything you need."

"Well, I feel like I have both. Apparently, though, Nick doesn't have everything he needs, wants, whatever. A wedding ceremony must have meant more to him than he let on."

Eleanor took a sip of her coffee. "But, baby, I don't understand why now. I could see if you guys renewed your vows for, like, your tenth anniversary or something like that. Even had an anniversary party for your fifth. But the whole shebang of a wedding ceremony seems strange, if you ask me."

"Well, I didn't ask you." Lorain said it as respectfully as she could.

"Sure, you did. You asked me to help you plan a wedding for my future son-in-law, who happens to be my current son-in-law." She cut her eyes at Lorain. "Uh-huh. That sounded stupid, didn't it? Go on and admit it."

Lorain began to question why she'd ever decided to include her mother in this. After thinking about the idea all night, Lorain had finished getting herself dressed this morning and, as soon as the twins got on the bus, had headed straight to her mother's place. She'd wanted to call her mother last night, when the idea first entered her mind. But had she woken her mother up out of her sleep, Eleanor might have shot more words than just *stupid* at her. So she had anxiously waited to share with her mother what she thought was a bright idea.

Lorain had thought Eleanor would be as excited as she was, considering Eleanor hadn't been too pleased about being robbed of the opportunity to plan her only child's wedding when Nicholas and Lorain eloped. Perhaps too much time had elapsed and the novelty of it all was gone as far as Eleanor was concerned. So why couldn't Nicholas get over it just as easily? That was one of the reasons why Lorain thought there might be more to Nicholas's comment about their wedding.

"Forget I even asked, Mother," Lorain said, standing to leave.

The white, hard plastic, contemporary bar stool spun slightly after Lorain lifted herself off it. Eleanor had copied the whole black-and-white kitchen theme at the main house. She loved her black- and white-checkered flooring. Her kitchen could substitute as a fifties malt shop. It was just more updated.

"If I can plan a monthly meeting for the wives," Lorain said, "then a wedding can't be that much more difficult.

Besides, I can have Sister Tamarra's company do the catering. Unique will be my maid of honor, of course, so she can't do any cooking. Sister Deborah is married to a *New York Times* bestselling author. I'll have her get him to write an original poem to recite at our wedding, kind of like what Oprah had Pearl Cleage do at that all-women's Legends Ball thing she had. Ooh, and Sister Paige knows she can blow. She definitely has to sing."

"Hold up." Eleanor held up her hand. "Weren't Paige and Tamarra on some basketball wives' type of mess at Mother Doreen's wedding? I heard them two got into it bad right in the church kitchen. I wouldn't have those two nowhere in the same vicinity . . . or at least not near the wedding cake. From what Unique said, I think half the bridesmaids ended up wearing that cake."

Lorain thought for a moment. "Yeah, you're right. Oh, well, I'll think of something." Lorain tapped her foot. "Sister Helen can—"

"Crazy Sister Helen? The one that has to take happy pills? The one I can't even believe you got twitching up in front of your husband from nine to five as his receptionist?"

"Come on, Mom. Everybody has a story. Don't judge her."

"It's hard not to when she stood right there in the middle of the singles' ministry meeting and told all her business. Do you know that girl used to be a stripper?" Eleanor shook her head in disgust.

"No, but I know a couple of first ladies who used to be one, and a prostitute too," Lorain retorted. "Anyway, if I want to get this done in the next four months, I better start making phone calls. I haven't talked to some of the women from New Day in a minute. That's why I thought you could help by reaching out to a couple of them for me."

Although Lorain had chosen to leave New Day, Eleanor had remained a faithful member. She swore up and down that attending New Day was like being part of the cast of a real-life soap opera.

"I guess I can help you out in that area," Eleanor said, giving in. "You calling those women up that you barely keep in touch with wouldn't seem right. But then again, this whole wedding business don't seem right." Eleanor put her hands on her hips. "What's really going on?"

"Nothing. I just want to give my husband something I've never given him before."

"I get that, but does it have to be a wedding that's going to cost an arm and a leg and cause so much work? Wouldn't oral pleasure be cheaper? Now that is something I'm sure you've never given him before that he'd much rather prefer . . . or not given him enough of, anyway. A man can never get enough—"

"Mother, please!" Lorain spat in disgust. "I'm trying to talk to you about my wedding, not my sex life." Lorain stormed off toward the kitchen door that led to the path to the main house. Before opening the door, she stopped in her tracks and turned to face her mother. "But for your information, I take great care of my husband, both in the bed and out. Thank you very much."

"And you are very welcome," Eleanor replied. "'Cause like they say, you get it from your mama." Eleanor began to do this little grinding dance move, gyrating her hips as she rose up off her stool.

"Ugh, there is no talking to you sometimes."

"Then perhaps you should try talking to that husband of yours instead. Talk is cheap, but in this case, that would be a good thing, because it would be cheaper than throwing a wedding that probably isn't even going to resolve whatever it is that's going on over there under your roof, anyway."

"There's nothing going on, Mother. Now, I've got a lot of work to do, and a little bit of time to do it in, if I want to pull this off by July. I wanted you to be a part of this, but obviously, that's not going to happen. But I am having this wedding, with or without you." Lorain walked out the door.

Eleanor stood there, staring at the door, shaking her head and then saying, "Child, it ain't me you need to be a part of this whole shenanigan of a wedding. It's God."

Chapter 12

"I can't thank you first ladies enough for the support you've shown me," Unique said, almost in tears as she packed up her Mary Kay products. She couldn't believe these ten women had ordered almost three thousand dollars' worth of products from her. Not bad at all for the first Mary Kay party she'd hosted since returning to Malvonia two weeks ago. The bar was set high now, and Unique could only go higher.

"Child, it's you we should be thanking," said First Lady Duncan, the president of the Malvonia First Ladies' Club. "It's hard out here for a first lady who is trying to keep a good grip on her earthly Lord with all these hoochies running around, trying to get their claws into him. We gotta do all we can do to keep it together." She began to pat her hair, and the other first ladies giggled.

The first ladies ranged in age from the early thirties to the late seventies. Besides being the wives of pastors, they all had something in common: they all secretly wanted to be the best-looking woman in the church come Sunday morning. Unique was glad to help them look their best with her skin-care and beauty enhancement products. However, Unique didn't really consider these products beauty enhancements; she believed they merely helped draw attention to the women's natural beauty. No enhancements were needed for what God had created.

"I know how exclusive your quarterly get-togethers are, so letting me be a part of it is an honor," Unique said. "Thank you, First Lady Duncan, for allowing me into your home."

"Baby, if we can keep you in that pink Cadillac of yours you're driving, then we'll have you at every meeting." First Lady Duncan laughed. "We gotta support our sisters and their crafts."

Unique turned and looked out the picture window in First Lady Duncan's living room. There were a couple of Cadillacs parked outside, but the pearl-pink one parked at the end of the driveway belonged to Unique. She'd earned it free and clear with her hard work and dedication to the Mary Kay brand. She'd come a long way since selling the products while living in her sister's basement, trying to take care of three children. But she'd never given up. She'd never lost the faith, not even when she was behind bars.

"Well, I sure do appreciate it," Unique said. "And for those of you who ordered products that I didn't have on hand, I'm going to put in the order first thing in the morning. When the products come in, I'll contact you about delivery. And thank you all again."

Unique carried her items out to the car. Once everything was loaded, she climbed behind the wheel and started the ignition, but before pulling off, she sat there for a moment. She ran her hand across the dashboard, admiring the leather interior of her car. Even though she'd had the car for a year now, she swore it still had that new car smell. She inhaled. She could recall leaving a Mary Kay party several years ago and having to lug her totes down the street to the nearest bus stop. She exhaled.

"I am a child of the King," Unique said out loud to all the proverbial naysayers. She smiled, pulled out of the driveway, and headed for home.

It was two o'clock in the afternoon. That gave Unique four hours to get home and rest up before she had to be at the reception hall where she was catering a wedding that evening.

As Unique was about to turn onto her street, her cell phone rang. The caller's name appeared across the digital screen on her dash. Her lips spread into a smile as she pressed the button on her steering wheel that allowed her to answer the call.

"Hello," she said, still smiling.

"Hey, love." The male voice rang through the car speakers. "How was your session?"

"It was a blessing, indeed. Those first ladies ordered up some stuff," Unique revealed.

"That's good to hear."

"How's your mom?"

"She's doing pretty good. I actually just left from having lunch with her. She sends her love."

"Aw, I'm sending mine right back."

After a moment of silence Unique's beau brought up the inevitable topic of discussion. "So, when am I going to get to see you? It's been about two weeks since you left, and it feels more like two years."

Unique exhaled. "I don't know. Between scheduling consultations with my Malvonia customers and catering, baby, I barely get to sleep."

"Then it doesn't sound like you'll make it back to West Virginia any time soon." Disappointment laced his voice.

"I'm afraid not."

Another moment of silence. "But that doesn't mean I can't come to Malvonia to see you. After all, I haven't been there since . . . well, you know . . . the wedding. There's still a couple people I'm sure I need to apologize to while I'm there. My behavior was . . ." His words trailed off.

"Baby, please don't beat yourself up," Unique said as she turned into the parking lot of her apartment complex. "Besides, that was years ago. Everyone has gotten over it and has long moved on. Mother Doreen and her husband forgave you, and those are the only people you need to be worried about. And they aren't even here. They live in Kentucky," Unique said. "Besides, once we all learned the full story, we kind of understood where you were coming from. If it had been my mother, Lord, have mercy, I probably would have done worse. Besides, the wedding ended up taking place, anyway, and now the lovely couple is living happily ever after. All is well, trust me. We talked about you like a dog, ran you into the ground, and were about to sic God on you, but we forgave you." Unique laughed as she pulled in front of her apartment door, then turned the car off.

"And I'm glad you did. Otherwise, you wouldn't have given me the time of day. Now, that is something I'd truly never be able to forgive myself for, losing the woman I love."

Now there was dead silence. If Unique hadn't already turned the car off, she probably would have driven it right into her living room. Had the person she'd fallen head over heels for confessed his love for her?

"You there?" he asked.

There was no response.

"Hello?"

"Oh, yeah, I'm here." Unique regained her composure, but in the forefront of her mind, she wondered if she should respond to the L bomb that had just been dropped. "I just pulled up at my place, and I'm gathering my stuff." She punked out. It didn't feel right to say anything about how she felt after having paused for so long to think about it. The fact that she had to think about whether or not she loved someone back meant that any expression of love on her part would not seem genuine. It wasn't as if she had to think about how she *truly* felt about this person. It was the fact that he had expressed his feelings first that had thrown her off, and nothing more. She prayed that God would give her a second chance to respond. And if Unique knew anything about God, it was that He was definitely a God of second chances.

"There are no second chances here," the twins' dance coach said as all the girls and their mothers stood in the dressing room at the competition site, getting ready for their group performance. All the solo dancers had already performed. "If you don't nail it out there, that's it. The judges don't let you do it twice," she continued. "When you go out there, you are representing me. I'm a winner, which means you have to be winners. Anyone who taints my name, my record, will suffer the consequences."

The way the dance teacher spoke to the kids took some getting used to on Lorain's part. Her manner seemed so dramatic and over the top, but oddly enough, most of the girls seemed to respond positively to it and dance their butts off every time. When Lorain snapped the first time the dance teacher was out of pocket when addressing Victoria and Heaven, another mother had to remove her from the room and calm her down.

"You can't take it personally," the mother had told Lorain. "It's how she is. It's how all these dance teachers are. They're here to make our little angels stars, even if it means giving 'em hell. But it builds character. Makes them tough. You and I both know life is not rainbows and penny candy. Our kids are going to come across some not-so-nice characters in this world. But you know what? They won't be broken. After dealing with this . . ." She'd nodded toward the studio where the kids were rehearsing. "They'll be able to withstand anything."

Lorain had taken the mother's words in, and as much as she'd wanted to snatch her girls out of that dance school, the other mother had made good sense. After all, the girls hadn't flinched once when their teacher fussed at them. It was almost as if they had been told about her antics and couldn't wait to experience them firsthand.

"If she's not fussing at us and calling us out, that's when we should worry," a very mature Victoria had told Lorain after class that day.

Lorain had almost forgotten she'd raised such smart, strong girls. They had a wonderful relationship. If they ever felt some kind of way about the treatment they were receiving, she prayed that they would let her know. So Lorain toughened up and allowed the girls to remain in dance.

"Now, on the count of three," the dance teacher said as she continued preparing the girls for the group competition, which was only moments away, "I want everybody to say what we came here to do. All right?"

The eight girls on the group competition dance team nodded.

"One, two, three."

"We're Malvonia's best. We came here to beat the rest. Broadway Babes Dance Studio number one!" the girls chanted in unison, then screamed, cheered, and clapped.

"Now, let's go." The dance teacher led the way as the mothers checked to see if there were any last-minute costume details that needed to be taken care of and made sure the girls had everything they needed.

After checking the girls in backstage, the adults went and found seats in the audience so that they could watch the girls perform. They watched the current performers onstage and then another group before their girls performed. The eight young girls did a lyrical dance to a song the dance teacher's husband had composed in his studio basement. The dance told the story of a girl who never seemed to fit in with the others.

The audience was enthralled. It was as if an ice-cold draft had come through the door and frozen everyone stiff in their seats. The judges barely took their eyes off the dancers long enough to write down any notes. They, too, didn't want to miss a thing. By the time the girls finished their routine, it was clear they were going to be the highest-scoring group, regardless of how many performed after them. The standing ovation and the minute-long applause they received, not to mention the fact that a judge wiped a tear from her eye, were the dead giveaways.

An hour later, when it was time for the trophies to be awarded, Broadway Babes did a clean sweep, receiving first place in their solos and group performance.

"Congratulations, ladies," was heard all around as the girls entered the dressing room to change back into their street clothes after receiving their awards.

"Thank you," the girls said in unison, hugging their dance teacher first and then their moms.

"Mommy's little angels were perfect," Lorain said to the twins as each one hugged a leg. "I'm so proud of you."

"Thank you," they chorused.

"Yes, you two did quite well," Lorain heard a voice say.

Lorain closed her eyes and took a deep breath. Given that she was beefing with the doctors' wives, dealing with the fact that Unique was back in town, and planning a surprise wedding, the last thing she needed was to have this woman try to get up under her skin. Because in all honesty, right about now, it wouldn't take much to do so.

"Thank you, Ivy," Lorain said. "Gabby did a wonderful job as well."

"With as much money as my boyfriend spends on privates for her, she better." Ivy laughed that irritating laugh of hers. In all actuality, it was a regular-sounding laugh, but to Lorain, because it was Ivy who was laughing, that laugh was irritating.

Lorain simply smiled.

"Mommy, we want to take privates too," Victoria said.

"Yeah, so we can dance as good as Gabby," Heaven agreed.

"As well as," Victoria said, correcting her twin.

"Oh, even the children know star quality when they see it." Ivy bent down to address Heaven and Victoria. "Keep working hard, darlings, and one day you'll earn a solo because of your skills."

The twins frowned. They weren't quite sure what Ivy meant exactly, but they could tell that whatever it was, it wasn't nice, otherwise Jacquelyn wouldn't have quickly jumped in between their mother and Ivy as Lorain was reaching for Ivy's hair.

"Lorain. The bus will be pulling off in a few," Jacquelyn said, out of breath from having to make it halfway across the room at the speed of lightning in order to keep Lorain from doing a Sheree Whitfield when she pulled Kim Zolciak's hair. "Let me help you get the twins back in their street clothes."

"Why, thank you," Lorain said to Jacquelyn as her eyes shot invisible daggers at Ivy. "Street clothes are appropriate, because something tells me I'm going to have to get street."

Ivy walked away with a smug look on her face, leaving Lorain standing there and boiling all by herself. But that didn't mean that eventually, Ivy wouldn't get burned.

Chapter 13

Eugene stepped outside and inhaled deeply. Although the air itself didn't have a smell, this particular breath he had taken in did. It smelled like freedom.

For four years Eugene hadn't breathed the fresh air of freedom. Yeah, he'd had his time in the prison yard, but that wasn't freedom. That was him in a bullring, having to constantly watch his back. A bullring that was surrounded by a barbed-wire fence that would bite at his skin like a school of piranhas if his flesh came into contact with it.

Eugene exhaled and then breathed in one more whiff, closing his eyes as he took it all in. "Ahhh," he said, releasing his breath with a huge smile on his face. He was free and clear. No halfway house, either, because his mother had agreed to allow him to move back home with her, for at least ninety days, anyway. After that, Eugene knew what he had to do; he had to hit them streets again and make that paper. He wasn't about to be thirty-something years old and talking about how he lived in his mama's basement. But for now, he would enjoy the ninety-day vacay. Then he'd connect with his homies to see where he could get that candy to sell to those with a sweet tooth.

Wearing an outfit that resembled army fatigues—pants that hung loosely around his waist, an army jacket, and military-style boots—Eugene looked more like a new recruit who was finishing up basic training in the

National Guard than a newly released felon. Six feet, six inches tall, he could easily be an NBA baller rather than a street baller.

He opened his eyes and began walking out to the parking lot, but then he stopped in his tracks. "Miss Korica?" he said, confused to see her standing there.

"Call me Mom," Korica said. "After all, you are the father of my grandkids." Korica opened her arms wide.

Eugene just stood there, looking at Korica like she was crazy.

"Come on here, boy, and show me some love." She waved him to her with her hands, like she was directing traffic.

Eugene slowly moved toward Korica. He didn't want to hug her, but he didn't want to leave her hanging, either. This woman was one firecracker, and he didn't want to give her any reason to pop off. But at the same time, he was clueless as to why she'd want a hug from him. She'd always hated his guts. The only times she'd ever been nice to him was when she wanted to be hooked up with a bag of weed . . . if she wanted something from him, period.

"Why you standing there, looking crazy? Give me a hug." Korica opened her arms even wider.

With Korica blocking his path to the parking lot, there was only one other direction in which Eugene could go. He looked over his shoulder at the prison gate, which had closed behind him. That was definitely the worst of two evils. So, afraid not to follow her orders and to cause a situation, Eugene slowly walked over to Korica and leaned in. In his mind he was going to get this hug over with and keep it moving.

Korica threw her arms around Eugene and hugged him tightly. He didn't return the gesture. He stood there and allowed her to embrace him like he was her long-lost son. Before she released him, she gave him a wet kiss on the cheek. He wasn't a churchgoing fella. He had read the Bible in prison only because finding Jesus or Allah seemed like something to do to pass the time while locked up. He couldn't recall too many Bible stories, but one that clearly came to mind at this point in time was the kiss of Judas, the one Judas gave Jesus right before he threw Him to the wolves. Eugene could almost hear howling in the distance.

"Now, come on and let's go get you something to eat. I'm parked this way." Korica pulled on Eugene's arm, but his feet stayed planted where they were. "What? What is it, son?"

"Son?" Eugene asked out loud. Anytime she'd ever called him son, she'd called his mother a female dog afterward. Eugene couldn't bite his tongue any longer. He was liable to get in that car with Korica and never be seen alive again. "What gives?" he asked. "You've shot digs at me and you've belittled me since the day Unique brought me to your doorstep and introduced me as her dude. Now, all of a sudden, you're my best friend."

He shook his head. "Uh-uh. I'm not buying it. What do you want from me, Miss Korica? I don't have no money, and I ain't got no weed, so you can stop pretending you like me, you can go on about your business, and you can let me catch the bus home." Eugene attempted to walk around Korica.

"Wait. Hold up." Korica grabbed Eugene by the arms. "Look . . ." Korica took a deep breath and then exhaled, as if she was giving in to something. "I know I've been a witch to you all these years. What mother is going to like the boy who knocks her teenage daughter up?"

Eugene gave her a look, as if to say, "Yeah, keep going." There had to be something more. Certainly, she'd gotten over that after all these years.

"With all that's happened, none of that matters any-more. You're just the father of my grandkids. I want to make things right. I can't change the past, but I can admit and atone for my wrongdoings now and be able to move on with my life. So please forgive me. I know it may not mean much to you, but it would be the world to me." Korica finished her little spiel and then waited on Eugene to reply. She was hopeful he would come around, as with each word she'd spoken, she'd appeared to chip away some of the ice. She could tell by the way his facial muscles relaxed.

Eugene looked her up and down. He even tried to look around her to see if she was concealing any weap-ons. Korica was real good at patting a person on the back with one hand, while preparing to stab them in that very same spot with the other. During the course of his relationship with Unique, Eugene had seen firsthand how Korica manipulated people in so many situations and lied to Unique so many times. Korica had made it almost impossible for him to believe anything she said. But so much time had gone by. They'd each suffered a tremendous loss. Perhaps Korica really did want to move on. After all, that was all he want to do.

Finally, Eugene replied, "I forgive you." He exhaled, as if that had been the hardest thing he'd ever had to do in life. He'd never even forgiven his own mama for how badly she'd treated him while he was coming up, yet he'd forgiven this woman with whom he shared no bloodline. Anything was possible.

Korica's face lit up, and she went to hug Eugene yet a third time.

"Hold up. Not so fast." Eugene held his hands up, blocking Korica from putting her arms around him. "I'll forgive you, but on one condition."

Korica looked puzzled. What could Eugene possibly want from her? "Sure . . . What . . . what is it?" If he wanted her to help him with anything illegal, he was wasting his breath. Not that Korica hadn't done illegal things in her day. But in Korica's opinion, Eugene didn't always play with a full deck, and he sometimes even showed his hand to the other players. She had to be careful with this guy. But unbeknownst to him, she was a little bit at his mercy as well.

"I need you to get your daughter to forgive me." Eugene put his head down in shame. For years he'd harbored guilt and blamed himself for Unique being arrested for drug charges and for the death of all three of her children, one of whom was his child, namely, her oldest son. If it hadn't been for him, Unique wouldn't have been there when the drug house he was working in got raided, and her children certainly wouldn't have been out in that car and left for dead. He didn't know if he'd ever be able to forgive himself. The chaplain in the prison had told him that God had forgiven him. But the one person he was worried about forgiving him now was Unique.

He'd sent letters to Unique's sister's house while he was in jail, begging Unique for her forgiveness, but she had never replied to any of them. He took that as a sign that he wasn't forgiven. She probably blamed him as much as he blamed himself, if not more. If she hadn't tried to hunt him down after he ignored her calls and text messages for weeks, she never would have gotten mixed up in the raid. But he'd dipped and dodged her, knowing she was looking for him to try to get him to throw her some change for child support.

All his son's life he'd given Unique only what he felt he could break her off, and she'd always accepted it without a complaint. "Something was better than nothing" had been her attitude. She'd say that she knew from the jump what type of dude she was dealing with, which was a street pharmacist, so she couldn't complain about him. She'd chosen him as a father by lying down and having unprotected sex with him. Eugene had always taken advantage of Unique's acceptance of him and her passiveness toward him. But that last time around, his selfishness cost him more than money. It cost him the life of his son.

One might think that such a terrible tragedy would have been a turning point in Eugene's life, a reason for him to turn his life around for the better. If not for himself, then for the memory of his son. But now, with his only offspring buried six feet under, he had nothing to live for. Whatever happened to him while he got his hustle on, it happened. He was now a convicted felon, anyway. Copping that six-figure job on Wall Street was no longer an option. All he had was whatever it was the streets had to offer, and that was all he wanted. He knew there were only two ways out the game: death or jail. Well, he'd already done the jail thing, so all that was left was death. But what he needed before he left this earth was his baby mama's forgiveness. Not having it was too heavy a burden to bear. It messed with his mind. He needed to free his mind.

"So do you think you can do that for me? Get your daughter to forgive me?" Eugene asked calmly, though it was clear from his voice that he was pleading.

Korica paused for a minute. She'd always had a great deal of influence over Unique. Eugene was aware of this, as Korica had gotten Unique to forsake him at times and side with her or do what she suggested. Korica had somehow ended up being the closest with Unique, out of all her kids. Perhaps it was because young Unique had clung to Korica like pollen to a bee. The poor child had been thrown away so many times, she'd expected that Korica would ultimately do the same to her. Some nights Korica would wake up to find Unique sitting at the foot of her bed, struggling to stay awake so that she could watch her.

"Girl, what are you doing in here?" Korica would say once she spotted Unique in the middle of the night.

"Waiting for you to try to go away," a sleepy Unique would say, "so I can go with you."

"Child, I ain't going nowhere. Take your tail on back to bed."

Unique would stay planted where she was, as if Korica hadn't said a word.

"Did you hear me? Do you want a whuppin'?"

Unique would nod. "As long as you don't leave me. I don't want no more mommies."

Korica would have to do everything she could think of to keep from breaking down in tears. And every time she'd end up allowing Unique to climb in bed and sleep with her. Unique would hold on to Korica for dear life while they slept, trying with all her might to make sure Korica didn't get away from her. Korica would often wake with little Unique's nail impressions deep in her skin. It hurt to some degree, but not nearly as much as the impression that abandonment had left on the young girl's heart.

It would break Korica's own heart, causing her to overcompensate Unique in love and attention in an attempt to make up for what the girl hadn't received earlier in her life. Korica had an idea of what it felt like not to be wanted, to be thought of as nothing but trash that could be easily thrown out. This forged an unbreakable bond between the two, a bond that couldn't have been stronger had they been related by blood.

Once Unique got older, she realized the sacrifices
Korica had made for her. She'd always felt indebted to
the woman who had once lived next door but then had
taken her in as her own. She'd always obeyed Korica, respected her, and tried to follow everything she said. She
had never wanted to give Korica a reason not to want
her around. While she knew that Unique would change
over the years, Korica hoped that the younger woman's
sense of obligation toward her wouldn't. Korica was almost certain that it hadn't and wouldn't, considering
that she wouldn't be living in the house she lived in now
if it weren't for Unique. Korica would hate to have to
take advantage of Unique's sense of obligation toward
her, but she would if it meant that she'd get what she
wanted.

Korica put aside these thoughts and focused on Eugene. "I can talk to her," she told him.

"Good, because I know she always listens to you," Eugene said. His facial expression was hopeful because
he'd witnessed what he referred to as the "power" Korica
had over Unique. As far as he was concerned, he was as
good as forgiven.

"So come on." Korica grabbed him by the arm, and the
two started walking toward her car.

Eugene stopped. "One more thing," he said to Korica.
"You keep saying I'm the father of your grandkids. For
one, my son is gone, so technically, I'm not anybody's
father anymore. And two, you keep saying grandkids,
with an s. What's that about?"

A wicked grin spread across Korica's face. "I'll tell you
all about it in the car."

Chapter 14

"Surprise!"

"Oh, my God. Honey, what are you doing here?" Unique was surprised, all right.

"I was in the neighborhood and decided to stop in," he replied.

"In the neighborhood? All the way from West Virginia, huh?" Unique said as she stood in her doorway with her fist on her hip, bouncing as she waited for a reply.

"Yep, and I picked these up along the way." He whipped a bouquet of flowers from behind his back and extended it to Unique.

"Get in here, you." Unique pulled him into her apartment and closed the door behind him.

She'd ordered a pizza, so when there was a knock on the door, she'd simply dug for a twenty-dollar bill in her purse, taking so long that she flung the door open in a hurry after grabbing the money. Instead of finding the pizza man, she'd found her man . . . all the way from West Virginia.

Unique shot him a naughty look before stepping up to him, taking the bouquet, and hugging him.

"Mmmm," he said, relishing the comforting arms of the woman he'd fallen in love with over the past few months. "So you are glad that I'm here?"

"Yes, I am," Unique said. "And obviously, you are too." She made googly eyes at him.

"Girl, cut it out." He playfully pushed her away. "You know I'm celibate, so don't try to lure me into a life of sin with them ole sexy eyes of yours." He looked her up and down. "And them sexy legs." He stared at Unique's legs, which were hanging out of the pajama shorts she'd been lounging in.

"Those you can forget about getting in between until we're married."

Dead silence. First came *love,* and now the word *marriage* had been put out there.

The knock on the door couldn't have come a second sooner.

"I'll get it!" Unique said quickly, and a little loudly. She handed the flowers to her beau to hold while she opened the door.

This time it was the pizza man. "Keep the change," Unique told him after taking the pizza and giving him the twenty. "Mmmm. Smells good." Unique rushed into the kitchen, making no eye contact at all. She grabbed a couple plates. "Looks like you're in time."

Unique slapped a couple slices of pizza on each plate and carried them into the living room. She sat down on the tan tweed La-Z-Boy chair, which was across from the navy leather couch, while simultaneously placing the plates on the coffee table. She gobbled a bite, still making no eye contact.

"Sit, sit." She motioned at the couch with a hand. Good thing she used hand signals, because her mouth was so full, he wouldn't have understood a word she was saying if she'd spoken.

The second he sat, she stood, while biting off another huge hunk of pizza. She mumbled something that was unintelligible, then used her hand to lift an invisible glass to her mouth to signify that she was going to fetch something to drink. Once again, had she not demonstrated her intent, he would have had no idea what she was talking about, because her mouth was so full.

Unique went into the small kitchen. The refrigerator, stove, and sink occupied most of the space, leaving room for only a two-seater table with an extension leaf, which she never used. The space was tight enough as it was. But Unique didn't need much space. It was just her. She opened the fridge and pulled out two bottled waters. She made it halfway out of the kitchen before turning back around and exchanging the water for two cans of soda, figuring those would go much better with the pizza than some tasteless water.

"Ahhh, here we go," she said upon returning to her chair in the living room. She placed one soda can on the opposite side of the coffee table and the other in front of her. She opened the can and began to chug down the soda. Then she placed the can back down on the coffee table and wiped the soda that was dripping down the side of her mouth with the back of her hand. "Napkins!"

She stood again, picking up her half-eaten slice of pizza as she did so.

"Please!"

The sound of his loud plea made Unique freeze in her tracks.

"Please." He lowered his tone this time. "Allow me." He stood. He slowly walked toward the kitchen. Once there he stood in the small space and scanned it. This was his first time ever at Unique's place, so he wasn't familiar with where things were.

From Unique's vantage point, she could see him standing there and looking around, confused. "Over by the microwave." She pointed. "There is a roll of paper towels."

His eyes landed on the microwave, which sat in a corner of the counter, and as Unique had stated, there was a roll of paper towels on a wooden holder next to it. He walked over, tore a couple paper towels off the roll, and then returned to the living room. He sat and handed Unique a paper towel, eyeing her the entire time.

"Oh, thank you." Her mouth was still full, but he could understand what she was saying this time.

Unique took the paper towel, wiped her mouth, and then quickly finished off the crust of her first slice of pizza. She hadn't even swallowed the last bite before she was picking up the second slice she'd placed on her plate. Her mouth was wide open, prepared to take a bite, when she felt a pair of eyes staring at her. She looked up over her pizza and locked eyes with him.

"What? What's wrong?" she asked, keeping the pizza near her mouth.

"Oh, nothing," he replied, leaning back with his arms spread-eagle on the couch. "Figured I'd wait for you to stop with your nervous antics, unless you really are that hungry and thirsty. Then we'll talk about the nice, big elephant in the room."

"Elephant? I don't know what you're talking about. There's no elephant."

"You're right. There's two. One's called love, and the other's called marriage, and you've managed to avoid them both. But not to worry. I booked a hotel around the corner." He crossed his leg over his knee and snidely added, "So I've got all night."

Unique looked as though all of a sudden she'd lost her appetite. She laid the slice of pizza back down on the plate.

"Go ahead. Eat up . . . before the elephant gets it."

"Sister Unique, have I told you how glad I am that you are back for good?" Paige said, kissing Unique on the cheek as they stood in the church vestibule.

"Thank you, Sister Paige. I'm glad to be back." She looked Paige up and down. "And you looking good . . . and after having two babies. Girl, you da bomb!"

A huge smile covered Paige's face, causing her dimples to swallow up her cheeks. Then, suddenly, the smile vanished into thin air. "What are you doing here?"

Unique was baffled as to why Paige's attitude had changed and her voice had gotten louder. A second ago she'd been expressing in this tender, loving voice how happy she was that Unique was back. Now she was yelling at her, asking her why she was even there.

"Excuse me?" Unique said, being demure and keeping her cool, because she was genuinely confused about the sudden change in Paige's attitude.

Paige was looking past Unique at the church's entrance. "Not you," Paige said to Unique. "Him." She pointed her index finger at the gentleman who had just entered the church.

Unique turned around and recognized the man Paige was talking about. What was he doing there?

The man spotted Unique and started walking toward her and Paige. He went to open his mouth to say something to Unique, but Paige stepped around and in front of Unique.

"Why are you back here?" Paige asked. "I know the devil goes to church too, but—"

"Paige . . ." Unique tried to calm her sister in Christ, but to no avail.

"Did you think we wouldn't recognize you? Humph! We'll never forget the face of the man who tried to ruin our beloved church mother's wedding," Paige spat. "I thought we got all this settled the last time you were here." Although it had been some years since she'd last seen the man, Paige would never forget his face, not after all the drama he had caused. "We ended things on a pretty decent note, so if I were you, I'd leave it that way and go on back where you came from."

"I'm sorry," he said, looking from Unique to Paige, then back to Unique again. His eyes pleaded with Unique to jump in before Paige pounced on him again. "I uh, came to—"

"To what? Interrupt another wedding?" Paige interrupted him. "Well, there are no weddings going on here today, buddy, so you've wasted a trip."

The last time Paige had seen this man was back when Mother Doreen was about to say "I do." This joker had had the nerve to jump up and talk about how he had reasons why she and her soon-to-be husband shouldn't be married.

"I have a very good reason why no man in his right mind should marry that woman," were the exact words he'd uttered as he pointed at Mother Doreen. It was awful. No one had any idea why this stranger would show up and ruin one of the best days in the life of the church mother of New Day Temple of Faith.

They would all soon find out, though, that he was the son of the mistress of Mother Doreen's husband from years ago. He had actually been conceived as a result of the affair and thus had turned out to be Mother Doreen's deceased husband's son. He had blamed Mother Doreen for his mother's mental state and for the fact that she had had to live for years in a nursing home after the devastation she suffered at Mother Doreen's hands . . . literally.

When Mother Doreen had caught his mother and her husband, Willie, in a hotel room together many years prior, she'd jumped on the woman and beaten her to a bloody pulp. Mother Doreen hadn't realized that the mistress was pregnant until it was too late. The baby died, and Mother Doreen served time in jail. All the while Willie continued the affair. Mother Doreen serving a jail sentence wasn't enough punishment in the opinion of the son whom the mistress would later give birth to, the son of Mother Doreen's first husband, the son who was now standing in front of Paige and Unique. He'd wanted to sentence Mother Doreen to the same life of misery and loneliness that his mother was enduring, therefore destroying her chances of living happily ever after.

He'd caused such an uproar that day in the church that the women wanted to bash him upside his head with their bouquets. Unique, sure enough, practically had to be held back to prevent her from clocking him. Mother Doreen, always the peacemaker, hadn't blamed him for his actions. She'd apologized to him and asked that he take her to his mother in West Virginia so that she could give her, too, a long overdue apology. Reluctantly, he did so, and Mother Doreen was able to get the forgiveness she sought. After seeing the positive effect her encounter with Mother Doreen had had on his mother, he was able to let it go and forgive Mother Doreen as well. He also apologized to Mother Doreen for interrupting her wedding. Mother Doreen forgave him, returned to Malvonia, and proceeded with her wedding . . . all in one day.

As far as Paige was concerned, just because Mother Doreen had forgiven him didn't mean they had to keep company with him.

"No, I'm not here to interrupt another wedding," he said to Paige. He then looked at Unique. "But if I'm lucky, I'll be here having a wedding of my own."

All of a sudden Paige felt as if she was missing something. He and Unique were staring at each other, all starry-eyed. The two looked like long-lost lovers and were acting as if no one else was in the room except the two of them. Finally, Paige began to put two and two together.

"Hold up." She looked at him. "You live in West Virginia, right?"

He nodded, not taking his eyes off of Unique.

Paige turned to Unique. "And you were in West Virginia for some months." She didn't move her head once as her eyes darted back and forth between the two of them. "Wait a minute. Don't tell me that while you were in West Virginia, you two . . ." Now she was talking solely to Unique. "No way." She shook her head.

He cleared his throat. "Go ahead, Unique. Tell her."

Unique put her head down.

"Yeah, go ahead, Unique. Tell me," Paige said to Unique sternly, her hand on her hip and her foot tapping impatiently.

Unique was tired of being judged for the decisions she'd made in her life. It always seemed like someone was looking down on her for the choices she'd made. But she'd made a commitment to herself—one that she was trying to keep—that she would never let what other people thought about her keep her from doing what she thought was right for herself. She looked up at the man she'd fallen in love with. Her eyes lit up as a smile spread across her face. If loving him was wrong, no way did she want to be right.

"Yes," Unique said with confidence, pride, and authority. "Yes, Sister Paige, we did connect while I was in West Virginia. We've been seeing each other and . . ." Unique lost her courage for a moment but then found it. "And last night he proposed to me."

After he was finally able to get Unique to stop stuffing her face with pizza and soda, he'd put his feelings on the table, letting Unique know he wanted to spend the rest of his life with her as her husband. Unique hadn't answered him at the time, because thoughts of what others might think were taunting her.

Paige stood there, listening in awe.

But right now, as Unique considered the way this man had come into the church and declared his love for her once again, she knew she had made up her mind. "And this morning I'm accepting his proposal."

His eyes lit up in surprise. Last night, when she told him she had to think about it, he'd feared she was going to try to come up with the words to let him down gently. Well, obviously, she was done thinking about it. His fears, which had had him tossing and turning all night, nearly regretting having worn his heart on his sleeve, had been in vain.

Unique walked over to him, looked him in the eyes, and said, "About last night . . . about what you asked me. In case you need me to spell it out, the answer is yes. Yes, Terrance Casinoff, I will marry you!"

Chapter 15

Unique and Terrance sat side by side, hand in hand, in church. They were all smiles the entire time. After service the word spread about their engagement, and the couple was congratulated several times before they even exited the church doors. It pleased Unique to know that people seemed to be genuinely happy for her, but even if they weren't, she was still elated by her pending nuptials.

No, she hadn't been dating Terrance for more than six months. She hadn't even bumped into him in West Virginia until she'd been there for over a month. She'd literally bumped into him. She was taking his mother, who was a patient at the facility, her lunch one Saturday afternoon. He was leaving his mother's room after one of his afternoon visits. After opening the door, he remembered something he needed to tell his mother and turned back around to talk with her. After saying what he needed to say, he quickly spun back around and proceeded to walk away, not realizing Unique had walked up behind him. They bumped into each other, and the lunch tray she had in her hands went crashing to the floor.

Unique looked down at the floor where Ms. Casinoff's food lay. "Really?" Unique spat without even looking up. She had been having a bad day. Earlier she'd caught one patient's relatives eating up all his food, so she had waited for them to leave and then had taken the patient another tray of food. Now, for the second time that day, she'd have to fix a patient another tray of food. And the fact that it was that time of the month and she was cramping something awful only magnified things.

"I'm sorry," said the culprit responsible for the lunch tray being on the floor.

"You're sorry, and blind is what you are," Unique said without thinking. She'd been able to exercise self-control until now. She bent down and began picking up the mess. She still wore the plastic gloves all the kitchen workers used to cover their hands when around food. As she placed the food on the tray, it took only a few seconds for her to start feeling guilty for speaking such venom. It was an accident, one that she herself could have easily caused. She had no right to take her crappy day out on this man.

The man bent down to help her. That was kind of him. Even though he was the one responsible for the mess, after the way Unique had just spoken to him, she could understand if he left her there to fend for herself. So now she felt that she was the one who owed an apology.

"I'm sorry," Unique said as she reached for the milk carton. He reached for the milk carton a split second later, so his hand landed atop of hers. "Oh," she said at his touch and then looked up.

The two locked eyes and immediately fireworks went off . . . or more like grenades.

"You!" they both shouted at each other, shooting each other vicious looks.

Unique looked down at his hand, which was still touching hers. He looked down and then immediately snatched his hand off of hers. They both stood up straight like sharp swords, ready to cut one another to pieces.

When Unique first drove down to the facility in West Virginia with Mother Doreen, she knew it only as the place where Terrance's mother was a resident during Mother Doreen's wedding fiasco. Unique didn't go inside with Mother Doreen to visit Terrance's mother, and when she returned later to the facility, she remembered only the outside. She had no idea who Terrance's mother was or if she still resided at the facility.

Brookside Residence was a little bit of everything: a nursing home, an assisted-living facility, a mental health care facility. They didn't discriminate against anyone and tried to meet the needs of all their elderly patients. Since doctors and nurses were available twenty-four hours a day, some would even call it a hospital too. Brookside had really taken care of Ms. Casinoff. It had become like her home. So even when her health improved tremendously over time, compared to how it was when she was initially admitted, with Terrance always traveling out of town as an auditor, both he and his mother were 100 percent in favor of her utilizing their assisted-living facility. The staff was like family, and in the short period of time Unique had worked there, she'd become like family to Ms. Casinoff as well. But when she had that first encounter with Terrance years ago back at New Day, he was far from family. He wasn't even a friend. He was a foe if she'd ever had one.

"I remember you," Terrance said to Unique. "You're that fresh-mouthed ghetto girl from Malvonia."

"And I remember you too," Unique spat back. "You're that tight-tail, wedding-ruining revenge seeker who tried to wreak havoc in Mother Doreen's life."

"What are you even doing here?" he asked Unique, looking her up and down like she belonged in a doghouse somewhere. After all, she did remind him of a feisty puppy.

"What's it look like I'm doing?" Unique replied. "I'm doing what I've been doing for the past month. I'm bringing your mother her food."

"Oh, Lord. Rhoda at the front desk told me they had a new company servicing the kitchen, but I had no idea . . ." His words trailed off, and then a look of horror crossed his face. "My mother is eating *your* cooking? Hopefully, no desserts with powdered sugar on them. I've heard of that little trick."

Was this man really insinuating that Unique would sprinkle some kind of rat poison powder on the desserts instead of powdered sugar? Unique took great offense. "You . . ." She had to catch herself from calling him a name that would make even the devil blush. "You are lucky that I'm saved."

"No, you're lucky, because Jesus is probably the only man who would ever know how to deal with you, anyhow."

"Oh yeah?" Unique said, throwing her hands on her hips. "And what makes you think I don't already have a man?"

"Because your lips are moving. That alone will send any man packing. You're as beautiful as can be, but then you open that mouth, and your beauty is only skin deep, for sure, because your surface is pretty bland."

Although his intention was to insult her, Unique wasn't the least bit insulted. She did not miss the fact that he'd complimented her by calling her beautiful. This was the first time in Unique's life that a man had called her beautiful without trying to get down her pants. This man had said it out of anger. He could have called her the bad B word, but instead he'd chosen the other B word, the one that no woman minded being called—*beautiful.*

Korica had always told Unique that when people were angry, they tended to tell the truth. That meant he must have told the truth. He thought Unique was beautiful. As Terrance stood there, continuing his rant, his comments reflecting his dislike for Unique, she stood there, smiling self-consciously.

"You're not even listening to me," Terrance said. "Figures. With all the talking you do, I'm not surprised you can't force yourself to listen to someone else."

"I was listening," Unique told him. "And I heard everything you said." She was still smiling, and on top of that, she was staring at him, all glossy eyed.

Observing the smile still plastered on Unique's face, Terrance tilted his head from left to right, trying to figure out this woman. "Are you okay?" he asked.

"Yes, yes, I am." Unique snapped out of her daze. "By the way, I don't know if you remember, but I'm beautiful . . . I mean, Unique."

"Beautiful and Unique. Let me guess. Your first name is Beautiful, and your last name is Unique. Middle name is Alize'."

Not even that wiped the smile off of Unique's face. "You know what, Mr. Casinoff? If I wasn't a Christian, I'd tell you what a stuffy, rude, classless wad of snot you are, but since I'm saved, I'll just say, 'Have a blessed day, because I know I will,'" Unique said, meaning every word. After all, this was a milestone for her. She was definitely going to write this down in her journal. *Beautiful.* "Now, if you'll excuse me, I need to finish cleaning the floor, and then I'll go get your mother another tray."

Terrance watched for a moment as Unique cleaned up the mess. As badly as he wanted to leave her there to do it alone, he couldn't. He'd caused it. So he swallowed his pride and bent back down to help her. "You go ahead and get the other tray. I'll clean this up. It's my fault."

Unique stood. "A man who knows how to accept blame, especially when he should . . . I like that."

"Was that supposed to be a compliment?" Terrance asked.

"Take it however you want, but while you figure it out, I'm going to go back and get that other tray." Unique turned to walk away.

Terrance continued cleaning up the mess, but at a very slow pace. Whether he was doing it consciously or subconsciously, it didn't matter. All he knew was that he wanted to still be there when Beautiful Alize' Unique returned.

And now, as they walked side by side out of the church where they'd met and into the church parking lot, Terrance never wanted to leave Unique's side again.

"So where to?" Terrance asked. "I figured we'd grab a bite to eat or something before I head back to West Virginia. I have a flight to catch from the HTS in the morning."

"Well, with all these folks knowing about our pending nuptials, it would be a good idea if I told my family. Grandma Eleanor wasn't in church today, but she has eyes and ears up in New Day. I say we have about twenty minutes before word gets to her. I think it would be nice if they could hear the news from me first."

Terrance raised his arms and allowed them to drop down at his sides. "Well, then, let's go tell Grandma Eleanor the good news!"

"Follow me in your car, Mr. Fiancé," Unique said, and then the two of them headed to their separate vehicles.

As Unique drove, Terrance followed close behind. En route she decided to give Korica a call to share the news with her as well. She instructed her vehicle to "Call Mommy," then listened as the rings bellowed through the car speakers.

"Hello," Korica said upon picking up.

"Hey, Mommy." Unique was smiling so hard, it could probably be heard through the phone line.

"Hey, girl. You just getting out of church?"

"You know it."

"Why you sound like the Lord Himself came and sat next to you in church today?" Korica laughed at her own funny.

"Well, because that's what it felt like. As a matter of fact, I think my earthly Lord did."

Unique lost Korica with that line. She didn't do church or hang around a lot of church folks, so she didn't know that some women referred to their husband as their earthly Lord. "Unique Emerald Gray, what are you talking about?"

"I have something to tell you, but you know what? I think I'll wait." Just then Unique decided that she didn't want to tell Korica over the phone that she was getting married to a man Korica had never met before. That was like a double whammy. Although Korica wouldn't have any issues with Terrance, Unique thought she should at least have the decency of introducing the two first. That was the same courtesy she was about to extend to Lorain.

"So why you call me up and tease me?" Korica huffed. "But you know what? I'm 'bout to pay you back, because I've got something to tell you too."

Now it was Unique who was intrigued. "What is it?"

"Oh, no, you don't. See what it's like to get a taste of your own medicine?"

"Okay, okay," Unique said.

"So when do I get to hear whatever it is you have to tell me?"

"Umm." Unique looked at the clock on her dashboard. It was 1:40 p.m. "Can I swoop by there at about three-thirty or four o'clock?"

"That's perfect!" Korica said with far too much excitement in her voice.

"Mommy, what have you got going on?"

"Whatcho mean?" Korica was playing coy.

"I know you. I can tell by that little sneaky tone in your voice that you've got something up your sleeve."

"You do know me well." Korica laughed. "But you'll see. You'll see. The same way you are making me wait, you have to wait too. I'll see you around four."

"All right. Love you," Unique said, surrendering.

"I love you too."

Unique ended the call, shaking her head, knowing that no matter what Korica had to tell, she couldn't possibly trump what she had to share. But if Unique knew Korica as well as she claimed to, then a red flag should have definitely been waving in her head.

Chapter 16

"Married! How wonderful. Does that mean you'll be moving back to West Virginia to live with your husband?" Lorain hoped she didn't sound too anxious for Unique to get out of Dodge, but this news was like music to her ears.

Having Unique back in town had been too stressful. Lorain had had nightmares about Unique coming over and ripping the twins right out of her arms. If Unique was going to get married and move back to West Virginia permanently, that meant Lorain's biggest worries would be no more. She wouldn't even have to pack for her guilt trip over keeping a distance between herself and Unique. Unique would be the one putting the distance between them . . . literally! This also meant that Lorain wouldn't have to have that dreaded conversation with Unique. Why should she waste her breath now, when it didn't even matter?

"Well, we . . . I . . . uh . . . ," Unique stammered. She looked at Terrance. The two were sitting side by side at the dining room table, across from Lorain and Eleanor. Nicholas was at his parents' house with the twins.

Unique had called Lorain to let her know she was going to drop by only a few minutes before Nicholas headed out the door. Lorain had convinced her husband to take the twins with him. This would allow her some time alone with Unique to have the heart-to-heart talk she'd planned on having before Unique shared the news of her marriage. And she had to be honest; she had been up to her usual antics and had shipped the girls off to keep Unique away from them. But none of that mattered now. Lorain was so happy . . . for Unique. Needless to say, Lorain couldn't be happier. "Out of sight, out of mind" was how she saw it. Unique would be far too busy tending to her new husband to worry about the girls. And due to the fact that he was older than her, he'd probably start pressuring her about having kids of their own.

Seeing that Unique was struggling to reply to Lorain's inquiry about whether she'd be moving back to West Virginia, Terrance jumped in to save her. "We haven't talked about that yet, Mrs. Wright."

"Yeah, girl," Eleanor said, jumping in and directing her comment to Lorain. "They ain't been engaged but ten minutes. Dang. I'm sure you and Mr. Nick didn't have everything all figured out before you hopped on that plane and ran off to Vegas to get married without telling a soul." Eleanor rolled her eyes at Lorain. She faced Unique and Terrance, allowing a big smile to cover her face. "I'm so happy for you, granddaughter."

"Thank you, Gran," Unique said.

"But for the record," Terrance said, "I get sent all over the map to audit banks and corporations. It doesn't matter where I live. I want to be wherever my wife is going to be." He lifted Unique's hand to his mouth and kissed it. "So if that means packing up and moving to Malvonia, then—"

"But what about your mother?" Lorain was quick to ask Terrance. "You can't up and leave her in West Virginia for dead, can you?" Lorain made it sound so morbid. Her words actually made everyone in the room a little uncomfortable.

Terrance cleared his throat. "My mother is under the best care possible back in West Virginia, but if need be, I'm sure we can find just as fine a facility here." He looked at Eleanor. "Or even have some type of setup like you and Ms. Eleanor have, where my mother will be just feet away."

Unique nodded. "Yes, we could find a place that has a mother-in-law suite. We can hire the best nurses and home health-care providers. And of course, I can still cook for her."

"By the way," Terrance said to Unique, "my mother told me to tell you that she misses your cooking. She misses you, too, but you know Mama loves to eat."

"Awww. How sweet," Unique said. "But Patsy uses the same recipes as I do, and the food tastes pretty much like mine, if I don't say so myself."

"I don't think it's so much the food as it is the delivery." Terrance ran his finger down Unique's nose and smiled. "Even before you and I started dating, you treated my mother well. I appreciate that. Thank you." Terrance kissed Unique on the lips.

"Have you no respect, young man?" Eleanor asked Terrance.

He automatically got nervous. "Oh, I'm sorry. No disrespect was intended."

"Well, you can't go getting all fresh in front of somebody who ain't had no lovin' of their own since Columbus set sail," Eleanor huffed. "That's like eating a large pizza in front of somebody who you know is on a spiritual food fast. Just rude."

Everyone in the room but Eleanor laughed. She was as serious as a heart attack as she smacked her hand on the table.

"You told me she was a hoot," Terrance said to Unique.

"I ain't a hoot. I'm keeping it real," Eleanor told Unique. "Unlike you and your mama's phony selves." She glared at Unique. "I knew you were keeping something from us. I told your mother that time you drove back in town, before moving back for good. I should have known you were hiding a man."

"Can't get a thing past you, can I, Gran?" Unique asked Eleanor.

"Nope, not you or your mammy," Eleanor replied.

"Oh, then what was it that Mom was being phony about?" Unique asked.

"Huh?" Lorain was stumped.

"Gran said we were phony, and she knew I was hiding something," Unique said. "So what was it that you were hiding?"

"The kids," Eleanor said.

"What?" Lorain and Unique asked in unison. Lorain had a look of horror on her face.

"The kids." Eleanor pointed out the window. "Them and Nick are back. I just saw them pull up in the drive."

"So soon?" Lorain stood. "But they left not too long ago."

"Yeah, right before Unique showed up," Eleanor said knowingly, mean mugging her daughter.

"Oh, the infamous twins," Terrance said and smiled. "I'll get to meet them, after all."

Terrance had been as disappointed as Unique when they arrived at the house and were told the girls were not at home. Unique had told him so much about them that he couldn't wait to see the unique little pair.

As they sat there, waiting for the twins to enter the house, Lorain couldn't help but wonder exactly what Unique had told Terrance about them. Did he know the truth? The whole truth? Nothing but the truth? Even if she hadn't told him yet, it was probably only a matter of time. Would he be the person in Unique's life who convinced her that it was a good idea to tell the girls the truth about being adopted and to reveal to them the identity of their biological mother? If the girls knew that their big sister, whom they adored, was really their mother, would they want to spend all their time getting to know Unique, abandoning Lorain in the process?

Moments later everyone gravitated to the front door in anticipation of the twins' arrival.

"There's Mommy's little angels," Lorain said as soon as the girls made it through the door. She made it a point to be the first one to pounce on them. "What are you guys doing back so soon?" she asked Nicholas.

He was too busy greeting everyone to reply to his wife.

"Hey, Mom Eleanor." Nicholas greeted his mother-in-law with a kiss on the cheek. "Unique, my girl." He gave her a hug. He then pulled away and looked at the male stranger in his house.

"Oh, yes, Nick, this is Terrance. And, Terrance, this is Nick," Unique said, making the introductions.

"Her fiancé," Eleanor added proudly.

Nicholas paused and looked at Lorain. He had to make sure Eleanor wasn't joshing him. There was no telling with his mother-in-law.

Lorain nodded the confirmation. "Yep. Unique, here, is engaged."

"Well, congratulations." Nicholas gave Unique another hug. He then walked over to Terrance. "Nice to meet you, man." He gave him a hard, excited handshake.

"Thank you," Terrance said.

"So you two are getting married, huh?" Nicholas asked like a proud papa.

Just then Terrance froze. "Oh, my! I'm so sorry," Terrance said to Nicholas. "With you being Unique's stepfather and all, I definitely should have come to you before I—"

"Oh, don't worry about that, man," Nicholas said, waving his hands. "It's all good. Love don't wait on no one. If you felt the time was right to propose, as long as you checked with God and got His blessing, you get no mouth from me."

Terrance relaxed.

"Where did you two meet, anyway?" Nicholas asked. "When did you meet?"

"Well, we met some years ago," Terrance answered.

"Not under such great circumstances," Unique added.

"But then we reconnected closer to a year ago," Terrance continued.

"Again, not under such great circumstances," Unique said.

"Yeah, I kind of ran into Unique, knocking a tray of food out of her hands, causing a huge mess."

There were some chuckles.

"But I was able to look past all that and ask her to be my lady," Terrance said.

"You mean *I* was able to get past all that." Unique took her finger and ran it up and down the length of Terrance, like she was reading him.

"From the looks of it," Eleanor said, "you have each met your match."

"So when is the wedding?" Lorain asked, getting right to the point.

"And can we be the flower girls, sissy?" Heaven asked.

"Absolutely." Unique walked over to the girls and hugged them. She'd been sidetracked by all the talk of her and Terrance's engagement.

"And can we wear real pretty dresses?" Victoria asked.

Unique bent down to their level. "I'm sure we won't be able to find dresses as pretty as you two, but yes, we'll find pretty dresses for you two to wear."

"So that's going to be your husbfriend," Heaven asked.

"Husband," Victoria said, correcting her sister.

Unique laughed. "Yes, girls, this is Terrance, and he's going to be your mom's . . . I mean your sister's . . ." Unique had to catch herself and make a quick correction. "He's going to be my husband." She stood up and walked over to Terrance to formally introduce him to the girls. She couldn't believe she had slipped up and had almost referred to herself as the girls' mother. Where on earth had that come from? Probably from all the badgering Korica had done.

Unique had become so used to the life they'd chosen to live—with Lorain as the girls' mother and she as their sister—that in all honesty, she didn't even look at the girls as her own daughters. She couldn't. It was far too painful. She wasn't a mother anymore. After the loss of the boys, people had tried to tell her that she was still a mommy, but it didn't feel the same. If she had motherly love for the twins, she would feel like she was betraying her boys.

That was why she hated when Korica pushed the subject with her. She didn't try to explain how she felt, because only a mother who'd walked that mile in her shoes could understand. And perhaps even then, such a mother wouldn't understand. It was different with some mothers. Even when they lost their child, in their heart, body, and soul, they felt like they weren't finished with motherhood and they were able to rekindle that maternal feeling with another offspring. But Unique couldn't. It hurt too much. It was like being stung by a bee and never removing the stinger. She'd rather be allergic to the stinger and die than hold on to it and live with that pain.

Unique took her fiancé by the hand and pulled him over to the twins. "Terrance, this is Heaven and Victoria, my little sisters."

"Pleased to meet you," the girls greeted with their perfect little manners.

"Same here," Terrance said, shaking their hands.

"I thought you were going to visit your parents," Lorain said to Nicholas, getting back on that subject.

"I went by there," Nicholas told her, "but they weren't home. Probably having Sunday dinner somewhere." He turned to face Unique. "But it all worked out. The girls and I got to meet the newest member of the family."

Terrance smiled. "The pleasure is all mine, sir."

"Sir," Nicholas said, scrunching up his face. "You can't be too much younger than the doctor himself." He began to play with the hairs on his chin in a *GQ* manner.

Nicholas was right about that. Terrance was Unique's senior by a few years, but he was who someone like Unique needed to tame her. She'd eat one of those young boys alive. She'd lived a long, hard life in a short amount of time. She'd been broken, but she'd healed, and it would take a certain kind of man to handle her, to handle her heart. She didn't think the guys she was used to entertaining, namely, young street dudes, could provide her with that.

"Pardon me," Terrance said. "Just trying to show some respect for the man of the house, is all."

"Oh, I'm messing with you," Nicholas joked, then patted Terrance on the shoulder.

"Well, I'm glad you guys made it back to see us and hear the good news from the horse's mouth," Unique said. "But now we have to head over to Mommy's to tell her the news as well."

"Oh, she doesn't know yet?" Lorain asked, feeling elated inside that Unique had come to share the news with her first.

"No, not yet." Unique shook her head.

"Well, I'm sure she'll be just as excited for you as we are," Lorain said.

"Hopefully." Terrance sounded nervous. "I hear Ms. Korica is something else."

"Oh, she's something else, all right," Lorain said under her breath in an unflattering way.

Nicholas gently elbowed her. "Be nice." He gave her a stern look as Unique shot her a similar one.

"Okay, okay." Lorain held her hands up in surrender. "Thank you for stopping by."

Hugs and kisses were given, and good-byes were said. And then Unique and Terrance were on their way.

"Well, I better go get dinner finished up," Lorain said after closing the front door. She looked at her daughters. "Girls, do you want to help me?"

"That depends," Victoria said.

"On what?" Lorain asked.

"On if they're any bowls to lick."

"Why you little . . ." Lorain tickled Victoria all the way into the kitchen, while Heaven followed, giggling.

"I guess I'm going to head on over to my place until dinner is ready," Eleanor announced. "Then I'll be back."

"All right," Nicholas said as he headed upstairs. "I'm about to go get my mind right, because I'm sure I'm going to get bombarded with ideas for the wedding by my wife soon."

"Oh, you are going to get bombarded about a wedding, all right," Eleanor said as she watched her son-in-law scale the steps. "You wait and see."

Eleanor headed into the kitchen, where she found Lorain at the counter, about to give the girls orders. "Y'all just came in from outside the house and didn't wash them little paws," Eleanor said to the girls. "Y'all know better. Go get them hands washed, and then come back and help your mama."

Heaven and Victoria did what they were told. They exited the kitchen and headed to the nearest bathroom.

Eleanor walked over to Lorain and jumped right in. She knew she had only two minutes, tops, to speak to her before the girls returned to the kitchen. And that was only if they fought over who was taking up too much space at the sink.

"Viola Lorain!" Eleanor said. Viola was Lorain's first name, but she hadn't gone by that name since her college days. But Eleanor chose to use it whenever she was good and livid with her only child. "Next time why don't you go hire two men and a truck and go help her pack," she said to Lorain, her eyes filled with disappointment. "Why don't you talk to the dang girl? Let it go. Then you won't have to act like this anymore. You will both know where the other stands, what each other's intentions are." Eleanor shook her head. "I don't get you, baby. You and Nick legally adopted the girls. Unique signed off on all the paperwork. There is no way on earth any judge would take them from you and give them to her." Eleanor gave her the evil eye. "Unless you did something totally off the charts."

"I know I should talk to her," Lorain admitted.

"I'm telling you, the guilt is going to eat you alive."

"The guilt wasn't here when Unique was in West Virginia, and now there's a possibility she might go back."

"That's because she wasn't a threat to you while she was out of town." Eleanor put her hand on Lorain's shoulder. "Honey, your own daughter should not be a threat to you." Lorain put her head down. Eleanor put her hands on both her daughter's shoulders and lightly shook her. "God is giving you a second chance with the baby girl you thought was dead. He can't be pleased right now."

Lorain backed up and turned away from her mother. Everything Eleanor was saying was true. God couldn't possibly be pleased, which was why Lorain had tried to stay as far away from Him as she had from Unique. She didn't even pray anymore, because she didn't want to hear what God had to say. She wasn't talking to God, and she wasn't talking to Unique. She felt trapped and just needed to be free. But knowing that freedom was found in truth, for now Lorain would opt to remain a prisoner of her own secrets.

Chapter 17

"Unique, my baby girl. Come on in." Korica kissed Unique on the cheek after opening the door for her. She then immediately took her by the hand and began to lead her into the kitchen, where she was finishing up dinner.

After finding out that Unique was going to drop by her house, Korica had hung up the phone and had got busy. This was the perfect opportunity to put her plan in motion. The timing couldn't be more perfect, because there wasn't any time to waste as far as Korica was concerned. She hoped that all parties involved would be pleased with her bright idea, otherwise she feared she might end up left alone in the dark.

"Mommy, I . . ." Unique couldn't say any more, as she was being dragged into the kitchen of Korica's home, which had been built from the ground up just for Korica. It wasn't a five-level dwelling or anything like that, but it was bigger than any place Korica had ever lived in before, and it wasn't an apartment, which was what she had lived in all her life. This dwelling had made her a first-time home owner, and the fact that it was a new build made it even better. It had three bedrooms, two and a half baths, and a finished basement that had a half bath and a bar area. The home had plenty of room for Korica to entertain her grandchildren and to house one or two of her own children if ever they were down on their luck and needed a place to stay.

"I know, I know. You have something to tell me," Korica said, pulling Unique by the hand. "But you're in my house, so me first."

They reached the kitchen, where there was a huge spread on the counter. There was spaghetti with meat seasoned with taco seasoning. There was corn bread. Korica always added sugar to the batter, so the corn bread was sweet. It was still warm, and slivers of butter were melting on top. Korica had also made a tomato and cucumber salad and fried chicken wings with hot sauce on the side. The hot sauce was for both the wings and the spaghetti. Unique's stomach started to grumble at the sight and the smell of all those foods on the counter. But the sight at the kitchen table made Unique suddenly lose her appetite.

"Eugene!" Unique said, her blood instantly beginning to boil.

"Unique." Eugene stood up from the table. His half smile quickly turned into no smile at all when Unique's reaction to him registered.

"What are you doing here?" Unique's tone was not one of surprise, but of disdain. Her entire demeanor had changed. She began to clam up like that younger, bitter, hurt Unique, who was starting to engulf her and take over.

Eugene opened his mouth, slightly stunned. He looked at Korica, who was looking at the ceiling while whistling Dixie. He then looked back at Unique.

"Who is that?" Eugene uttered these three words as he pointed over Unique's shoulder. And so did Terrance, who had been trailing behind and had finally caught up with Korica and Unique in the kitchen.

At the sound of the two male voices, Korica turned and, for the first time, noticed the male stranger standing in her modestly decorated modern kitchen. Korica had been so busy trying to get Unique into the kitchen to see Eugene that she hadn't even noticed poor Terrance and certainly hadn't given Unique the opportunity to introduce him.

"Who is he?" Terrance demanded to know, nodding at Eugene.

"I'm Eugene, Unique's baby daddy," Eugene answered, his chest all puffed out, flexing his muscles. He stood there in his baggy jeans, Timberland boots, and a double T-shirt. Both of his ears were pierced. "Who are you?" He looked Terrance up and down, sizing him up.

After hearing his name, Terrance knew exactly who this thug standing in front of him was. Even before he knew the guy's name, he could tell that his presence had a negative effect on Unique. Now this chump was trying to flex on Terrance as well. *Oh, heck no!* All bets were off as Terrance waited for Unique to share the news of their pending nuptials with her mother.

When she remained silent for what seemed like an eternity, Terrance pulled Unique to him, hugged her tightly, and announced, "I'm her fiancé."

"Fiancé!" both Korica and Eugene said in unison. Their voices bounced off the pearl-colored kitchen walls and the glass see-through cabinets, which protected all the brand-new dishes Korica had purchased for the house. When she was moving into the house, her children had refused to allow her to pack up the mismatched cups the grandkids had once drunk out of and the old jelly jars that Korica had drunk her daily Pepsi out of. Those plastic plates from the dollar store had been replaced with a nice set from Bed Bath & Beyond that Unique had given her.

Eugene instantly shot Korica a side-eye look. This time she didn't have enough time to look around and whistle, like she was none the wiser. "What's really going on here? When you called me, you said that Unique wanted to—"

"Look, I'm sorry." Korica cut Eugene off, walked over to him, and placed her hand on his shoulder.

She didn't necessarily want to be rude and cut Eugene off like that, but Korica hadn't been sure exactly what was about to come out of Eugene's mouth. She knew one thing, though: she didn't want it to be the wrong thing. Heck, for that matter, she didn't want it to be the right thing, either. She could not afford for him to mess up everything she'd been strategically lining up. In other words, if his dumb butt showed his hand during their game of Spades, with them being partners, they could go set and not make the bid.

Five minutes ago Korica had felt certain her plan was foolproof, but that was before Unique had strolled in with Superman himself, who was willing, ready, and able to leap tall buildings in a single bound if it meant protecting Lois Lane.

"You trying to play me, Miss Korica?" Eugene spat. "All I wanted is for Unique to—"

This time it was Unique who did the cutting off. "All *you* wanted?" They could see Unique's chest rising up and down. "All *you* wanted?" She pointed a finger and started walking up on Eugene. "You think I care what *you* wanted? Why should I? You never cared about what *I* wanted!" Now Unique was right up on him. "Like when I wanted *you* to help take care of your son." Unique poked him in the chest when she said the word *you*. "Remember that, Eugene?" Her eyes began to fill with tears.

Terrance reached out to grab Unique's arm. She snatched it away angrily.

"No," she told Terrance, all the while glaring at Eugene. "He needs to hear this. Besides, I think I've earned the right to say what I need to say to him."

"And you do have that right." Eugene sounded sympathetic. "That's why I wrote you and tried to call—"

Korica walked in between Unique and Eugene. "You
two, please. Not in front of company." She nodded at
Terrance. "Company that I had no idea we were going
to have." She looked at Eugene sympathetically. "Honestly."

Eugene rolled his eyes at Korica and twisted up his
lips in doubt. At this point he didn't know if he could
believe a word she said. He had tried to give her the benefit of the doubt, but now he felt stupid. He was kicking
himself inside. He should have known better. A leopard
never changed its spots, only its location. Korica was
still a lying, manipulative, aging hood rat . . . just in a
better house now. Eugene was feeling set up by Korica,
who was supposed to be his playing buddy. He turned
his attention back to Unique.

"I wanted you to write me, take my call just once, so
you could let me have it. Let me have everything I deserved," he told her. "This is exactly what I didn't want
to happen—you holding on to it like this."

"You mean *you* didn't want to have to hold on to the
guilt," Unique snapped. "Forgiveness from me would
mean you could sleep a lot easier at night. Forgiveness
from me would let you off the hook from feeling like
the piece of—"

"Unique, baby." This time Terrance was successful in
pulling Unique away from Eugene and back toward him.

Unique pursed her trembling lips. Her eyes were still
filled with tears of rage, but she did not let one teardrop
fall. At this point, if she didn't get out of there, things were
going to get ugly. She turned and looked at Korica. She
shook her head at her. She felt so betrayed. Korica knew
how Unique felt about Eugene. How dare she invite him
into her home to break bread with them?

Korica had never seen her daughter look at her that way before. The look Unique was giving her went beyond disappointment. It read the B word—*betrayal.* Korica honestly hadn't anticipated this type of reaction from Unique. Regardless of Korica's antics and actions, Unique usually turned a blind eye and loved Korica for who she was, anyway. Unique's reaction now made Korica feel sick inside. She needed to fix this with her baby girl.

"Unique, I'm—"

"Come on, Terrance. Let's go." Unique turned sharply and exited the kitchen, not waiting on a response from Terrance, but hoping he was right behind her.

Terrance and Unique had driven together to Korica's house. After visiting Lorain's house, they had gone back to Unique's apartment to drop off her car. It didn't make sense for Terrance to keep following her around town, especially with the high price of gas. So after leaving Korica's house, they jumped in Terrance's car and headed back to Unique's place.

"He was trying to be slick," Unique told Terrance as they drove. "Telling me what he thinks I wanted to hear."

Terrance simply listened and didn't talk, as he'd done for the past ten minutes of their drive. He didn't completely understand the situation, and it was so complicated that he didn't need to add his own two cents. Right now Unique was going through so many emotions, and all she needed was someone to vent to, a listening ear. Terrance would be that for her.

She went on. "That's what he's always done in order to get what he wants from me—tell me exactly what he thinks I want to hear. And it usually works. That's what he did the night we conceived the girls, but not this time, sucker."

"The girls?" Terrance had a confused look on his face. "I thought you said he was your son's father, and just one of your sons."

Unique thought she would die. In all her ranting and raving, had she really let it slip that the twins were actually her daughters and not her little sisters? She was not supposed to tell Terrance about the girls. She was not supposed to tell anybody. Of course, eventually, she would have had to; after all, she was about to marry the man. She absolutely did not want to go into a marriage without sharing something as serious as that with him. But this wasn't how she wanted to tell him. She wanted to share this with him on purpose, not by accident, and certainly not when she was having an angry fit.

Terrance didn't say another word. He wasn't about to discuss something of this magnitude while driving a three-thousand-pound vehicle. What had started off as a beautiful day, one lit up by the sun's rays, was now a cloudy afternoon. Terrance looked in the rearview mirror, saw that he was free to pull over, and did so, easing to a stop on the side of the road. The sound of the gravel underneath the tires was intensified by the thick silence inside the car. It sounded like the crackling sounds of thunder before a loud boom rumbled across the heavens and a streak of lightning danced in the sky.

He put the car in park, then turned to face Unique.

Unique figured she'd better go ahead and finish what she'd started. "Terrance, I'm—"

He held up his hand, closed his eyes, and then shook his head. Confused, he gathered his thoughts, trying to sort out the truths and misperceptions. He loved Unique. He was in love with Unique. But was there a side of her that he didn't know about? A side that would keep things from him? He took a deep breath, then opened his eyes. "Unique, I get that we've been with each other only a few months, not even a year. I get that we still have a great deal to learn about each other. We can't share our entire life story in a few months, so I'm being as understanding as I possibly can right now. I suspect things might come up in my life that make you feel some kind of way. Over time I'll try my best to give you all of me. I'm expecting reciprocity from your end."

Unique sat there, listening intently. While in jail, she used to watch the daytime court show *Judge Judy*. She had learned from that show that sometimes if you shut up and let the other person do all the talking, you could win the case. Unique was praying that this theory would prove true in this current scenario.

"Whatever you ask me, I will give you the truth, the whole truth, and nothing but," Terrance continued. "I will answer you honestly and will not lie by omission."

Unique twisted her face in confusion. She wasn't quite sure what Terrance was saying, what he meant by *omission*.

Noticing the expression on her face, Terrance said, "Lying by omission—that's when you don't tell someone something in order to keep from having to say the truth. You don't lie and say it didn't happen. You just don't tell the truth and say that it did happen."

"Oh, I see." Unique nodded her understanding.

"Can I expect the same from you?"

"Of course," Unique replied wholeheartedly.

"Great." He took another breath. "I know you've been through a lot, Unique, so I don't want you to feel like I'm putting you on trial or badgering you. So feel free to give me yes or no answers or even just say you don't want to talk about it. But I do think some talking is in order. Fair?"

"Fair," she replied. Did she want to talk about all this now? No. But she'd opened the can of worms, and she'd be the one doing the squirming if she didn't hurry up, let the worms free, and close the empty jar, with nothing left to be said.

"Okay, good, then," Terrance said before he dived right in. "Are Heaven and Victoria your daughters?"

"Yes." That was all Unique offered. She'd also learned from the *Judge Judy* courtroom television show that sometimes when people offered more details than they were asked to supply, they ended up losing the case.

"Is Eugene their father?"

"Yes." Unique was in between a boulder and a place that wasn't so soft. This was when she could have shared more information, offered more than a yes, but she didn't want to jeopardize the case. On the other hand, she feared that her response could be considered lying by omission. So she decided to go against what she'd learned from Judge Judy and offer more. "But—"

She'd taken too long to decide to be more forthcoming. Terrance was already on to his next inquiry. "The girls call you sissy. But do they know that you are really their mother?"

Unique shook her head. "Lorain and Nick adopted them. They call Lorain Mommy and Nick Daddy. As far as the girls are concerned, Lorain is their mother and I'm their big sister."

Terrance fell back into his seat and exhaled, as if the wind had been knocked out of him. "So another man will be raising my stepdaughters? My stepdaughters will be calling another man Daddy?"

"No, your sisters-in-law will be calling the man they know to be their father Daddy."

"But, Unique—"

"You are not their father, Terrance," Unique said. "And I am not their mother. Nick and Lorain have legally adopted the girls."

Unique went on to tell Terrance about the initial plan of having Lorain be the girls' legal custodian. Then she revealed that after the death of her sons, she didn't feel fit to be a mother and wanted Lorain and Nick to adopt and take care of the twins permanently. She explained how she felt it was in the best interest of the girls to be raised to adulthood by the newlyweds and to know Unique only as their sister.

"Who knows? Maybe one day we'll share everything with them. But maybe not." She shrugged. "I have no idea what the future holds when it comes to this. But what I do know is that for now, this is how it is, and my mother, Nick, and I . . . we are all in agreement. Now, down the road, with you being my husband, of course, you will have a say if we want for things to change. But if we don't want for things to change, you are going to have to accept that, Terrance. And what I don't want is you ever trying to change my mind for me. Because right now I'm content with the way things are, and I honestly don't foresee ever wanting the situation to change."

The expression on Terrance's face was not lining up with what Unique was saying, and he was shaking his head.

Unique turned her whole body toward Terrance. "You are being thrown into this. I get that basically, you'll have to live with the consequences of the decisions I've made. And if you feel that's not something you can live with . . ." Her words trailed off. She'd let Terrance speak for himself.

Terrance took Unique's hands in his. "Look, I'm not trying to come into your life and change things," he said. "I'm trying to understand them."

Unique exhaled. "That's good to hear, Terrance, because if you think Annie had a life of hard knocks, then you should take a look at my past. There is so much that can't be changed. But you know what? My past is just that, my past. I love you. And I know you love me. And when you really love somebody, you meet them right where they are in life, and you don't try continually to revisit their past."

Terrance nodded his head and smiled. His little Unique knew a lot, even though she was much younger than his forty-year-old self. She was smart beyond her years. Here, he thought he'd have to school her on some things in life, and already she was schooling him.

"So, can we agree to move forward?" Unique asked. "There's nothing we can do about past decisions that have been made, anyway."

"I understand that. The past is the past, and I agree. But I don't want to be in a situation like today, where your past comes back and confronts me in the face . . . literally."

Unique shrugged. "I can't promise you that. Today was not my doing. That was all my mother's doing."

And Unique couldn't wait to have a one-on-one with Korica to find out what the heck she was thinking by inviting Eugene to have dinner with them. While standing in that kitchen back at Korica's, though, she'd felt it was neither the time nor the place to have that discussion, not with Eugene and Terrance there. Korica had the most unfiltered tongue of anybody she knew. Nothing could be caught before it fell off her tongue, so Unique didn't want Terrance, or Eugene, for that matter, to be within earshot when Korica spoke.

"I'm sorry that you were put in an awkward position today," she continued. "And trust me when I say I will definitely be having a conversation with my mother about it." Unique squeezed Terrance's hands. "Just know that there is nothing in my past that I would ever hide that I know could intentionally come back to hurt you."

Terrance stared at Unique for a moment. He then pulled her to him. He placed his lips on hers, and the two kissed passionately.

"It's hard to believe that once upon a time I thought very little of you," Terrance said once they broke the kiss.

"And once upon a time, I wanted to take off my earrings, my shoes, put Vaseline on my face, and fight you."

"And now we're in love."

Unique smiled. "Yes, in love, till death do us part."

The couple shared yet another passionate kiss before Terrance put the car in drive and pulled back onto the road, which was once again dappled with sunlight.

Korica's middle name had to be Death, because little did the happy couple know that she was going to make it her business to see to it that they parted before they ever even came together in holy matrimony.

Chapter 18

"What do you think about this dress?" Lorain asked Eleanor. The two women had dropped the girls off at dance practice and then had walked over to a bridal shop in the same strip mall as the dance studio. Lorain held out the white mermaid-cut dress she'd found, like a needle in a haystack, among the rows of dresses in the small specialty boutique.

"It's white," Eleanor said with a frown.

"It's beautiful," Lorain said.

Eleanor looked at the dress again and then at Lorain. "But it's white."

"And what's wrong with my dress being white?" Lorain asked. "This is my first time having a wedding, so it's kind of like my first time getting married." Lorain placed the dress against herself and admired it in the mirror, imagining what it would look like on.

"It might be your first time having a real wedding, but, honey, white is for virgins." Eleanor let out a chuckle. "And it sure ain't your first time—"

"Mom, dang! Really? Can't a bride wear white if she wants to?"

Eleanor shot Lorain a look. "Do you really want to have that conversation with me, of all people?"

"Mom, you are so old-fashioned. Besides, you wore white when you married Daddy, and you were pregnant with me at the time."

"Only a month. Heck, I didn't even know I was pregnant."

"But you knew you weren't no virgin." Lorain raised an eyebrow.

"Child, I'm not 'bout to sit here and go tit for tat with you. If you want to wear white, by all means, wear white." Eleanor walked over to a rack and began looking through the dresses. "Ooh, look at this." She pulled a tiny white dress off the rack.

"That would be cute . . . if I was five years old." Lorain smacked her lips.

"Not for you. For the girls . . . to wear in Unique's wedding."

Lorain's entire demeanor changed, and this didn't go unnoticed by her mother. She went from being jolly to joyless.

"Oh, Lord, here we go," Eleanor sighed.

"What?" Lorain said.

"Don't 'what' me. You know what. This thing with you and Unique. Can't you see that girl is trying to move on with her life, get married, and maybe start another family with that soon-to-be husband of hers? The last thing she's thinking about is trying to come and take Heaven and Victoria away from you. Besides, it was her idea in the first place for you and Nick to adopt and raise them as your own. It's not like you had to convince her or go to her house and steal 'em out of their crib."

"I know you are trying to make me feel better, Mom, but please don't stand there and try to pretend like you didn't hear it," Lorain said.

"Hear what?" Eleanor looked around. "Did you fart or something? No, I didn't hear it. But let me get my little bottle of air freshener I carry with me from out my purse. Those silent ones are the most deadly." Eleanor began to dig in her purse.

"I did not pass gas. That's not what I'm talking about," Lorain said. "You mean to tell me you didn't hear Unique slip up and almost refer to herself as the girls' mother that day she introduced them to Terrance?" Lorain said.

Eleanor looked up from her purse. She then turned, put the little dress back on the rack, and shuffled around, looking some more. She was trying to avoid answering Lorain's question. Clearly, her actions showed that she'd caught Unique's slipup too, that and the fact that she hadn't yet denied hearing what Lorain had heard.

"I knew it. See? I told you." Lorain went and flopped down on a bench, placing the dress in her lap. "The more time she spends with them, the more . . . I don't know. . . . The more that mother thing is going to kick in." Lorain's knees began to shake. Worry covered her face.

Eleanor went and sat down next to her daughter. "Baby girl, I truly wish I had the answer for all this, but I don't. It's too much. I've already told you what I think you should do, and that's talk to Unique. She'll tell you what I'm telling you, that she wants those girls with you and Nick. But maybe you should talk to God first. Have you tried that?"

Lorain shook her head. "I'm too ashamed."

"To talk to Unique or to talk to God?"

"How about both."

"Well, daughter, I can't blame you. You should be ashamed."

"Mom!" Lorain stood to her feet. "Forget it. Let's keep looking for a dress." Lorain took the dress she'd selected and placed it back on the rack, and then she began to look through the other dresses. "We have to find something, because the clock is ticking."

Eleanor stood and began to help her daughter in her search.

The clock was ticking, all right, and if Lorain didn't move fast enough, she just might run out of time. To make things right not only with Unique, but with her husband as well.

"Lorain, I want to thank you for agreeing to have lunch with me."

Lorain simply smiled. No "You're welcome" or anything came from her mouth. She hadn't agreed to have lunch with Tabby because she wanted to. Nicholas had done everything but put a gun to her head to get her to go and reconcile with his friend's wife.

"This isn't high school, Lorain," Nicholas had told her. "And besides, Lance and I don't want what's going on between our wives to affect our professional relationship or our friendship. They've invited us to their house for dinner next week, and I accepted."

"But—"

Nicholas had put his hand up, halting her words. "I will not walk through the doors of their home yet again without my wife on my arm. Period. So between now and then, do what you need to do to fix it. Lance is having the same conversation with his wife, so I'm sure she'll be reaching out to you to get together. Take the credit card and go pick out something nice to wear." Nicholas had then entered the bathroom and had closed the door before Lorain could even refuse.

Nicholas had never asked Lorain for much. He'd always gone with the flow. So for him to interfere in her social dealings and put his foot down meant this was really something he wanted and expected from her. Considering that Nicholas had done everything in his power to give Lorain and the girls the world, she felt she could at least fulfill this one little request.

So the next day, when Tabby sent her a text inviting her to lunch, she had had no other choice but to reply and ask when, where, and at what time she wanted to meet. Now the two of them were sitting across from each other at Brio in Easton Town Center in Columbus. It was a nice, cozy, upscale Italian eatery with a classy atmosphere.

"I just wanted to tell you face-to-face how sorry I am about what happened at last month's wives' meeting," Tabby said, apologizing. "I should be and I am ashamed of my behavior. Not even in high school did I ever get caught up in the rumor mill."

"And now here you are, blowing the hot air that keeps it spinning." Lorain raised an eyebrow at Tabby.

"I deserved that. You have every right to be angry with me. I'm willing to take whatever you dish out and swallow it. Even if we're not the best of friends, our husbands are friends. Lance truly admires Nick, and I think it's safe to say that the feeling is mutual. I don't want my childish behavior to come between our husbands and damage their relationship. So what do you say? Can we at least be cordial?" Tabby waited in anticipation.

Lorain had no problem keeping her waiting, either. She did not want to make this comfortable for Tabby, as she hadn't been the least bit comfortable standing in Tabby's dining room last month, being the topic of rumors. Lorain took a sip of her seltzer, then looked at Tabby.

Tabby's words had sounded genuine enough, and the expression on her face matched. Behind those eyes of hers, it looked as though regret had pitched a tent. Not one to get off on holding grudges and having people at her mercy, Lorain decided to go ahead and set Tabby free.

"I forgive you, Tabby." Lorain exhaled.

Tabby's shoulders lifted, her eyes filled with happiness, and she opened her mouth to speak, only Lorain cut her off.

"On one condition," Lorain added.

Tabby slowly closed her mouth, her joy quickly evaporating. She hadn't foreseen that a condition would be attached.

"If there is anything, *anything at all*," Lorain stressed, "that you want to know about me, please do not hesitate to come directly to me. I might tell you that it's none of your darn business, and I might spill my guts."

"Hmm. Funny that you should say that," Tabby said.

Now Lorain was the one with a sour look on her face. "What makes you say that?"

Tabby opened her mouth, then closed it again. "Oh, nothing. It would just be me blowing the hot air that keeps the rumor mill running. And you wouldn't want me to do that, now would you?" Tabby shrugged and then picked up the menu. Just that quickly Tabby was making Lorain eat her words. "Eat up," Tabby said. "I'm buying."

Chapter 19

"I know you're mad, but before you say anything, let me explain," Korica said to Unique as Unique sat down in the booth at Captain Souls. Korica had called and invited Unique to her favorite restaurant to make a truce. Unique had immediately accepted, because for one, she couldn't wait to have a conversation with her mother and get to the bottom of the whole Eugene situation, and two, Captain Souls was her favorite restaurant.

"Is this why on the reality shows the women are always out somewhere eating?" Unique asked. "Because they think that because they are out in public, a person won't clown? Or is it because they think they can calm the roaring lion with food?"

"Both," Korica said.

Unique shook her head. "Mommy, how could—"

Korica put her hands up. "Wait, now, honey. I said to let Mommy talk first."

Unique settled herself back in the booth and nodded. While Unique was known for her stubbornness and attitude, she'd never aimed them at Korica. She'd always had the utmost respect for the woman who had raised her. "Okay, shoot."

"That boy is hurting too. That boy lost his son too."

Unique was quick to lean forward again. "It's because—"

"Wait. Now, you said you'd let me talk," Korica reminded Unique.

Being a woman of her word, as hard as it was, Unique willed herself not to speak until she heard what Korica had to say for herself.

"First off," Korica said, leaning in, "I don't want you to think for one minute this is about that boy. I don't give a rat's a—"

The waitress walked up to their booth. "Ladies, can I get your drink order?" she asked the mother and daughter. It was a tense and inopportune moment, indeed. Slightly annoyed, as they were ready to get into the meat of the conversation, the women placed their drink orders. Then Korica continued.

"Unique, I see how angry you are at Eugene."

"And you should be angry at him too," Unique spat. "But instead, you're trying to feed that Negro. You're supposed to be on my side. You're supposed to have my back. Any other time, even if I'm wrong, I could always count on you to be there and be wrong right along with me, as I have always been for you. But now it's like you're on his side."

"You know I've got you through thick and thin. I'm not even about to let you question my loyalty to you, Unique. But this isn't about sides. This is about you getting right. Now, your religion has helped you deal with and heal from the death of the boys, but the anger you have for Eugene is going to be the death of you. You have to forgive him."

Unique stared out the window. "I have forgiven him, Mommy. But I'm still mad. I have forgiven him, but I haven't forgotten. If I hadn't forgiven him, I'd be waging war."

"And you are, in your own heart. You have to free yourself completely from all the residue of pain when it comes to your boys. Eugene is part of that pain. You want to heal completely and move on? Then tell that boy to his face that you have forgiven him. He don't deserve to hold that kind of power over you."

Unique took in Korica's words and allowed them to penetrate her heart. They were so true. For years she'd been harboring anger toward Eugene, anger that she felt she'd managed to keep hidden and under control, but God knew her heart, and obviously, so did the woman who'd raised her. Unique had been too grateful to God for giving her the strength she needed and for keeping her mind sound while she was going through her ordeal of being in jail and at the same time dealing with the loss of her sons. Had she not had Jesus on her side, it could have been a lot more painful.

People had wanted to see Unique broken, battered, crying, and beaten down, because they thought that was how a woman who'd lost all three of her sons at the same time should look. They had wanted to see her fainting and falling out, crying out and wailing while clutching her heart. Pulling her hair out. Not looking good, not smelling good, her hair nappy, and unable to get out of bed. When people didn't see her acting that way—when her pain didn't look like what they wanted it to look—they couldn't muster up any sympathy for her. Well, if they had taken a closer look, they would have seen that Jesus had overtaken her, and not the pain. They would have seen in the sand the footprints of God as He carried her through the pain. If only they'd looked a little closer.

But thank God, they hadn't. If they'd looked too close, they would have seen that scab on her heart with Eugene's name on it. But perhaps Korica was right. It had been there long enough and was now serving no purpose. Maybe that scab needed finally to be peeled off. Yes, it would leave a scar, but that would reflect the healing that had taken place.

"You're right."

Korica sat shocked after hearing the words that had escaped from Unique's mouth. She had been expecting the feisty, "I don't care if I'm wrong, as long as you ain't right" attitude that Unique used to have. A smile teased the corners of Korica's mouth. This had been far too easy. The waitress hadn't even taken their food orders yet. Korica had been certain it would take dessert and all to get Unique to see eye to eye with her.

"I appreciate you setting up a meeting with Eugene for me," Unique said. "I now understand that you were only trying to help. I think it would have been better if it had not been a surprise. That was something I needed to prepare for."

"I agree, and I'm sorry," Korica said as the waitress brought their beverages.

The women had almost forgotten about their drink orders. It had taken this waitress longer than usual to return with their beverages. Having sensed the two women's agitation when she took their drink orders, the waitress had waited until it looked like the coast was clear to return to their table. Kind of like how motorcyclists had to stop underneath an overpass when the rain started to come down harder. They could handle a little sprinkle, but they had to be smart enough to know when it was time to wait out the storm. It looked like sunshine was now in the forecast, so it was safe for her to address the women again. The waitress took their food orders. A couple minutes later she walked away, leaving mother and daughter alone to continue their conversation.

"So what do you say you two try it again?" Korica asked, hopeful.

Unique stared out the window and thought for a moment. She then looked back at Korica and nodded. "I think it's a good idea that Eugene and I have a one-on-one."

Korica clasped her hands together in excitement. "Good. I can—"

"No, Mommy, you don't have to do anything. This is between Eugene and me, so I'll set everything up when I'm ready. I'm pretty busy next week. Perhaps I can set something up with him on Friday. I have a luncheon to cater earlier in the day, but then I'm free after that. I'll see if he can stop by later that evening."

"Well, good. I have his number, and I'll text it to you."

Unique turned and looked out the window again, as if she was having second thoughts.

"You're doing the right thing, baby," Korica said, encouraging her and patting her hand.

"I know. This is truly something I need closure to before I go embarking on a new beginning with Terrance."

Korica's ears perked up. "Yes, this Terrance character," she said, getting serious. "I know I ruined your surprise with that so-called surprise of my own. But please tell me everything there is to know about him." Korica was all ears, indeed. She wanted to know everything about the man who had said he was going to marry her daughter. He was the only one who could possibly mess up her plans, so the more she knew about her potential enemy, the easier it would be to take him down, if need be. "The same way an apology was in order for you, I believe I owe one to Terrance. So if you don't mind, text me his number."

"I'm sure he'd appreciate that," Unique said, smiling at her mother.

"Oh, darling, trust me, the pleasure will be all mine."

At that moment the waitress brought out some biscuits for the ladies to indulge in, steering Unique's attention away from Korica and causing her to miss the mischievous grin that was resting on Korica's lips.

***

"Thank you for inviting me over," Eugene said as he entered Unique's apartment.

It had taken Unique a couple days, but she had done what she promised Korica she would do and had called Eugene up and arranged for them to talk that Friday. She'd invited him over to her place because she had some things of her oldest son that she wanted to give him for memory's sake. Like Unique, Eugene had been in jail at the time of the triple funeral. Both of them had been denied a release to attend the funeral. For Unique, not being there for their home going was almost harder than her sons' deaths. Not being able to say good-bye. She imagined it had been as difficult for Eugene.

"Thank you for coming," Unique said.

Eugene was from the streets, so he was always on the lookout for the okey doke, for dudes to leap out of closets and try to jump him or something. He looked around. Everything appeared to be kosher.

His hesitation didn't go unnoticed by Unique, though. "Boy, quit that. What you think I invited you over here for? To beat you up or something?"

"No, but how am I supposed to know whether or not that dude who tried to get all up in my grill at your mom's ain't gon' try to come at me again?"

Unique threw her hands on her hips and tilted her head. "You know me better than that."

"I don't know . . . between you and that mama of yours . . ." Eugene shook his head.

"Please." Unique wagged her hand. She left the front door open to let in a little sunshine before the sun went down. There was only about an hour left before the sky darkened. "Whatever Mommy said to you, that has nothing to do with me. I asked you over so that we can talk."

"I hear you. I hear you." Eugene was much more relaxed now. He didn't feel that Unique was trying to play him, but the verdict was definitely still out on her mama.

"Can we go talk in the kitchen?"

"Sure," Eugene agreed, and then he followed Unique into her kitchen, where she had some mini bottles of water and little finger sandwiches laid out on her petite kitchen table. There were chocolate-covered strawberries, as well as some nacho chips. This spread wasn't something special that she'd prepared for Eugene. She'd catered a corporate luncheon earlier that day, and these were some of the items that were left over.

"Help yourself to whatever you want," Unique told Eugene as she handed him a plate.

He did just that. He picked up a sandwich and bit into it, then grabbed some nachos, more sandwiches, and several other items.

"Hungry, are we?" Unique joked.

"Girl, I've been staying with my moms for the last month," Eugene told her. "You know the only thing she knows how to cook is—"

"Grilled cheese." Unique finished his sentence, and they both laughed. Unique remembered clearly how back when she first met Eugene, whenever she went to his house, his mother was always cooking the same thing for dinner—grilled cheese with potato chips and dill pickles on the side.

"I have some meatballs left over, too, if you want something hot," Unique offered. "They're in the refrigerator, but I can warm them up."

"No, I'm good. I appreciate this. Anything but grilled cheese." He ate another sandwich. There was a variety of sandwiches, including tuna, chicken, and turkey. A couple of the turkey ones even had bacon on them. He was sampling them all.

"Please, have a seat." Unique extended her hand toward one of the chairs at the table. After he sat down, she sat in the chair across from him.

There was silence, broken only by the crunching sound Eugene made as he devoured the nachos on his plate.

"Oh, my bad," he said after realizing Unique was staring at him, waiting on him to slow down so that she could talk to him. He washed down the food he'd eaten with water, wiped his mouth, then sat up straight in his chair, with his hands folded. "All right, shoot."

"What I have to say won't take long," Unique began. "I basically wanted to do something that I should have done a long time ago. It would have set both you and me free."

Eugene waited for Unique to continue with a puzzled look on his face, as it was not clear to him if she meant free from jail or what.

"I should have forgiven you completely, without anger, Eugene, and freed both our minds, hearts, and spirits," Unique told him.

"You . . . you forgive me?"

Unique paused for a moment and then nodded. "Yes, Eugene, I forgive you."

Eugene breathed as if a pillow held down over his face by someone trying to force him to say "Uncle" had finally been lifted. He didn't even know what to say. He was afraid that if he said something, and it was the wrong something, Unique might take it back. So he said nothing. He nodded as his eyes filled with tears.

"Please don't," Unique said, looking down. "If you start, then I'm going to start."

"I don't want to make you cry, Nique," Eugene said. "I guess I want to know why. Why now?" Eugene had written Unique several letters while he was in jail. The last address he had for her had been her sister's house, so he'd sent them there. He'd even tried calling her collect, but to no avail. He'd felt that she would not forgive him until the day he died. And maybe not even then. Maybe she'd do nothing more than spit on his grave.

"It's time, Eugene, you know. I mean, my moms may not go about things the right way, but she was right when she told me I needed to let go of all this anger I had for you inside my heart." Unique shook her head. "And I'd had a death grip on that anger. I don't know. . . . I felt like if I let go of that anger, then what would be left? There would be nobody left to blame and nobody to be mad at. That meant all that would be left was happiness and joy."

"And what's wrong with that?" Eugene shrugged, and a look of confusion covered his face. "Isn't that what you women want? Didn't Mary J. Blige sing the anthem for y'all? I just wanna be happy? So why not just be happy?"

"Because I don't deserve to be!" Unique snapped as her eyes flooded with tears.

Dang it, Eugene thought. Had he done it? Had he made Unique angry at him all over again, and was she now going to *unforgive* him?

"Don't you get it, Eugene? If I don't have you to blame and be mad at, and if I refuse to be happy and joyful, then that means one thing." She got up and walked away, then stood with her back to Eugene as a wave of tears took over.

Eugene got up out of his chair and walked over to Unique. He stood behind her. Slowly, he reached his hand out to touch her, hesitated, then decided against it. Eugene felt so bad as he watched Unique's shoulders heaving. But everything was all making sense now; it was now apparent why she'd been hell-bent on harboring this hatred and animosity toward him.

"If you didn't blame me, then you'd have only yourself to blame." That was it. Eugene had hit the nail on the head.

Unique's shoulders heaved uncontrollably.

This time when Eugene raised his hand, he placed it on her shoulder. "It's not your fault, Unique."

"But I left them in the car. I left my babies in the car on the hottest day of the year. And they died, Eugene. Had I not—"

"Had I and those other two loser baby daddies not been sorry fathers, you wouldn't have had to spend your day riding around town, trying to hunt us down for child support. We can play the blame game all day, Unique, and it will never lead back to you. You are not the domino that started the whole horrible effect. So if blaming me for the rest of my life is what you need to do, I'll take that. I can live with that, but what I can't live with is watching you blame yourself. Not after you did for my son what I didn't do. You fed him, clothed him, and made sure he had whatever it was he needed. My little man was brilliant, smart, and intelligent. He didn't get that from my dumb a—" Eugene stopped. He knew Unique was a Christian, and he didn't want to offend her by using foul language.

"Eugene, you're not dumb," Unique said, looking straight ahead, wiping her tears.

"Tell that to my mama." He snickered. "For a minute I used to think dummy was my name. That's all she ever called me. The one smart thing I know I did was getting with you. But even after all was said and done, my moms was right. When I messed things up with you, she told me I was a dummy for doing so."

Unique turned around and faced Eugene. "We've both made a lot of mistakes, Eugene. The first was thinking we could raise a kid when we were only kids . . . doing grown-up things."

"Yeah, but you grew up. I stayed in a state of perpetual childhood."

Unique raised her eyebrows at Eugene's use of words.

"I learned about that in jail, at some meeting. Dude said that society wants us to continue to think, talk, and act like we thirteen, even though we thirty. If we stay in that mind-set, then we never grow up and become real men." He shrugged. "Guess I got trapped in that. Just never wanted to admit it until now."

Unique smiled. "I know you lost a son too, and I'm sorry. And because your relationship with our son didn't look like what I wanted it to look like, I guess I felt there was no way his death could have hurt you as much as it was hurting me. And I'm a hypocrite for thinking that. Because I had a problem with people who thought I should have been acting and looking a certain way after losing my boys."

"It's okay." Eugene looked down.

"It's not okay. I judged how you might have been feeling based on what I thought your relationship with our son should have looked like, and that wasn't fair." Unique took a step toward Eugene. "Will you forgive me?"

Eugene stood there, speechless. He felt as if he was the only one who should have been apologizing, yet here Unique was apologizing to him. He didn't know what to say.

"Please, will you forgive me?" Unique extended her hands.

Eugene looked down at her hands and shook his head. "You don't need forgiveness."

"Please, Eugene, I've forgiven you. Now you forgive me."

Eugene stood there, looking as if there was more he needed to say. "Before you really forgive me, let me explain myself first."

Unique nodded for him to proceed, putting her hands back down to her side.

"I messed up." Eugene's voice began to crack. "I was so busy stacking loot, thinking the entire time, *My son ain't gon' have to hit these streets on no grind. I'ma grind enough for the both of us.*" Tears threatened to fall from his eyes, but he fought them off. "That money I meant to hand you from the freezer that day, but instead, I handed you those drugs. . . ."

Unique nodded. She remembered just fine that brown bag he'd handed her from the freezer right before the police raided the place. Unique had insisted he break her off some child support money. After a couple minutes of fighting her on the issue, Eugene had given in, had told her to hold on, and had gone and grabbed a bag out of the freezer. He'd thought he was giving her a bag of money he kept hidden in the freezer, but instead, he'd handed her a bag of dope. The worst timing in the world.

Eugene went on. "That money was part of the stash I'd been saving. The reason why I had been avoiding your calls was that I was on my hustle for real. I knew once you got at me, you was gon' cuss me out. But it was going to be worth it when I handed you over that big payday. I had gotten involved with these new cats and was making money hand over foot and had a big deal set up that was going to make me more money than I'd ever seen. But it was all a setup . . . as we all found out the hard way. Turns out that shortcut to riches was a quicker way to nowhere but hell and jail. And in the process, I lost my son."

Tears filled Eugene's eyes and began to flow. There didn't seem to be anything he could do to stop them. Although he didn't want to offend her, the F-bomb dropped from his mouth. Frustration, hurt, anger, and regret had all created a fire inside of him. Eugene turned his back to Unique. He'd never cried in front of a woman before. All those times when his mother was insulting and humiliating him by cussing at him and calling him all sorts of dummies, he'd wanted to cry. The words had cut so deep, he'd wanted nothing more than to bleed tears, but he hadn't. Being the little street soldier that he was, he'd simply puffed out his chest and held it all in. Well, right now every tear he'd held in over the years poured out as he shook uncontrollably.

"Eugene." Unique came up from behind him. She slowly opened her arms and embrace him from behind.

He pulled away. Unique's feelings weren't hurt. She figured he was embarrassed and ashamed to be crying in front of a female.

"It's okay, Eugene. I felt the same pain. I know it hurts. Let it out. It's okay. It's okay to cry." Once again Unique slowly wrapped her arms around Eugene from behind. This time he allowed her to comfort him.

The genuine love and warmth Eugene was feeling from Unique was something he'd never felt before in his life. His own mother had never even been the hugging type. She wasn't the kind of mother who told her children she loved them every night at bedtime. Even when Eugene had thought making the basketball team would make her proud, she'd never come to any of the games to show her support. His mother had given him the bare minimum: clothes, food, and a roof. Then, when she'd learned Eugene was a dope boy, all she'd done was hold her hand out. It had hurt him and had affected him negatively while he was growing up. At this moment, it all just took over him, the years of heartbreak, anger, and pain, and he broke down even more. His shoulders heaved as the sound of his cries bounced off the walls.

Several minutes went by before Eugene regained his composure. He lifted his head and began to speak. "'You ever seen a grown man cry? You ever seen that look in his eye? Than to let that first tear drop, he'd rather die. He can't keep the others from flowing, no matter how hard he tries.'"

By now Unique realized that he was reciting a poem.

He continued. "'Following these drops are arrays of "whys." His weep lasts forever as time goes by. Your witnessing shrinks him to the size of a fly. I don't mean to get personal and I don't mean to pry. Just wondering if you ever seen a grown man cry.'" Eugene turned to Unique with red eyes. "The short story 'You Ever Seen a Grown Man Cry,' from the book *Please Tell Me if the Grass Is Greener*, by Joylynn M. Jossel. I read it when I was locked up."

Unique tenderly turned Eugene around to face her. He didn't resist her direction. He didn't resist her touch. A lone tear slid down Unique's cheek as she witnessed Eugene's breakthrough.

"I'm sorry," he said, breaking down once again.

This time Unique wrapped her arms around him from the front. He was taller than she was, so he simply rested his head on hers and let his tears fall. This time there was no shame and no embarrassment.

"It's okay," Unique assured him. "You can cry in front of me. It's okay, Eugene. Let it out."

And that was what he did for the next couple of minutes. Unique held him as if he were a small child in need of love and affection, something she was sure he'd never gotten from his mother, who, Unique knew, was cold and standoffish. It was never too late to make that little boy inside of him feel loved. Finally, he pulled away and looked down at Unique. For a moment they looked into each other's eyes, for the first time seeing something more in each other than just a young teenage kid. The two of them had been through a lot. The birth of their son had connected them, the challenges of being so young and trying to take care of him had made them drift apart, and now his death was bringing them closer than ever.

"Thank you," Eugene whispered to Unique, taking his thumb and wiping her tears away. "Although I don't feel like you owed me an apology, I thank you for it and I forgive you."

"And I forgive you too . . . really forgive you." Unique smiled.

The longer the two of them stood there and stared into each other's eyes, the closer their faces seemed to come, until finally their lips were locked. Eugene caressed the back of Unique's head, allowing his fingers to play in her hair. She held his arms as the kiss became more passionate.

"Sur . . . prise."

Unique and Eugene were engulfed in one another's arms, sharing a kiss, when the voice startled them. They broke apart. They looked over to see Terrance standing in Unique's kitchen doorway with a bouquet of roses in his hand.

Before Unique could even catch her breath from the kiss, the roses were lying on the floor and Terrance was out the door.

Chapter 20

It took Unique a couple of seconds to let everything that had happened sink in. Had it all been real? Had Terrance really shown up and found her and Eugene in an embrace, kissing? Terrance, her fiancé?

"Oh, God," Unique said as she immediately fled from the kitchen and dashed through the living room and out the screen door. "Terrance, wait!" she called out as she ran down the walkway, toward where Terrance was parked.

Terrance ignored Unique's call as he clicked his key fob to unlock his car.

"Baby, please wait," Unique said when she caught up with Terrance before he could open the car door and get in.

"Baby?" Terrance turned to face Unique. "Is that what you called him before you stuck your tongue down his throat?" Terrance had said it with such venom.

Unique opened her mouth, but no words fell out. What could she say to defend herself? He'd seen what he'd seen. She couldn't even utter the infamous words "It's not what it looked like," because it was absolutely what it looked like. She'd been caught kissing her babies' daddy.

Unique swallowed and this time forced the words out of her throat. "I know you're angry right now, and you have every right to be," she said. "Eugene and I were just talking, and then I apologized to him, he apologized to

me, and then . . . I don't know. Things got emotional.
I was crying. He was crying. We were both trying to
comfort each other, and . . . I got lost. I don't know how
else to explain it."

Unique's eyes pleaded with Terrance to understand where she was coming from. "What you saw
was nothing more than me getting caught up. There
is nothing going on between Eugene and me. It's just
that we had never mourned the loss of our son with
each other and . . ." Unique ran out of words. Even
to her own ears, everything she said sounded like
babble. Why hadn't she followed her *Judge Judy*
rules? This babbling on went against everything
she'd learned.

"You can't even finish, can you?" Terrance shook his
head. "Even you can't stand to eat that bologna you're
trying to feed me, huh?"

"Terrance . . ." Unique went to step toward Terrance
to touch him, but the look he shot her let her know
not to come any closer, let alone put her hands on
him. She hadn't seen that look of hate on his face since
the day he stood up in the sanctuary to stop Mother
Doreen's wedding.

"I drive all the way here to surprise you. To make it
official. To get down on one knee." Terrance reached
into his pocket and pulled out a small red-leather box.
"To give you this."

Unique looked down at the box. Terrance didn't even
need to open it. She knew a ring was inside. "Terrance."
She shook her head in shame. "I'm so sorry. I didn't
mean for this to happen. I didn't plan it."

"Well, you planned something. He's over at your house,
which means you must have invited him. Certainly, he
wasn't an unexpected and uninvited guest, because it
sure looked like you were expecting him. What were
those? All his favorite foods you had laid out?"

"It isn't what it looked like." *Darn.* Unique had let those ridiculous-sounding words escape her mouth.

Terrance looked at her like he was insulted by the fact that she had even said those words.

"What I mean is that those were leftovers from . . ." Unique stopped herself. There was no use explaining. Where the food came from didn't matter nearly as much as where all those emotions had come from that had led her to share a kiss with her ex. And at the time of the kiss, she'd been totally in—mind, body, and soul. Not only had she forgotten about Terrance, but she'd also forgotten about the whole frickin' world! It had felt like she and Eugene were the only two people on the planet. All the hate and anger she'd had for him for so many years seemed to have vanished with just two little things—forgiveness and a kiss.

"I thought you said you hadn't seen Eugene since that day. . . ." Terrance didn't want to sound insensitive by bringing up the day of her sons' deaths. But he'd told Unique that he didn't want her past coming back to mess up his future. He didn't want her lies to hurt him. He didn't want to suffer the consequences of her mistakes.

"That's the truth," Unique confirmed. "Except for that day at my mother's, I hadn't seen Eugene since the day . . . since the day at the drug house."

"Your mother," Terrance said in a tone that Unique couldn't read.

"What about my mother?"

"She was wrong."

"I know she was wrong to invite Eugene over to her house that day," Unique agreed. "She said she was going to call and apologize to you and—"

"She did call. That's what I meant by her being wrong. She called and apologized to me about putting me in that predicament with Eugene being at the house and all. I understood. It's not like you'd told anybody you were seeing me, so how was she to know I'd show up with you that day? So of course, I accepted her apology. What I meant by her being wrong was that she was wrong about you."

Unique shook her head. "I still don't get what you're saying."

"You always say how close you and your mother are, how she knows you better than anybody," Terrance said. "So when she told me it would be a great idea to actually buy you a ring and propose to you, ring in hand and down on one knee, like you'd dreamed of since you were a little girl, I didn't argue with her. She even suggested I do it today. 'The sooner the better,' she'd said."

"Wait. My mother told you to surprise me? On this particular day?"

Terrance thought back. He wanted to be sure he was giving Unique the correct information. He recalled the conversation he'd had with Korica the day she called him up to apologize to him for the whole Eugene incident. She'd been adamant about doing it Friday evening. Even when Terrance told her he had a dinner appointment scheduled, she'd insisted he cancel it. Terrance had assumed that Unique must have mentioned something to her mother about not yet having a ring. Not wanting Unique to have a change of heart for any reason, he had listened to his future mother-in-law, had hit the jewelry store to get Unique a nice stone, and had canceled his dinner appointment so that his Friday evening would be open and he could go propose to Unique properly.

"Yes." Terrance nodded with certainty. "She said she knew for a fact you would be home Friday evening."

"Are you sure?" Unique was not willing to accept that answer. Unique remembered specifically mentioning to her mother that she was going to invite Eugene over to her place to talk with him on Friday evening. So why would her mother deliberately tell Terrance to drop by her place that same evening? She should have known this was going to cause drama. Then again, maybe that was exactly what Korica had wanted. But why on earth?

"Terrance, for some reason, I feel like we were both set up, and I really need to get to the bottom of this," Unique said, now unable to even think straight with all the thoughts running through her head. "Do you mind if I call you later so that we can talk or if I come by your hotel? Where are you staying? There is something I have to look into."

"Unique, honestly, I don't think we have anything left to say. You've made your decision. You don't want me. It's clear that I was someone who you were going to settle for until you fixed things with . . . him." He pointed angrily at Unique's apartment.

"Terrance, that truly is not the case. I have to straighten some things out, and then I promise—"

"You don't need to make me any promises, Unique," Terrance said. "Look, you go on and get back with 50 Cent in there and try to start another family with him." As if on cue, 50 Cent came ambling down Unique's walkway and approached Terrance and Unique.

"Unique, is everything okay?" Eugene asked her.

"Yes, Eugene, everything is fine. Why don't you go, and I'll talk to you later?"

"No, Eugene, why don't you stay? Because I'm leaving." Terrance looked at Unique. "For good."

"Please, Terrance," Unique pleaded.

"Unique, don't beg this Negro to stay. Let him go. We don't need him," Eugene spat.

"We?" Terrance mocked.

"Eugene!" Unique said. She couldn't believe he was standing there, using the word *we,* as if they were an actual couple. Didn't he realize that what they'd shared inside was nothing more than a heat-of-the-moment kiss? It was not an attempt to rekindle their relationship, at least not on her part, anyway.

"No, he's right," Terrance said, opening his car door. "You and Lil Wayne should go start y'all a nice little family together or even get married, get back the twin daughters you conceived during your little one-night stand, raise them, and live happily ever after."

Eugene appeared stunned. "What? What did you say, man?" Eugene looked at Unique. "Twin daughters? The ones you were a surrogate for? What's he talking about, Unique?"

Unique buried her head in her hands in shame. The throbbing caused a streak of pain to fill her head.

"Was Miss Korica right?" Eugene said under his breath as he looked off in wonderment. This was why Korica had kept saying that he was the father of her grandchildren. But again, Eugene took everything that Korica said with a grain of salt.

Unique lifted her head and looked at Terrance. Her eyes questioned why he'd said that in front of Eugene, but of course, Unique hadn't gotten the chance to tell Eugene the whole truth, so he was clueless.

Terrance looked at Unique and saw pain written all over her face, but the biggest word was stamped right across her forehead: BUSTED! In all capital letters.

"Wow, Unique," Terrance said, shaking his head. "He didn't even know." He let out a tsk. "I can see now I dodged a bullet. Girl, your past is deadly. I'd need to marry you in a bulletproof vest instead of a tux." On that note, Terrance got into his car and drove off.

Unique's eyes began to water as she watched Terrance drive away. She didn't know if it was because she was so angry or so hurt, but the river was flowing.

"It's all right, baby girl," Eugene said, wrapping his arms around Unique.

Now, all of a sudden, Eugene's touch didn't feel like it had felt twenty minutes ago inside her kitchen. Unique was no longer caught up in her emotions. She pulled away.

"What's the matter? You okay?" Eugene said, rubbing Unique's cheek with the back of his hand.

Unique shooed his hand off her cheek like it was a mosquito about to bite her. "No, Eugene, I'm not." Unique looked up at him. "How did you get here?"

"Caught the bus."

"I need to take you home," Unique said. "But first, we have a stop to make."

Chapter 21

"Slow down," Eugene said to Unique as she drove way above the speed limit.

"I can't," Unique said, making a tight turn after almost driving through the intersection. The car screeched, and it felt as if it was up on two wheels. "I can't get to my mother's fast enough." She gritted her teeth and hit the steering wheel. "I'm not going to believe my mother tried to set me up."

Unique wasn't going to let another moment pass without confronting her mother. Here, she'd gotten her in another fix involving Eugene. Well, this time Unique was bringing Eugene along with her. Since he was always the one caught up in everything, it only seemed fitting that he was present. Clearly, Korica had been communicating with Eugene. Perhaps he could corroborate any story or call out a lie if Korica got to telling fibs.

"What are you talking about?" Eugene asked nervously.

"Terrance said she told him to go over to my house this evening." Unique shook her head and hit the steering wheel again. If Korica was behind the demise of her and Terrance's relationship, Unique didn't know how long it would take for her to forgive Korica, if ever. "She knew darn well I was having you over."

"Maybe she forgot. You know Miss Korica be smoking all that weed," Eugene said in Korica's defense.

"My gut tells me this has everything to do with some green stuff, but weed ain't it."

Eugene thought for a moment. "Listen, Nique, if you and Miss Korica are about to go at it, take me home first. I ain't been out the joint too long. She living over there in a nice neighborhood. Y'all get to wildin' out, them folks gon' call the police. I ain't got time for all that. Besides, you know your moms always got your back. She would never put you in a position like that. What reason would she have to do that? What would she get out of that? You know she only half can stand me, and the other half wishes I were dead. So she certainly wouldn't be trying to hook you and me up." Eugene let out a snort.

Unique looked at him as if she couldn't believe he was making sense.

Seeing that he was actually reasoning with Unique, Eugene continued. "I might not like Miss Korica a whole lot, but I know this much about her. If she ain't got nobody else's back in this world, she dang sure got yours." Eugene let out a little laugh and shook his head. "Nobody better not mess with her Unique."

Unique allowed Eugene's words to settle in her spirit. Within seconds, she had to admit, he was probably right. In all Korica's excitement over calling Terrance to apologize, Eugene had surely been the last person on her mind. Once again, Unique felt that Korica had probably been trying to look out for her. She had probably been making sure her baby girl got an appropriate proposal with a wedding ring. Unique even smiled when she recalled that Terrance had mentioned that Korica had shared with him the thoughts about marriage proposals that Unique had had way back when she was a little girl. Her Prince Charming would come rescue her from the hood.

"You're probably right," Unique said. "I don't know what I was thinking. This is all a mess, bad timing. The story of my life." She threw her hands up and then let them land back on the steering wheel.

"Don't do that, Unique." Eugene put his hand on Unique's shoulder. "The story of your life ain't nowheres near written."

Unique briefly looked over at Eugene and then put her eyes back on the road. She had calmed down and was back to doing speed limit. "I thought jail was supposed to roughen you up, not make you all soft and poetic," Unique joked with Eugene.

"Girl, what you talking about? Just 'cause a brotha shed a little tear, read a little poem and whatnot, why he gotta be soft?"

The two shared a laugh.

"So you still going to Miss Korica's house?" Eugene asked.

"No." Unique shook her head. "But before I take you home, there's still one stop I have to make."

Unique took a quick right and then drove for about five more minutes before she went through a large, white open gate.

When he realized where they were and what they were probably going to see, Eugene immediately sat up, his body stiff.

Unique sensed Eugene's uneasiness. "You never been here before?"

He shook his head.

"I didn't think so." Unique kept driving along the gravel road. When she finally parked and turned off the car, she quickly opened her car door, but Eugene remained frozen in place.

Unique held out her hand. "Come on."

Eugene looked down at Unique's hand and then over her shoulder and out the window. He caught sight of three large headstones in the near distance. He knew exactly who those headstones belonged to. He felt as if guilt was attempting to swallow him up whole. "I can't." He shook his head and stared straight ahead.

"Please, Eugene," Unique pleaded. "I think you need to do this. *We* need to do this."

Not only had Eugene never visited his son's grave site, but he also hadn't even known where his own child was buried. He'd said a prayer once in jail that he'd see his little man someday in heaven, but not in a graveyard. But at this point in his life, Eugene wasn't too sure God would let him into heaven, so he figured he'd better take advantage of the opportunity to see his son now.

"I think Junior would love to see his mommy and daddy together, coming to see about him." Unique smiled at Eugene, her hand still extended.

Eugene looked down at Unique's hand again. He stared at it for a moment. Could he do this? Was he strong enough, was he man enough, and did he even deserve the opportunity to pay his respects to his son? He'd failed him so much in life. He didn't even feel worthy of this visit. Then Eugene thought about his boy's smiling face. Given that Unique had never bad talked their fathers in front of the boys, they had been none the wiser about what losers their fathers were. Whenever Eugene's boy had come around him, it had always been with open arms and a smile. The boy hadn't even known what child support was, and he'd been unaware that he wasn't getting it on the regular. When his boy had looked at him, all he'd seen was Daddy. Eugene hadn't been able to even say his final good-byes. His boy at least deserved that from him now. With that last thought, Eugene placed his hand in Unique's.

Unique squeezed it tightly. "I'll be right here with you."

Eugene nodded, then opened the car door. He walked around and met Unique over on the driver's side. Hand in hand, Unique and Eugene walked over to the grave sites, where they sat for the next hour, reminiscing about what had been and contemplating what could have been. As Unique sat curled up under Eugene's arm, she couldn't help but wonder what could possibly still be.

This time was all about their son. There were no thoughts of Terrance and what had just happened. That was all a distant memory now. No suspicions about Korica having set Unique up came to mind. They neither thought nor spoke of any other man, woman, or child, not even the twins. This moment was dedicated to their fond memories of the boys. After all, that was all that was left of them . . . memories.

Chapter 22

"I watched the recorded episode of *Mary Mary* last night. Ole girl is going through the motions after finding out her husband had been cheating on her for years with multiple women and she'd been absolutely clueless!" Lorain said. She sat in the first row of the three-tiered bench seating in the viewing room at the dance school. "Guess that's two points for the chicks who go through cell phones and look in wallets and at credit card statements. At least they ain't clueless."

There were a couple chuckles from other parents who were watching their children through the glass the separated them.

A mother named Taina asked, "Which one of the girls found that out?" She'd been engrossed in a book but was now focused on Lorain.

"Tina, the one that just had the baby," Jacquelyn said, jumping in.

Another mother, named Makasha, who was sitting directly behind Lorain, shook her head. "The worst feeling in the world is to find out you're clueless."

"Is her husband a stay-at-home dad?" Ayanna, another mother, asked.

A mother named Michelle jumped in. "He's always at home every time they show him, but I think he's actually the music director for one of those late-night talk shows, *American Idol,* or something like that."

Lorain said, "I know she travels a lot, and some men will say she probably wasn't giving him enough sex. Well, they got quite a few babies to prove otherwise. And I'm sorry, but not being satisfied sexually is not grounds to cheat. Otherwise, there are a lot of women walking around who would have grounds to cheat, because men always get theirs during sex, but women can't say the same . . . but all those women don't hop out of the bed and go find somebody to finish the job."

"You said a mouthful, Lorain!" Makasha said.

Lorain turned and exchanged high fives with Makasha and a couple of the other mothers.

"Preach! You ain't never lied!" Ayanna exclaimed, and then she and Lorain high-fived as well.

Sharon, one of the dancer's grandmother, added her two cents. "He's not a househusband. He's a cheater with no redeeming qualities in my book!"

Dance mom Cerise, who was also a private investigator, said to Lorain, "You made every point I would have made. Well said!"

"I wonder which one of them makes the most money," Ayanna thought out loud. "I'm sorry, but cheating and being supported by my income is a double whammy. We can talk all we want about 'what's yours is mine' in marriage, but we all know to wait until her pain turns bitter. If she holds the purse strings, he'll have to ask for money to buy a Happy Meal. A woman scorned is a force!"

The women nodded in agreement.

"He does contribute," Sharon said. "He's a lowlife!"

Lorain turned to Sharon and chuckled. "Sharon, I don't see you sympathizing with him anytime soon."

Sharon shook her head. "Nope. I was a little upset that several episodes ago, when they were doing the cover shoot for *Ebony,* she 'accepted' responsibility for not being there for him. I couldn't see her being responsible for his actions, and now that he has admitted that there were numerous affairs over a long period of time, she realizes how deceived she really was." You could see in her eyes that Sharon felt the reality star's pain. It was as if she was speaking from experience.

Lorain turned to Ayanna. "I hear you about that woman scorned being a force. I know initially, when she thought he'd cheated on her with one woman, she wanted to forgive him. She felt that everybody makes mistakes. But, honey, he was cheating with the same woman for years. That ain't a mistake. That's a *relationship!*"

Some of the women nodded to show they agreed.

"And besides," Lorain added, "I'll have to agree with Iyanla Vanzant on this one. You can forgive somebody from a different address!"

"Now you preaching again," said someone sitting in the row behind Lorain.

"No question she needs to become a force—a force for putting him behind her!" It was clear Sharon was not going to give a cheating man any slack or any room for excuses.

Cerise jumped back into the conversation. "I don't watch the show, but every woman has intuition. She didn't lose hers, and something in the pit of her stomach said that he's not right. That's why their marriage has issues. They just aren't saying it on camera. Maybe this is the private investigator in me. To this day I haven't had a client hire me to prove their husband is cheating who didn't already know it. They tell me exactly where to find his cheating behind. She's no fool! This is why I stay in my man's business, and if he's doing what he's supposed to be doing, that should never be a problem for him."

Ayanna shook her head in disgust. "The violation . . . raw, unprotected sex . . . you know it was. All I can say is this will make for quite an album. You know, as an artist, that pain has to come out."

Sharon addressed the last comment Cerise had made. "I think if I was at the point of hiring a PI, I would certainly know something was up, but some people think they are doing all the right things and really don't have a clue until it smacks them in the face. In so many cases, love truly is blind."

Lorain said to Cerise, "I'm glad to hear that I'm not the only woman who gets in her man's business. I'm not obsessed, but this girl keeps her eyes and ears wide open. It's not a matter of distrust. I'm the kind of person who asks questions when I don't have answers. I refuse to run around in my marriage with a question mark on my forehead—afraid to ask my husband anything that is on my mind."

Lorain had to pause, because she'd caught her own self in a lie. Something had been bothering Nicholas about their wedding, or rather, about not having had a wedding. She could see it in his eyes every time he mentioned the wedding. But instead of coming right out and asking him about it, she'd just assumed she knew what was bothering him, and now she thought she could make it better by giving him a surprise wedding.

Lorain quickly changed the subject, addressing a comment Ayanna had made. "Ayanna, like you said, especially unprotected sex. That's attempted murder. 'AIDS kills. . . . Negro, you tried to kill me? For real?' Oh, it would be on in my house. I would be one of those women who started a bogus lawsuit, you know, the kind of women people were always talking about. I would absolutely try to hire a lawyer to help me with my attempted murder case."

"You and me both," someone agreed.

Cerise said to Sharon, "I respectfully disagree with what you said a minute ago, Sharon. It's not that love is blind, and frankly, men are not that good. I love my man, the father of my children, to the moon and back, but I do that with my eyes wide open. I give no woman credit for playing the fool, and believe me, it's an act. However, if it helps her sleep better at night, then sleep on."

One of the dads, who had been quietly tucked into a corner in the top row of the bench seating, finally spoke up. "Wow, he cheated with a *woman,* and yet it seems that all this faultfinding is aimed at the *man.* And you've made up excuses to search through a man's things without cause. If there is no reason to do so, please do not make one up. This goes both ways. That's just my view." He immediately buried his head back in his iPhone, where it had been. But of course, that hadn't kept him from hearing the hens peck.

Sharon addressed Cerise first. "I do understand where you're coming from, but I also have to believe there are exceptions to every rule." She turned and addressed the dance dad. "And certainly what's good for the goose is also good for the gander."

Lorain turned to the dance dad. "I hear you, but we ain't talking about a case on the ID Channel over here or about the O. J. Simpson case, where you need just cause and all that business. We're talking about matrimonial vows here."

Cerise jumped in to back up Lorain. "As long as we share an address and a bed, there's my reason. I agree, this also goes both ways. I have no quarrels with checking something out. If I'm wrong, great, but if I'm not, please believe I better be."

Sharon said, "I wish Tina could hear this conversation her situation has started and know she's not alone and there is light at the end of the tunnel. My second husband and I will celebrate thirty-seven very happy years together this year. I just learned that the wife of my first husband—the cheater—just filed for divorce. It seems she caught him with his umpteenth girlfriend and had enough!" Clearly, Sharon had been speaking from her own pain and experience, which people tended to do.

"Good for you and the mister, Sharon," Lorain said, congratulating her. "That's awesome! I pray I can say that about me and Nick one day. But back to you, Cerise. I see you don't play." They laughed. "I hear you, though. You don't need a warrant for a search and seizure of your own property. . . I mean the house and its contents . . . not referring to men and women as each other's property. I wanted to clear that up."

Ayanna said to Sharon, "I'm also blessed to have a second marriage that is all I hoped for. I recall snooping when I got 'the feeling' something wasn't right with my first husband. I went so far as to act like his secretary and call the hotel for a receipt 'for his expense account' to get proof he was cheating. We women have all the evidence but require a confession. I should have left then, but by the time I did, I didn't even need proof. But I found out a lot about myself and what was good for me and what I must have in a relationship. Good love is amazing. Hopefully, Tina will pick up her self-worth and toss out the garbage."

Shelia, one of the mothers who up to this point had been very quiet and had been listening, decided to join the conversation. "With her going public about the affair, she's also dealing with shame. If I could talk to her directly, I would tell her not to concern herself with what others have to say. She's the one who has to live with her decision, and she should do what she needs to do so she'll be happy. She should forget worrying about what the public may think."

A couple of the women nodded.

"That's exactly what her sister told her," Lorain said to Shelia.

"Good. Hopefully, she'll listen," Shelia said.

"Let me go back to something Ayanna said," Lorain stated. "Why is it, do you think, that women need to hear that confession from the horse's mouth?"

Shelia replied first. "I think women like to see if their man will tell the truth . . . confess after all the lies. Women go through the trouble of finding evidence so that when they confront the man, he won't be able to deny the allegations. But as we know, even with concrete proof, some men will still act like they are not guilty or will turn it around to make it seem like the wife is the reason why they slept with another woman."

"Plus," Lorain said, "if I do decide to forgive you, I need to know exactly what it is I'm forgiving you for."

Ayanna thought for a second and then replied, "I can't say exactly why. Maybe the least they can do is take ownership of the pain they've caused. I can't stand a liar, so it also could be wanting a confession for all the trouble I went through gathering dirt on your lying tail." Ayanna's voice rose an octave as she continued, and she began pointing her finger. "Oh, you gon' own up to this, you trifling pig. . . . Shoot!"

"Whoa," Lorain said, trying to calm Ayanna down. "Reel it back in. I didn't mean to take you back there. Count to ten and think happy thoughts . . . rainbows, flowers, and penny candy. . . ."

Ayanna counted to ten and then let out a deep breath. "Okay. Deep breaths . . . I'm happy Mary again."

"I'm not married yet," Michelle said. "I don't forgive for cheating. The reason why I'm probably not married yet is that I don't forgive for cheating. Control yourself or tell me so I can let you go. I will know, I will find out, and I'm not snooping. Bless you ladies who do. I can't. My Spidey senses are really good. They're linked to my instincts, which are linked to prayer, which, yes, is linked to God!"

"Amen," someone shouted.

Michelle continued. "I've said this before, and I will say it again. Human behavior is a science, one of the few natural sciences that are pretty exact. Unless your husband is a psycho, in which case you'd see other kinds of behavior and probably wouldn't live to tell about it, he will always leave a trail. Now faith in God will ensure that you recognize that behavior."

Lorain turned to Michelle. "I have to add that snooping is done in secret. I don't snoop. I need you to know I'm watching. That's called accountability, and every marriage should have some sort of accountability. You are right, Michelle. God will not allow you to be ignorant of Satan's devices . . . at least not forever, anyway."

"I understand," Michelle said. "And more times than not, it's right away. Before the exchange of numbers, before the first date. . . ."

The dance dad decided to add his two cents again. He wasn't about to let the scent of all the different women's perfumes that was filling the enclosed space overpower the male testosterone that was now permeating the room. "Even though marriage is to be respected for the vows and morals, there is that part about 'for better or for worse.' The true question seems to be, will she forgive him now and hold her peace? Or will she part from him and keep it moving?"

Michelle jumped right on that comment. "Yeah, but *worse* means losing a job, coping with sickness, dealing with the death of a child maybe. I don't think *worse* means committing adultery. That's not what God meant. But again, I'm not married, so what do I know." She shrugged.

Lorain addressed the dance dad. "You are absolutely right. We can all have our say and our opinions. We can talk about what we would do, what we didn't do, or what we have already done in our own situation, but each case and each person is different. Kobe and Bill Cosby's wife stayed in their marriages, while Michael Jordan's wife and Tiger's wife threw up deuces and stepped." She turned to Michelle. "And, Michelle, you have a point there. God does not compromise His word about the sanctity of marriage, so I'm inclined to agree with you."

Michelle smiled and nodded.

The dance dad wasn't quite finished making his point yet. "When wives are on the road or away from home, a lot of them cheat on their husbands. I don't think it's fair to single out men as the only cheaters. I'm not defending what he did, but it's funny how women are always quick to suggest divorce. Families have to find a way to stay together. Divorce is the easy way out. It doesn't even address the issues within the marriage."

Lorain addressed the dance dad. "Nobody is singling out men. This conversation is about a specific couple, in which the man was the cheater, not the woman, so that's what this particular dialogue pertains to."

"Okay," someone said before Lorain continued.

"I think you are confusing this conversation with somebody else's. No one in this room has suggested divorce. Even Tina's sister suggested she leave her husband for a little while, to get her thoughts together."

The dance dad was about to say something, but Lorain cut him off in order to finish up what she had to say.

"I repeat. In this instance the *man* was the cheater. I'm sure there is a discussion going on somewhere where the wife was the cheater and everybody is bashing cheating women. This is not that conversation."

The dance dad responded, "I have to bring balance to conversations like these. Women tend to get off the subject and turn the conversation into a male bashing festival."

Lorain replied, "How about you keep balance in the whole universe by continuing to be a faithful husband?"

The women clapped and high-fived when they heard that.

"There's no male bashing here," Michelle confirmed. "It's about setting the precedent for how someone treats you. It's about trusting God and your instincts before, during, and after—if you make the choice to divorce. It's about knowing when enough is enough. It's about knowing why you're staying. It's about the differences between different women and what they will or won't accept. No, no male bashing here. Don't make the mistake of speaking for your entire gender when you're responsible only for your own actions, because some men do some unforgivable things."

"Exactly," Lorain said. "We are not bashing all men. Just talking trash about the low down, dirty, cheating ones. No excuse to defile marriage *ever* . . . man or woman."

A mother named Paulette, who had been quiet up to now, said, "We all deal with situations in our marriage or relationship the best we can, and a lot depends on our emotional stability. She is doing it her way, and you ladies have done it your ways. We must forgive and let God do the judging. Married with children can be a tough place to be. As a Christian, I don't know and can't imagine what that would be like for someone with such a public life, anyway. There are no secrets, and whether or not she knew or did not know is irrelevant. She has chosen to make it work 'her way,' and we, as human beings with compassion for others, are to ask for her strength, peace, understanding, and encouragement in the Lord. That is where her answers really will come from. I've been sitting back and listening because this is a very interesting discussion."

"I don't think anyone was judging," Michelle said to Paulette. "I think that God allows certain discussions so people learn how to deal with situations. We all sympathize with her situation. In my humble opinion, whether or not she did or didn't know is relevant. It shows her obedience to God or possible lack thereof. She chose to put her Christian journey in the public eye for the purpose of our walking in our own journey."

Jacquelyn, who had been quiet for a minute, joined the conversation. "There are always red flags and some evidence that we, as women, refuse to admit or acknowledge without lowering ourselves and tree boxing the man or searching through his cell. Women are very wise and intelligent beings."

"Tina repeated over and over how she was clueless. So even if it isn't irrelevant to some of us, it was very much relevant to her and her pain," Lorain noted. "*Judging* and *having an opinion* are not interchangeable terms. We all deal with things differently in our Christian walk . . . at least all of us who are, in fact, Christians. Fasting and praying may work for one person in a particular situation, while in the same situation plain old-fashioned wisdom may work for another. I respect everyone's opinion, though, even if it does differ from mine. I won't say she is lowering herself if she chooses to stay with him, and I won't say the woman who searches the cell phone is lowering herself."

Lorain paused for a moment. "Everybody has different standards by which they weigh things, so I won't put mine on anybody else. Now I might say, 'I won't lower myself,' because those are the standards by which I weigh my own actions. But I'm conscious about not offending others by saying that they are lowering themselves, since they may be weighing their own actions by standards that are different than mine."

Jacquelyn took a deep breath, as if deciding whether or not to share what was on her mind. "I know when my husband first started running with other women, I chose not to end my marriage because of our children. But in no way was he allowed to be comfortable in it. We as women need to learn how to love and respect each other, and we must stick together and refuse to hurt our sisters by dating or sleeping with somebody else's husband. I don't share my panties, nor do I believe we should share our husbands in that way with other women."

"You know you just said that, girl!" someone called out.

"You got an amen from this corner!" another shouted.

Michelle exhaled. "Jacquelyn, I agree, and one of the first things I tell a married man if he asks me out is, 'I don't share! No, I don't want to hear about how bad your wife is treating you. Go talk to her. No, I don't care if you're just there for the kids. If you are ever single and it's meant to be, it will be.' There's a saying . . . 'A woman can run faster with her skirt up than a man can with his pants down.' I love it and live by it. No excuses."

"So true, Michelle," Jacquelyn said. "I like that saying. My mom used to say that all the time, about the woman running with her dress up. No man bashing intended. The truth is, men are going to ask, but a real woman should know to say no. God made man physically to sin, but He made woman to please the man. From my talks with my father and my brother, who was seven years older than me, I learned that once a man gets aroused, it is very painful and difficult for him to calm it down. So, ladies, learn to just say no to married men."

"Just say no to married men!" someone called out.

Jacquelyn continued. "God is a God that deals in truth. No deceit, lies, or manipulation will ever be found in Him or in the way He deals with us. Any secret sin will be brought to light. We have to learn to accept and deal with the truth."

There was a pause before Lorain spoke. "Jacquelyn touched on something *huge,* by the way. These children and how they affect our decisions as women to get into and stay in relationships." Lorain shook her head. She had to admit that she'd talked Nicholas into rushing into marriage and skipping a big wedding because of the twins. "This is a hard one. I'm going to continue to pray for Miss Tina and other women in her shoes. I know she regrets going public, but she is helping folks. It's one thing to tell somebody your testimony, but for people to actually see you walk it out in the midst of it . . ."

"No excuses ever for cheating, but Tina can grate a nerve," someone named Dawn said. "Her personality was a bit over the top. As for going through the phone, I refuse to do it. Once you're to that point, your problems are far bigger than that. I have not watched the show this season, but it's hard to believe she had no clue."

"I hear you, Dawn," Lorain said. "But I'm not mad at the woman who doesn't want to go to court and say, 'I want a divorce, because I think he's doing this, I think he's doing that, and I have a women's intuition about this, and God told me that.' No, in the court of law I'm slamming proof on the table. 'Dis what dat Negro did.

Contest that!' Like when Tom Cruise's ex-wife got herself a secret cell phone to communicate with her attorney when filing for divorce. Some women are being
abused and have to gather info secretly. Nope. You gotta
know someone's story. And if I grate a nerve, leave me,
but please don't risk my health and sanity."

"Yeah, I see your point," Dawn said. "My thought is
cheating is wrong, and definitely, risking the other party's health is wrong. Unfortunately, the other side of
the coin is that she obviously still wants to be with him.
Grating on his nerves can't be helping the situation. She
either doesn't care that she's doing it or doesn't know
how to stop it. Either way, she's not gonna have healthy
relationships unless she changes that. Notice I said *relationships,* not just marriage, because I think her personality negatively impacts her singing career as well."

All of a sudden, the conversation changed directions.
"So why is it that I seem to be the only woman who does
not support the illicit affair on *Scandal?* Am I missing
something?" someone said out of the blue.

"I have a girlfriend who refuses to watch the show for
just that reason," someone replied. "She doesn't understand why people are fascinated by that home-wrecking
scenario . . . practically rooting for Olivia to get somebody else's husband."

"No way. I don't support her affair," Michelle said.
"The show is more than the affair. I personally could do
without it, but it goes to a deeper place. Besides, she's
not the only one who has an affair on the show. The
main issues are the underhanded schemes the govern-
ment engages in every day."

"I was captivated by Olivia's business acumen during the first few episodes, but when everyone started
rooting for her because she was sleeping with the
president . . . I had to turn it off," said someone be-

hind Lorain. "I believe every woman can attest to this act one way or another, but it should never be condoned . . . lesson learned."

Just then Lorain's cell phone began to vibrate. She looked down at her caller ID screen, only to see the word restricted. She hated to be torn away from the very interesting and deep conversation at hand, but she needed to answer the call.

"Hello," Lorain greeted. For the next thirty seconds she listened as the caller spoke. With each second that passed and with every word she took in, the blood drained from her.

"Lorain, honey, are you okay?" someone whispered, placing their hand on her shoulder.

At that point, Lorain didn't even recognize the voice. She didn't even look up to see who it was that was trying to comfort her. The words that were entering her ear paralyzed her. After another few seconds of listening to the caller, Lorain heard a click in her ear. Moments after that her phone alerted her that she'd received a text from a restricted number. There was a date, time, and address.

"Lorain. Lorain." A different voice was calling her now.

Lorain couldn't speak. Even though the bench she sat on was hard, she felt as though she was sinking into a mound of pillows. She could feel the contents of her stomach rising to her throat. She jumped up and headed for the girls' locker room. She made it into a bathroom stall in time to puke into the toilet.

Lorain remained with her head over the toilet bowl to make sure everything had come up. Once she was certain she was finished, she flushed the toilet and then went to one of the sinks. She looked at herself in the mirror and saw that she was sweating profusely. She was clammy, and her stomach was still slightly queasy.

The smell of the sweaty locker room, which probably
contained garments that had been danced in all week
without being washed, made her want to puke again.
The taste of what had risen from her stomach to her
throat made her gag. Lorain turned on the water and began to rinse her mouth out and splash water on her face
to cool herself down. She had no idea how the dancers
tolerated this closed-in space, which didn't have a single
window, after having rehearsed for so many hours. The
permanent humidity in the locker room surely didn't
help them dry the sweat they'd worked up while rehearsing.

"Having a hot flash?"

Lorain looked into the mirror to see Ivy coming out of
a stall behind her. It wasn't until then that she realized
Ivy hadn't been in the viewing room, taking part in the
discussion they'd all just had.

"Something like that," Lorain said, grabbing a paper
towel and patting her face dry.

Ivy walked over to one of the sinks and began washing
her hands. She eyed a visibly discombobulated Lorain
the entire time.

"Are you okay?" Ivy almost sounded sincere.

Lorain nodded.

Ivy then grabbed herself a paper towel and began
drying her hands, all the while staring at Lorain, who
looked like a wreck.

"Look, Lorain, I know I can be a witch sometimes to
you," Ivy said. "Well, actually, to everybody." She chuckled.

Lorain didn't respond. She balled up her paper towel
and listened.

"I don't want you to take it personally," Ivy said. "It's
who I am. The way I come at people is pretty much a
conscious decision. In other words, I'm a witch on pur-

pose." Ivy said it without an ounce of shame. She was totally unapologetic. "I love my Gabby, and my other two kids as well. I'm a mother lion. And my own mother taught me that whenever I feel like my cubs are being threatened, I should attack. But you know what? She was wrong. What good mother waits around for her child to be attacked?"

Ivy's voice was intense as she continued. "You gotta let people know up front whose child not to mess with. You gotta attack first. I call it preventative maintenance. I show up with my claws and fangs showing, ready to battle out of the gate. I need people to know exactly what I'm working with so that they'll know that under no circumstances do they mess with mine. What they might be able to get away with, with the next child, they better think twice about when it comes to mine."

Lorain turned and faced her.

Ivy went on. "I watch Animal Planet enough to know that look in a mother lioness's eyes. That look that dares anyone to mess with her babies. I've seen it in my own eyes enough as well. And right now, for the first time, I think I see it in yours too." She snickered. "I knew that nice little Christian lady, 'kill 'em with kindness' garbage was an act." Ivy put the tip of her index finger between her front teeth, in thought. "Someone must have really done it now to finally bring out the beast in you. I feel like such a failure, considering for months I was incapable of doing so. I must be losing my touch."

"What are you getting at, Ivy?" Lorain came out and asked.

"I know we're not the best of friends. But we are a lot alike, you and me. I'm sure you don't take that as a compliment. But from one lioness to another, if you ever need anything from me, if anybody ever tries to screw with your cubs . . . you just say the word." Ivy balled up her paper towel, pitched it in the trash, and headed for the door. "But do me a favor, and don't let anyone know I said all that. They might think I care and have feelings. I got a reputation to keep around here, got a cub of my own to protect." Ivy winked and then walked out.

Lorain shook her head at the thought that she was anything at all like Ivy. Ivy was the type of mother who pounced before she even smelled danger. She looked over at the door that had closed behind Ivy seconds ago. Maybe that wasn't a bad thing, Ivy letting folks know that if they messed with her Gabby, they were messing with the wrong one. *Preventative maintenance.*

Lorain looked at herself in the mirror, staring into her own eyes. In the past, she'd tried the "kill 'em with kindness" thing, but obviously, someone like Ivy could see right through it, and so she'd chanced being eaten alive. She'd bitten her tongue and hidden her fists in her pockets one time too many. Was it possible that Ivy had given her that little golden nugget at the perfect time? Because God knew that Lorain was about to enter the wild and be in the fight of her life in an attempt to protect her baby cubs. Well, this time tomorrow, she'd find out.

Chapter 23

"Where have you been?"

"Oh, God!" Lorain almost jumped out of her skin as she grabbed her heart. "Jesus Christ, Nicholas! You scared me." It was late into the evening, and Lorain was just now walking in the front door of her home.

"Not as much as you scared me, I'm sure," Nicholas said as he walked through the foyer toward Lorain. He was in his pajamas. "It's ten o'clock at night. Your mom said that you weren't here when she got the girls off the bus and that you hadn't been back home since."

"I, uh, well, yeah," Lorain said. "I was doing wedding stuff." She wasn't lying completely. She had been doing wedding stuff, stuff for the surprise ceremony she was planning for Nicholas. But that wasn't the only activity that had occupied her into the late hours of the night.

"Really?" Nicholas shot her a peculiar look. "With Unique?"

Lorain thought for a moment as Nicholas stood, glaring her down, waiting for much-deserved answers. No answers were coming fast enough. At least not truthful ones.

"Yes, Unique."

"That's funny, because your mother called Unique, looking for you. She said she hadn't talked to you all day."

Lorain was so busted, but she'd started down the path of lying, and now she had to stay on it. "Well, I didn't actually do wedding stuff *with* Unique. Perhaps I should reword it. I did wedding stuff *for* Unique. Stuff for Unique's wedding."

Nicholas slowly nodded his head. "Oh, I see. Stuff like what?"

"Well, you know. Girl stuff. Wedding stuff. It's late. I'm sure you don't want to hear about that kind of thing." Lorain wagged her hand as she headed for the steps.

Nicholas grabbed her by the arm. Lorain stopped in her tracks and looked down at Nicholas's hand around her arm. It wasn't a tight grip or anything. But the look in his eyes told the story that he was not about to be played for a fool.

"Sure I do. I love hearing about your day. Come on. Let's go over to the couch and talk."

Lorain looked back up, and Nicholas pulled his hand away. "It's late," Lorain reiterated. I'm tired. I had a long day. I don't want to sit down here and talk on the couch. If you want, we can engage in our usual pillow talk." Lorain didn't want to give Nicholas the opportunity to insist they remain downstairs to talk. She proceeded up the steps.

Nicholas followed behind her. "Aren't you going to eat?" he asked.

"No. I'm not hungry."

"So you've had dinner already?"

"Yes, no . . . Well, I, uh, grabbed something earlier," Lorain said nervously as she arrived at the top of the steps.

"What did you eat?" Nicholas continued to question his wife, but to Lorain, it felt more like being badgered by cops in an interrogation room. Well, call her a hostile witness, because she wasn't having it!

Lorain turned around abruptly, almost causing Nicholas to run into her. "What is it with the hundred and one questions?" Lorain asked. "If there is something you want to ask me, come right out and ask."

"Okay. Fine," Nicholas said. "Are you having an affair?"

Lorain stared at Nicholas to see if he was serious about the question he'd posed. He looked dead serious.

"Nicholas Leon Wright, I can't even believe you fixed your mouth to ask me that!"

"Why not? We've always had the kind of relationship where we can ask each other whatever is on our mind. And we've always told each other the truth. I hope that hasn't changed."

"Of course not."

"Of course not what? You are not having an affair, or we have changed and we've stopped telling each other the truth?"

"Both," Lorain said. "I don't know whether to be mad at you right now, insulted, or what."

Lorain headed into the bedroom. She couldn't believe Nicholas actually had suspicions that she was cheating on him. The only other man she'd looked at with the least bit of desire since marrying Nicholas was the chocolate hunk from her doctors' wives' meeting who had greeted the women upon entering her home. But she'd only looked and certainly had not touched, or even thought of touching for that matter. A liar she might have been, with good reason as far as she was concerned. But a cheat she wasn't. No way was anybody going to be holding a conversation about her defiling her marriage the way they were doing at the twins' dance rehearsal that day regarding the famous gospel singer's cheating husband. Could Lorain blame her husband, though? After all, she had been acting suspicious.

As the women had pointed out in that conversation at the dance studio, Lorain knew that what was good for the goose was good for the gander. If it was okay for her to be in Nicholas's business in the name of marital accountability, then he darn sure had every right to be in hers.

"It's a reasonable question, you know, considering that in the past week you haven't answered your cell phone a couple times when I've called you," Nicholas said. "Ordinarily, you'd at least call me back once you'd seen that I'd called. In addition to that, some of your time has been unaccounted for."

Lorain turned around and faced Nicholas. The two of them stood in the middle of their bedroom. "My time has been unaccounted for? Since when do you keep tabs on my time?"

"Since you stopped answering or returning my calls. Since this is the second time in a week you've come home late. We've always lived a pretty predictable life, and now, all of a sudden, things are changing. I want to know what's going on. That way we can nip things in the bud."

"Well, believe me when I say there is no bud to nip. Trust me."

"Can I?"

Lorain looked at Nicholas sideways. "I'm going to pretend you didn't say that to me."

"We can pretend when we are role-playing with Leon, but right now this is Nicholas, and I'm dead serious. Is our marriage okay? Is there anything you are not telling me? Hiding from me?"

Lorain looked into the eyes of a man who was genuinely and sincerely concerned about her . . . about them. She respected him so much more for calling her out on her mess, rather than ignoring it and letting their marriage get out of control. She was blessed that he wasn't a man who allowed his ego to keep him from showing concern about his marriage. She wished to God she could share with Nicholas everything that was going on, but she couldn't. She hated lying to him, but hopefully, she wouldn't have to lie to him for long. But in the meantime, she needed all the help she could get to keep the truth from him.

"You coming down for dinner?" Lorain asked as she peeked into Nicholas's home office. The relationship had been a tad bit strained since their argument a couple days ago, but Lorain was hopeful that things would be back on track soon.

"Sure. In a minute," he said to her over his shoulder, not bothering to turn around and look at her. His desk sat facing the wall. His back was to the door. Nicholas was very much absorbed in the spreadsheet he was working on, on his computer, that and the checkbook on his desk.

"All right, then. I'll see you downstairs in a minute." Lorain went to close his office door behind her. Before she could do so, Nicholas posed a question to her.

"Baby, you haven't been doing any more shopping than usual, have you?" Nicholas asked.

Lorain swallowed hard. "Uh, no, not really."

"I didn't think so. I mean, I haven't seen you carrying in any bags or anything. I haven't noticed any new major purchases around the house."

"Why do you ask?"

"Nothing. I'll figure it out."

"Well, why don't you come on downstairs and eat? You've had a long day. Let me take a look at things and see if I can't figure it out. I'm sure you just switched a few numbers around or something."

"Yeah, maybe you're right," Nicholas agreed. "I've been looking at charts all day. I don't know what made me think I could come home and balance our checkbook and look at credit card statements. I'll figure it all out another time." Nicholas closed the document on the screen and stood up. "Right now I'm going to enjoy dinner with my beautiful wife and daughters."

Lorain smiled. She held the door open wide for her husband to walk through, allowing him to get ahead of her. Before following him, she turned and looked at the checkbook that lay open on Nicholas's desk. She might be a liar, but numbers didn't lie. It was only a matter of time before Lorain would have to come completely clean with her husband.

Chapter 24

"Baby, can you run my things to the cleaners for me?" Nicholas asked Lorain when he was about to walk out the door. "I kept forgetting to ask you, and I'm down to my last white coat."

"Sure, baby. I'll get them there before the cleaners closes today."

"Well, actually, I need them there before ten this morning in order to get next-day service," Nicholas stressed. "The one I'm wearing today I already wore yesterday. I managed not to stain it too badly, but who knows what today holds."

"But, honey, I . . ." Lorain stopped herself. If she told her husband she had somewhere she needed to rush off to the minute he walked out that door, he'd start asking questions . . . and then she'd have to start answering them. There was a light at the end of the tunnel, which meant that sooner rather than later she would no longer have to keep Nicholas in the dark when it came to her daily activities. But for now she had to keep the blindfold tied over his eyes.

Nicholas stood there with his hand on the doorknob, waiting for his wife to tell him that she couldn't make it to the cleaners before ten, which was very unusual. Usually, he never had to ask her twice to do anything, but today, for some reason, she seemed hesitant. Nicholas raised an eyebrow, an action that reflected his feelings of concern.

"Sure," Lorain said with a smile, although inside she was spitting fiery darts.

Nicholas kissed her on the lips and then headed out the door. "Have a good day," he called over his shoulder before he closed the door behind him.

That door wasn't even closed fast before Lorain started scaling the steps two at a time. She made it up to her bedroom in record time and quickly shed her robe and lifted her gown over her head. She kicked her house slippers off, and they went flying across the room. She washed up in the sink, saving time by eliminating her usual shower. She brushed her teeth and did her hair. She threw on an Old Navy long-sleeve tee and some jeans. She didn't even take time to put on earrings, which was something she'd taught her little darlings to never leave home without. Purse, earrings, lip gloss, and a nice scent were a girl's basic essentials before showing herself to the world.

Lorain grabbed her purse and raced down the steps. She got all the way out to her car before realizing she'd forgotten to grab the dry cleaning bag. "Snaps!" Lorain shouted as she got out of the car and went back into the house. By the time she got to the top of the steps, she had sweat beads on her forehead and she was breathing hard.

She went into the bathroom, opened the linen closet, and grabbed the dry cleaning bag from off the floor. Within one minute's time, she was back in her car and pulling out of her driveway like a bat out of hell. The driver of the car that was passing her driveway at that very moment lay on the horn, and that was what kept Lorain from driving out into traffic and possibly totaling her car.

"Jesus!" Lorain cried out. She then waved an apology to the driver through her rear window. She took a couple deep breaths, then looked at the clock on her car's dashboard. She had approximately twenty minutes to be in two places at one time. This time before she pulled out of her driveway, she made sure there were no oncoming cars.

When she neared a school, a couple of parents who were walking their children to school yelled and held up fingers—they were not making the peace sign—to let Lorain know that she was going a little faster than the law permitted in a school zone.

"I know we are supposed to follow God's laws and man's, but I'm sorry." Obedience was better than sacrifice, so surely Lorain should have obeyed the speed limit laws. But she was willing to sacrifice whatever she had to by not doing so.

It was 9:53 a.m. when she pulled into the parking lot of Lawson's Dry Cleaners. Lorain got out of the car and headed for the entrance. "Dang it!" She'd done it again. She'd forgotten to grab the bag of clothes to be dry-cleaned.

She went back to the car, retrieved the clothes, and then tried again. The chime that rang above her head let both her and Mr. Lawson know that she'd made it into the establishment.

"Hey, Mr. Lawson," Lorain called, greeting the owner of the only dry cleaners in Malvonia.

"Hey, Miss Lady. How are you?" He gave her a huge, toothless grin. He had the kind of smile that always made the jaw of everybody around him hurt.

"I'm actually doing pretty good." Lorain walked over to the counter and began emptying out the dry cleaning bag. As she placed Nicholas's items on the counter, she flipped his pockets inside out, like she always did, to make sure he hadn't left anything in them. She'd adopted this practice after he left his hospital ID in a pocket once.

"Well, that's good to hear, seeing that I don't see you over at New Day that much anymore." Mr. Lawson began going through the clothing as Lorain continued to place pieces on the counter.

"You know I got married. Had to follow the husband. We attend his family church now."

"Don't mean the both of you can't visit every now and then. If not as a guest of Jesus Christ, you can at least be a guest of your mother's." A huge grin spread across his face at the mention of Eleanor.

"Well, all right, then, Mr. Lawson. I have to go. I have somewhere I have to be." Most of the time Lorain would stand there and talk to Mr. Lawson for a few minutes, but today she didn't have the time.

"But you don't even have your receipt yet. Hold your horses." Mr. Lawson finished up counting the pieces, rang them up, and then handed Lorain the receipt.

Lorain snatched up the receipt and then headed for the door. It was customary for customers to pay for their items once they came and picked them up.

"Uh, Lorain, do you mind doing me a favor?"

"Goodness, man, did you not hear me say that I have somewhere I have to be?" That was what Lorain was screaming on the inside. But instead, she said, "What is it, Mr. Lawson?" between gritted teeth.

"Will you, uh, put in a good word on my behalf with that beautiful mother of yours? Woman won't pay me no never mind in church."

"Sure," Lorain said. She hated to be so short and rushed with Mr. Lawson. She was on the verge of being rude. "It was good seeing you, Mr. Lawson. I'll talk to you soon," Lorain said as she backed away hurriedly, almost tripping and falling.

"Watch it now, girl. Slow down, unless wherever it is you have to be is a matter of life and death."

Lorain simply smiled and then rushed out the door. She didn't want the person she had to meet to think she wasn't coming and to leave without the two handling their business. Because whether he knew it or not, Mr. Lawson was right. It was a matter of life and death. Her life with her twin girls and the death of her marriage.

Lorain pulled into the extended-stay hotel parking lot ten minutes later. She jumped out of the car and headed straight to the hotel room, where she had been expected to arrive ten minutes ago. It would now be her second time sneaking off to this hotel room, with only one other person knowing she was there. That was the person she was there to meet.

Lorain knocked on the door. There was no answer. "Come on," she pleaded to the invisible gods. She knocked again. When there was still no answer, she placed her ear against the door. "Please, please, God," she said, her voice breaking, on the verge of tears.

When Lorain was about to bury her face in the palms of her hands and stand there and cry, the door swung open. Standing there was a shirtless man, barefoot, wearing only a pair of jeans.

"Glad you could make it," he said to Lorain sarcastically. He looked behind his shoulder, over at the clock on the nightstand. "You're late. I thought you were going to let me get kicked out of here and put on the streets. If I were to get custody of my daughters, I would hate for the three of us to have to live on the streets."

Lorain stood there, wishing she could snap this jive turkey's neck and deep-fry him for Thanksgiving dinner. But she didn't know much about him. She didn't know how he operated. Unique had never talked much about any of her sons' fathers. The only thing Lorain knew was that they were all, in a nutshell, dope-slinging street thugs. Lorain had dated a street dude or two several years ago. She knew how ruthless some of them could be, so she had to feel this one out. Even though he had been locked up the past few years and had possibly lost his street connections, Lorain knew enough to know that serving time had given him that much more street credit, and it wouldn't be that hard for him to go out and find a little wannabe thug to do some dirty work for him. Especially one looking to gain some street cred of his own. She didn't want some gangbanger using her life to make a name for himself on the streets. She couldn't jeopardize her family by coming at him wrong. She couldn't jeopardize her girls by not coming at all.

"Come on in," Eugene said, inviting Lorain into the dimly lit hotel room.

Lorain peeked in and looked around as much as she could before stepping inside. But truthfully, she was going to enter that room even if there were a pack of lions sitting in there, waiting to devour her. She'd have to pray God would save her from the lion's den.

"Have a seat," Eugene said, locking the door behind her.

Lorain looked around the small, cluttered, and stuffy room. There was fast-food trash, snack packages, and beer bottles everywhere.

"I'll stand," Lorain said.

"Suit yourself." Eugene sat down on the double bed. He opened up the pizza box that was at the foot of the bed. He pulled out a cold slice. He took a bite and then looked at Lorain. While chewing, he said, "Want some?"

"No thank you," Lorain said. She wanted to throw up, and not just at the thought of eating pizza that she couldn't put a date on in a nasty hotel room. The fact that she was being blackmailed made her want to throw up too.

"So, you're here, which means you've thought about everything we talked about," Eugene said with a mouth full of food.

"Yes, I have thought about it . . . and . . ." Lorain had thought long and hard about everything Eugene had said since that day he called her while she was at the twins' dance rehearsal. His phone call was what had interrupted the discussion about cheating that she was having with the other dance moms and dads. His phone call was what had had her in the bathroom, puking her guts out.

Initially, he hadn't said much, just enough to make Lorain nervous.

"You don't know me, but I know you," Eugene had said through Lorain's cell phone receiver. "You're raising my daughters. Funny thing is, though, nobody even told me that I had twin daughters. I bet that wouldn't go over too well with the judge who signed the adoption papers. But I think I might have a solution to all this, and I'd like to discuss it in person. I'll text you about where you need to be, what day, and what time. Otherwise, I'll see you in court."

The line had gone dead, and Lorain didn't even have to think about who had been on the other end. When Unique got pregnant with the twins, she told Lorain that she hadn't even bothered telling Eugene he was the father. She couldn't come up with one reason why he needed to know. She was convinced he wouldn't take care of the twins any more than he'd taken care of the son she'd had by him. Unique knew the man far better than Lorain did, so she didn't argue with her. Now it was coming back to haunt her.

"Before we get started," Eugene said, "thanks for looking out and copping me this room. My moms was tripping. My ninety days was up, and she had my bags packed and at the door. So this was right on time."

"So you're doing this because you needed a place to stay?" Lorain asked him.

"No, no. Not just that, but it helped."

Lorain was a tad disappointed. If it was the thought of being homeless that had prompted him to seek her out, that was an easy fix. Lorain had done some volunteer work for Habitat for Humanity. That was her and Nicholas's adopted charity. They'd taken dollar houses and fixed them up, turning them into nice, livable homes for low-income families. It might be difficult to arrange a house for Eugene since he had a record, but Lorain could pull a few strings, make up a sob story about Eugene losing his son and needing society to give him a second chance, blah, blah, blah. She could get him hooked up and out of her hair. Could probably even get him a job with the organization. But it looked as though he wanted more.

"I got friends on the street who I can go stay with," Eugene told her. "I needed the space to get my mind right before I jump back in the game."

Lorain was all ears. If he planned on getting back into the game, that meant there was a chance this was a one-time thing, that if she gave him what he wanted, he would go on with life as usual and leave her be . . . her and the girls.

"So, anyway . . ." He threw the crust from the pizza slice he'd eaten back into the box, closed the lid, and brushed his hands together. "Let's get down to business. Just to reiterate from our first meeting . . ."

Eugene went on to repeat the terms he'd given Lorain at their first meeting at Captain Souls, where he had eaten everything on the menu and had stuck Lorain with the bill. Thank goodness she'd had her credit card on her, because she hadn't had the cash to cover all that he'd eaten, as well as all he had ordered to go.

He'd requested that she give him twenty-five thousand dollars, and he'd agreed to sign any paper she wanted him to sign that stated that he was giving up his paternal rights to the girls forever.

"Twenty-five thousand dollars!" Lorain had shouted so loudly that every head in the restaurant had turned in her direction. She'd leaned in and told Eugene, "I don't have that kind of money. I'm a stay-at-home mom."

"Yeah, with a husband who goes to work every day, as a doctor. I'm sure he wouldn't miss a few thousand here and a few thousand there. Besides, I've seen that reality show about doctors' wives. My moms watched it. Y'all spend that much money throwing parties to show off all the money y'all do have."

Lorain had cringed. He was right to some degree. The most she'd ever spent at once was ten thousand, but Tabby had peaked at twenty-five thousand with her winter wonderland theme last year. No wife would ever be able to outdo that all-white affair.

"So, in the meantime, while you think about it," Eugene had said after guzzling down the last of his Sprite and before signaling the waitress to get him a refill, "I'ma need a place to stay. Nothing fancy. A little hotel room or something. Oh yeah, and a few dollars to buy me some food until I can get on my feet, which will be real soon, depending on how soon you can get me that loot."

After their so-called meeting, Eugene had even had the nerve to ask Lorain for a ride to his mama's house. She'd obliged him, thinking the entire drive that she should take his black tail straight to the police station. Instead, she'd decided to play this thing out, having absolutely no idea how she would manage to take twenty-five thousand dollars from her and Nicholas's savings without him noticing.

Two days after that Lorain had gone to an extended-stay hotel and had booked Eugene a room for a week. She'd figured that was plenty of time for her to decide what she was going to do about Eugene and for her to gather the money, if that was what she decided to do.

This whole situation had been eating her up inside. This past week had certainly drained a decade of her life, at least it felt that way, anyhow. And having Nicholas on her back didn't make things any better. There had been so many times when Lorain wanted to tell him what was going on. But she didn't want to drag him into this ghetto mess of hers, which had started long before he ever said "I do" to her. He'd once asked about the twins' biological father. She'd simply told him it was some guy Unique had had a one-night stand with it. That wasn't the complete truth, but it wasn't a complete lie, either. She didn't want to get into all of that and have to explain herself if she didn't have to. She wanted everything to be done and over with, and she felt she could handle the situation.

Even at this moment, sitting in this hotel room with this thuggish blackmailer, she still felt confident that she could handle things alone. Telling Nicholas about her situation with Eugene would mean she'd have to tell him that she'd known who the twins' biological father was all along. Their marriage was already on shaky ground. She couldn't risk the ground crumbling completely. Besides that, Nicholas had a private practice to tend to. Taking time away from his work meant taking money from their bank accounts. She wanted everything to remain as normal as possible with her family and their lifestyle. She would not allow her family to suffer the consequences of her lies and mistakes. She had got into this mess by herself and she would fix it by herself, saving herself the embarrassment of being such a fool.

"I've got some money for you," Lorain said.

A gap-toothed grin spread across Eugene's face. He held out his hand. Lorain pulled a manila envelope out of her purse and placed it in Eugene's hand. He gave her a peculiar look and then looked at the envelope. He began to fondle the envelope.

"This don't feel like no twenty-five grand." He opened the envelope and looked through its contents. "Lady, what you trying to pull here?" He stood up angrily.

Lorain backed away. "Wait!" She put her hands up. "It's not twenty-five thousand. All I could get was ten."

"Ten?" Eugene spat. "Is that all those pretty little girls are worth to you? Ten thousand dollars? And all that money you and dude over there sitting on? Witch, you better go on with that mess."

"I told you, I don't work. You think my husband won't miss twenty-five thousand dollars? That's the best I can do."

"Then, trick, I'ma need you to go back and do all that you can do," Eugene said with authority as he stood. "I'm supposed to meet up with some people to get something from them today. I had business to handle." Eugene was furious, and spittle flung out of his mouth. "Them cats gon' think I'm playing games with them. Lady, I swear to God." He walked up on Lorain and used his hand to make the shape of a gun and put it to Lorain's head.

Lorain began to sweat when she felt Eugene's index finger press against her temple. "I'll get the rest. I promise. It's going to take a little more time."

"Time? Witch, I ain't got time. I got moves to make." Eugene began pacing.

"Then do what you need to do, then." Lorain had the nerve to get bold.

"No! You do what *you* need to do in order to have the rest of that money for me," Eugene snapped. "Look, you got two days."

"But—"

"Or you can kiss your little girls good-bye. You understand me?"

Lorain's lips tightened. She looked over at the lamp
on the nightstand and wanted to take it and bash his
head in with it and kill him dead. That was how much
anger she felt rising up inside of her. That would only
land her in jail, away from the girls. What good would
that do her? It would defeat the entire purpose of even
dealing with this joker in the first place.

"Okay, okay," Lorain grumbled, relenting. "I'll get you
the money, and I swear to God that better be the last I
hear from you, or—"

"Or what?"

Lorain had no words, to say, anyway. But in her head
a voice was speaking loud and clear. *If you ever try to
show your face and threaten to take my girls again, I
will have to take the chance of being away from my
girls for ten to fifteen years for manslaughter. Because
I will kill you and bury you myself.*

"Thought so," Eugene said. Then he went and sat back
down on the bed in anger. "Get on out of here and go get
my money. Two days! Two days!" He held up his index
finger and middle finger, not giving Lorain the peace
sign, but indicating the number of days she had to get
him his money.

Sweat poured from Lorain's face and ran down her
neck as she backed up toward the door.

"And stop at the front desk and extend my stay."

Lorain reached behind her and put her trembling
hand on the doorknob, not turning her back to Eugene for one second. She fumbled with the knob before
opening the door. She backed out of the room and then
closed the door behind her.

She leaned up against the door and exhaled. Her chest rose up and down as she breathed heavily. She went into her purse and pulled out a tissue. She began wiping away the perspiration. She ran her fingers through her hair. The roots were a little matted, and some of the edges were sticking straight up as a result of the perspiration. After a few seconds Lorain was able to gain her composure enough to walk over to the registration desk in the lobby and extend Eugene's stay by two more days.

Two days. That was all the time she had to come up with fifteen thousand dollars.

She climbed back into her car and sat there for a moment. She squeezed her eyes closed tightly in an attempt to keep the tears inside. Where was she going to get another fifteen thousand dollars? If only she'd taken Mary's advice a long time ago and kept her own bank account with her own money in it, this wouldn't be a problem. She would have easily made a withdrawal and paid Eugene off without a fuss. But now she was in a position where she was practically stealing from her husband in order to get Eugene the money he was demanding from her, practically stealing from her. Lorain was a liar turned thief.

She started the car. She looked in the rearview mirror to see if anything or anyone was behind her before she backed out. She locked eyes on herself in the mirror. "I'm going to hell for sure now," Lorain told herself as she pulled out of the parking spot. She left the parking lot and headed back home to try to figure out how she would come up with the money. As she drove, she looked down at her hands as they gripped the steering wheel, and that act alone gave her a good idea about just where she would start.

Chapter 25

An hour later Lorain pulled into her driveway. She got out of the car and headed straight into her house. When she opened the door and walked inside, she almost fell over all the suitcases that were sitting in the foyer, right inside the door.

"What the . . . ?" she said, looking down at her Louis Vuitton luggage set. She looked up to see Nicholas leaning against the fountain, legs crossed and arms folded. "Nicholas, baby? What's going on? What are you doing home? And are we going somewhere?"

Lorain thought for a moment, and then her eyes lit up. She knew exactly what was going on. Her man was sending her on a surprise vacation. He had probably seen how stressed out she'd been these past couple of months or so, and wanted to do something nice for her. This wouldn't be the first time, either. Once he'd sent her and Eleanor on a trip to Vegas for four days, while he actually cut his hours at work to tend to the girls . . . he and the nanny they got from a temp service.

"Oh, Nicholas, honey. You have no idea how much I need this." Lord knows, after these next two days were over with and she'd rid her life of Eugene, a vacation and time away would be well deserved. Lorain ran over and embraced her husband. "I can't go today, though, but I—"

"Yes, you are. You have to go today." Nicholas's voice was solemn.

Not only was her husband not hugging her back, but he also sounded very bitter, not like a husband who was sending his wife off on a surprise trip to the Bahamas, to stay at the Atlantis or something.

Lorain pulled back. "Excuse me?" She didn't even look Nicholas in the face. She was staring down at his chest. Lorain did not want to see the look in her husband's eyes. She could feel that something was wrong. She didn't want to see it. She'd already heard it.

"Lorain, you have to get out of this house today."

"What are you talking about?" Lorain could not have been more confused. She had to look up. She had to see for herself if this man was serious. Her eyes darted from one of his eyes to the other. After a few seconds of Nicholas just standing there, staring over Lorain's shoulder, she began to nod. A smile crept onto her face as she slipped her hands around his neck. "Oh, I get it. This is Leon talking." Lorain leaned up against him. "Well, listen here, Leon—"

"Lorain, I'ma need you to get your stuff and go . . . now . . . before I lose it. I'm trying to be calm, so just go." Nicholas pointed to the door.

Lorain could hear the beating of her heart, and it sounded like someone had taken a stick and was hitting something, such as a drum, with it right next to her ear. That was the way her heart felt too. The pain was piercing.

"There you are," Eleanor said as she came around the corner from the dining room. "I was trying to flag you down before you left earlier, but you drove off like a bat out of hell. Anyway . . ." Eleanor was about to continue before she realized that husband and wife were standing there, staring at one another, with serious looks on their faces. Neither had even turned in her direction. It was as if she hadn't even entered the foyer. "Did I interrupt something?"

Lorain didn't speak right away, and neither did Nicholas.

Eleanor spotted the luggage. "Is somebody going somewhere?"

Lorain cleared her throat. "Well, Ma, from the looks of it, I am." She gave Nicholas a questioning look. "Isn't that right, Nick?"

"Lorain, I'd rather not do this in front of your mother," Nicholas said.

"Oh, you don't want her to see the good doctor put her daughter and granddaughters out on the street like trash?"

"Whoa! What's really going on here?" Eleanor walked closer to them, now clearly concerned. "You putting my girls out?" Eleanor asked Nicholas. "Why? What is it?" Eleanor's mouth dropped open. "You got a new woman, huh, don't you?" Eleanor turned angrily to Lorain, pointing an accusing finger. "I told you not to let him hire that Helen. What man could resist that ba-dunka-dunk? Heck, I be wanting to reach out and squeeze it when she be walking down the aisle at church." Eleanor made a squeezing motion with her hands.

"Ma Eleanor, it's not that," Nicholas said.

Eleanor looked at Nicholas, trying to figure out what else it could be. She snapped a finger once another thought entered her head. "Uh-huh, I knew it." She turned to Lorain. "I told you what you should be doing with that mouth besides running it. Now look. You done run yourself right out of your own marriage." Eleanor shook her head. "I don't know what it is with you black women and not wanting to—"

"Ma Eleanor, please." Nicholas put his hand up. This was the most attitude he'd ever shown his mother-in-law. Usually, he was amused by her antics, but today wasn't a day he would be entertained by them.

Eleanor backed down. "Well, I'm sorry. I was trying to—"

"I know, I know," Nicholas told her in a more calming tone. "It's just that I really don't want to have this conversation in front of you."

"I get that, but you 'bout to put my child and grandchildren out on the streets. I think I deserve to know why."

"That's not true. I'm not putting your child and your grandchildren out on the streets," Nicholas said. Both women looked relieved. But that vanished within seconds, when Nicholas said, "Just your daughter."

Now Lorain was mad. What the heck was going on here to make her husband want to put her out of the house, and not only that, but keep the girls there with him . . . away from her? "You are talking crazy right now. I don't know what's going on, but I do know one thing. Wherever I go, my daughters go with me."

"Well, not this time, because I don't want my daughters staying in some motel with you and that lowlife you've been seeing behind my back."

Lorain's eyes bucked. "What are you talking about? What motel? What low—" Her words had no other choice but to trail off, as she realized what Nicholas was talking about. "Eugene," she said under her breath.

"And you've even got the nerve to say your lover's name in our house," Nicholas spat. "Go." Nicholas pointed at the door again.

Lorain put her hand over her face in relief. If Eugene was the reason Nicholas was putting her out, this was a mix-up. She could explain. She'd wanted to take care of the matter on her own and not drag Nicholas into it, but her hand was being forced. She was not about to lose her husband because he thought she was cheating on him with Unique's babies' daddy. "Honey, I can explain." She smiled, ready to come clean and clear her name.

"You don't need to explain. I have all the explanation I need right here." He pulled a paper out of his back pocket. "And right here." He held up his cell phone.

"What is that?" Eleanor couldn't help but ask out of curiosity.

Lorain shot her a look to silence her. She then turned back to Nicholas. "What is that?"

"Oh, just where you've been paying for the hotel room, buying food, taking out large sums of cash and a credit card advance. What? Is he making you pay for it?" He snickered. "Got you a real live gigolo. Guess Leon wasn't enough for you."

"Leon?" Eleanor said. "Not enough? What the heck you two freaks be doing over here?"

Eleanor was ignored once again as Nicholas stood there, hurt filling his eyes. "Guess I wasn't enough."

"Baby, if you'll let me explain," Lorain said, "you'll see that it's not what it looks like."

"You know, wife, I thought the same thing too, but then this right here is exactly what it looks like." He pushed a button on his phone, then held it up to display some pictures.

Lorain stepped in closer to get a good look at the pictures. As Nicholas scrolled through, she saw pictures of herself and Eugene. The worst was a picture that was taken just this morning, of her standing in the doorway of the hotel room with a shirtless man. The pictures of her standing in the threshold of the hotel room and closing the door behind her looked quite incriminating. But the most telling pictures were the ones of Lorain after she'd come back out of the hotel room. In one of them she was standing outside of the hotel room, all sweaty. And in another she was wiping the sweat away.

Lorain looked up at Nicholas with her mouth wide open. No words came out. After all, what could she say? The pictures said it all.

"The extended-stay hotel," Nicholas said. "And the Captain Souls charge to the credit card bill. A ton of food was charged. What? He convinced you to take him, *Tyrone*, and the rest of his posse out to what they consider fine dining?" Nicholas huffed, referring to the fictitious Tyrone that the talented Erykah Badu sang about. "Well, I guess you better call Tyrone, 'cause he can fool with you both. I'm done."

Lorain was still in shock at the pictures, and now Nicholas was adding salt to the wound with his words. She put her left hand over her mouth as tears filled her eyes.

Nicholas began walking toward her. He had always hated to see her cry, but today he wasn't fazed. He reached out and grabbed her hand. "Your wedding ring . . ." He looked at Lorain's vacant ring finger. "Guess you must have left it on the nightstand in his hotel room." He flung her hand away.

"Now like I said," he told Lorain, "you will be leaving, and you will be leaving the girls here. I will not have my daughters around this." He looked at Lorain with such disappointment and hurt in his eyes. "I wanted you so badly to be the person I thought you were. I even made the mistake of thinking that even if you weren't, eventually, God would change you. But I knew from the moment I had that conversation with Korica all those years ago that I was living a lie. That our entire marriage was a lie. That's why it pains me whenever the subject of our marriage even comes up." Nicholas turned his back. He couldn't even stand to look at Lorain anymore.

"Korica? What does she have to do with any of this?" Lorain asked.

"That's just what I was going to ask."

Both Lorain and Nicholas ignored Eleanor yet again, and then Nicholas relayed the conversation he'd had with Korica right after he and Lorain married.

"So, how's married life treating you thus far?" Korica had asked Nicholas.

"Better than I could have ever dreamed," Nicholas had answered.

"Yeah, Unique told me how you and Lorain ran off and got married on a whim."

"Well, not exactly on a whim," Nicholas had said, correcting her. "We'd already had plans to marry next spring. It's that we decided, 'Why wait?'" He'd shrugged. "So we did it."

"And let me guess. I bet it was all Lorain's idea not to delay the wedding." Korica was using that all too familiar knowing tone.

"Well, you know, she presented the idea, and eventually, I agreed."

"Well, that was definitely a good move on her part. That's definitely something the courts would take into consideration," Korica said.

"Courts? What are you talking about?" Nicholas's curiosity was piqued, and that was right where Korica wanted it.

She opened her mouth to speak but then paused on purpose. "No, I better not say anything."

"No, please, say it," Nicholas said, pressing her.

"Well, Lorain and I were talking, and she was a little worried about perhaps Unique wanting to take the twins back from her, you know, to fill the void left by the loss of the boys," Korica informed him. "I told her she shouldn't worry, but she got all worked up about the fact that she was not really in any better of a situation than Unique. I mean, her being single too and all."

Nicholas's brown complexion was now a shade of red.

"I'm sorry. It's obvious she hasn't discussed this with you," Korica said. "Please don't tell her I shared this with you. As Unique's mothers, she and I need to get along, and I don't want to throw a monkey wrench in that by speaking about something I perhaps shouldn't have."

"Oh, don't worry. I won't say anything," Nicholas assured Korica.

There had been a million things running through Nicholas's head at the time that conversation took place. He didn't know how to feel about the information Korica had shared with him. He didn't know if it mattered that Lorain might have convinced him to move their marriage up for her own selfish reasons, and he even wondered whether selfishness, not love, had motivated her to marry him in the first place. But life had been good for Nicholas, Lorain, and the girls. When Korica dropped that bombshell on him, he didn't want any of that to change. But something told him at the time that if he brought it up to Lorain, so much would, in fact, change. So he decided not to. For the sake of the girls, he removed himself and his feelings from the equation and became selfless. But thanks to the seed Korica had planted in his spirit, there had always been a nagging feeling inside of him about the sincerity of his and Lorain's nuptials. Lorain's actions of late had given him all the answers he needed.

"I didn't know what to think after hearing that," Nicholas told Lorain now. "Over the years I've questioned whether you loved me, whether you loved me in the beginning or grew to love me. But now, after knowing there is someone else in your life, I can't help but wonder if you ever loved me at all."

"Nicholas," Lorain said softly as tears flowed down her face.

"But you know what?" Nicholas continued. "Guess our marriage—what it was, wasn't, or is—doesn't matter anymore. Because it's over. So I guess I'll never know what your true intentions were." He turned to walk away.

E.N. Joy

"Nicholas, please, no—"

"Girl, you better not stand here and beg like some dog," Eleanor said. "When a man don't wantcha, child, if you insist on clinging to him, anyway, he gon' treat you like gum on the bottom of his shoe until ain't absolutely no flavor left in ya whatsoever. Then he gon' leave you, like your daddy did me." Eleanor had become emotional. She loved her son-in-law, but if he didn't want her daughter, the advice she'd pass on to her only child was not going to be for her to stay where she wasn't wanted.

At this point Lorain was drained, and she realized that she wasn't going to get anywhere with her husband, not right now. And that conversation Korica had had with him, which had been festering all these years, was the nail in the coffin of her dead marriage. Lorain looked at her mother, defeated.

"Come on, Mama. Let's go," Lorain said as she picked up one of the suitcases.

Eleanor looked at her child like she had two heads. "What do you mean, let's? You the one getting put out, not me. I ain't got nothing to do with this trifling mess. Y'all can do what y'all want to do. Stay married, get married twice, get divorced. My name is Bennet, and I ain't in it. And if anybody think about putting me out, you gon' have to go downtown and evict me. Ain't nobody got time for that. . . ." Eleanor shook her head and mumbled to herself the entire time as she walked away and headed back to her place.

The couple just stood there.

"I can't believe you're doing this to me," Lorain said.

"Baby, you did this to yourself," Nicholas said.

"My girls."

"They'll be fine, and you know it. Besides, enough people have been used already. You don't need to try to use them as well."

"How dare you say that?" Lorain snapped, offended.

"Do you blame me? Lorain, look at how far you went to make sure you got to be the one to raise Heaven and Victoria. You rushed into a marriage with me. You practically blackballed your firstborn, or did you not think I noticed?" Nicholas replied. "Just because I don't speak about a whole lot doesn't mean I'm clueless. Enough is enough. I've watched you—"

"Stop it. I know." Lorain buried her head in her hands. "You don't have to tell me what I've done. I've done wrong. I've done you wrong, and, baby, I'm sorry, but if you'd let me explain everything, it will all make sense." Lorain walked over and threw her arms around Nicholas. "You know I love you. You know my marrying you wasn't a lie. I loved you then, and I love you even more now."

Nicholas felt for his wife as she bared her soul and cried on his chest. He wanted nothing more than to put his arms around her and let her know that everything was going to be all right. But he wasn't sure if it was. She wasn't some toy that he'd picked up at the store and that had broken. She was broken when she came to him. Fixing her wasn't a job for him, Leon, or any handyman. This was a job for God. And there was one thing that as a doctor, Nicholas had vowed never to have—a God complex. People could not fix people—not their spirit, anyway.

"We'll discuss what we'll tell the girls later, but for now, good-bye." Nicholas walked away.

As drained as Lorain was, she couldn't give up without putting up more of a fight. "Baby, Eugene is—"

Nicholas stopped abruptly and turned in his tracks. He threw his hand up and shouted, "Stop it!" He was fed up and furious with his wife. He couldn't bear to hear her speak one more word.

Lorain tensed up. Never had Nicholas raised his voice that much and spoken with such authority. She was afraid, not of her husband and not that he would get violent. She was afraid that if she tried to explain the situation, Nicholas was so worked up, he wouldn't hear a word she was saying . . . or believe her. So with great reluctance, Lorain watched as Nicholas disappeared up the steps. She could hear their bedroom door close, as she'd heard in Nicholas's voice the sound of his heart closing her out.

Chapter 26

Eleanor was still fussing when she made it back over to her place. She went straight to her kitchen, opened her cupboard, and grabbed a bottle of Stella Rosa wine. She looked up while gripping the bottle. "See this, God?" She shook the bottle slightly. "They got me over here drinking, and not in the memory of your son's name."

Eleanor pulled out her kitchen drawer and grabbed the corkscrew. After opening the wine, she went into the cabinet and grabbed a long-stemmed wineglass with gold trim around the rim. She filled the glass with wine. She lifted the glass to her lips. As she was about to take a sip, her front doorbell rang. She sighed, placed the glass on the counter, and then went to answer the door.

The doorbell rang again as Eleanor was on her way. "I'm coming. I'm coming," she said. When she made it to the door, she looked out the peephole. She then sighed. "I knew I should have taken me a drink first."

Eleanor opened the door and found Lorain standing there, surrounded by her suitcases, which she'd struggled to carry.

"Dang, he wouldn't even let you wait there for the taxi to come pick you up and take you where you need to be?" Eleanor shook her head. "You must done really did it now." She stepped aside. "Come on in and wait for the taxi, 'cause I know if the man won't let you stay in his house, he sure as heck ain't gon' let you drive his car off into the sunset to be with another man."

"There is no other man," Lorain told her mother. She didn't move from her spot in the doorway.

"According to those pictures on the cell phone, there is," Eleanor retorted, begging to differ. "Now, I didn't get a good look, but it sho' nuff looked like a man to me . . . and without a shirt on." Eleanor began to squirm. "Then again, I might not be the best judge of that, seeing I ain't been that close to a shirtless man since forever. And the one in the pic looked like he had some muscles. Ooh, child, I don't blame ya for letting him get it."

"Nobody gets *it* but my husband. Like I said, there's so much more to this story than you could ever believe."

"It ain't me who needs to believe it."

"I know." Lorain slumped her shoulders. "If only he'd let me explain."

"Give him time. That's all I can say. Now, get on in here," Eleanor said, wrapping her arms around herself, signifying that she had a chill. "It's spring, not summer. And you know the weather here. Monday you got on shorts, Tuesday a rain jacket, and Wednesday your snow boots. Heck, I almost turned my heat on today."

Lorain started carrying her suitcases inside.

"Hold up!" Eleanor put her hand up. "Ain't no need for you to bring all that stuff in here. You can leave the luggage on the porch until the taxi comes. How long did they say they were going to be, anyway? I'm ready to get my Olivia Pope on and drink me a fishbowl full of wine and relax. "

"Mom, really? Your daughter's life is in shambles, and all you can think about is sending me off in a taxi so you can drink some wine?" Lorain brushed by her mother as she entered her home. "There is no taxi. I don't have anywhere to go. I figured I could stay here until . . ." Lorain didn't know until when. All she knew was that her husband had put her out, and she had nowhere to go.

She'd distanced herself so much from her grown daughter that she wasn't even comfortable in the same room with her for five minutes, let alone living with her. Besides, all of this would blow over once Nicholas calmed down and listened to reason. No, he wouldn't be happy about everything Lorain had gotten herself caught up in due to her own selfish actions, but he'd know that she loved him and was no cheat.

"Oh, heck to the naw. I don't do roommates." Eleanor shook her head adamantly. "Besides, Nick said you had to get out of his house." Eleanor looked around. "Well, the last time I checked, this was his house too. So humph, humph. You can't stay here. And besides, what am I gon' do with you when I got company?"

"Company?"

"You heard me. You think your mama ain't gon' ever get a man?" Eleanor put her hands on her hips and began twisting and turning, striking poses. "I been playing hard to get with that Mr. Lawson for years now. I've been thinking about finally giving in."

"Mr. Lawson?" Lorain said, recalling the favor he'd asked of her in the dry cleaners. But now wasn't the time to try to play matchmaker. Her own relationship was on the brink.

"Yeah. I know he ain't the finest man on the planet, but he's a nice guy, and he ain't half bad looking when he puts his teeth in. Besides, he owns his own business," Eleanor said. "Plus, I lost a hundred and fifty pounds with that bariatric surgery all them years ago, and I've managed to keep it off. Why let a hot body like this go to waste?" She made her best attempt to twerk.

"Mama, I can't right now. . . . I just can't." Lorain shook her head and put her hand up. "Are you going to let me stay here or not?"

"Sorry, but like I said, I don't do company." Eleanor was adamant. "You can stay here until your taxi comes."

Lorain couldn't believe her own mother was doing her this way. First, her husband, and now her own mother. She didn't know how much more of this she could take. "Mama, you wouldn't do your daughter like that, would you?" Her eyes moistened and her bottom lip trembled as she fought off the tears.

Eleanor pulled the door closed and glared at Lorain. "Absolutely not. I wanted you to see what it felt like for your own mama not to want to be bothered with you, is all." Eleanor cut her eyes so hard at her daughter that Lorain felt split in two. "You know where the second bedroom is," Eleanor said, walking toward the kitchen, mumbling. "Child think she V. C. Andrews on some *Flowers in the Attic* ish." Eleanor disappeared back into the kitchen to get her drink on.

Carrying two of her suitcases, Lorain headed to the second bedroom. She had to make two trips in order to get all of her luggage. She then started the task of going through her suitcases in order to find some pajamas. The first suitcase she looked into was full of outerwear. Next, she opened the medium-size trunk. She moved a couple items around, and then her eyes locked on the memory box the girls had made her in preschool. It was where she kept her most precious keepsakes. It was just like Nicholas to know what was important to her. But on the same note, that didn't sit too well with Lorain. Did the fact that he'd sent her packing with all her memories mean that this was the end of any memories the two of them could ever possibly make together?

That thought caused a lone tear to fall from Lorain's eye. She quickly brushed it away, opened the box, and went through it. There were pictures of her, Nicholas, and the girls from their trip to Vegas to get married.

It pained Lorain to think that Nicholas thought she'd married him only for her own selfish reasons and not for love. Korica had planted a seed in her husband's ear the same way she'd planted a seed in Lorain's to make her want to run off and marry Nicholas on a humbug in the first place. She would have married him eventually, though.

She remembered what Korica had said to her at the time. "Yeah, I know about that so-called doctor you've been dating. Got him running in and out of your house. What kind of example are you setting for Victoria and Heaven? Me, I don't have no man. My focus is my kids, even now that they're grown. So do you see now? That's the difference between you and me, boo. I'm a real chick who takes care of hers. While a ho like you spreads and dumps her baby for any ole body to take care of."

If Korica had been able to give the courts that kind of impression of Lorain, without a doubt, she wouldn't have been allowed to adopt the twins. What judge in his or her right mind would give a woman who had thrown one of her babies in the trash two new ones to take care of? But she'd been unstable back then, a young single mother. She wondered, though, if the courts still would have found her to be just as unstable when she was seeking custody of the twins. Lorain hadn't wanted to risk it, so she'd convinced Nicholas to elope in Vegas quick, fast, and in a hurry. She could admit that rushing the wedding was all about her being selfish, but the marriage itself was based on nothing but genuine love. Korica's manipulative words had carried so much power. It wasn't going to be easy to convince Nicholas of the truth.

Lorain wiped away a tear and continued looking through the box. There were special birthday cards, one that had touched her so much that she wanted to keep them and reread the words. There were little trinkets the girls had made in school for her for Mother's Day. She sifted through the box a little more and came across a drawing that completely took her breath away.

Lorain gasped and covered her mouth with her hand as her eyes filled with tears. The work of art shook in her trembling hand as she looked at the drawing her middle grandson had created before his passing. It was a picture he'd drawn of her and Unique. The two women were standing hand in hand and holding a Bible, and each was wearing a cross necklace. That was how he'd envisioned his mother and grandmother. Lorain's heart stung as she thought of the injustice she was doing to her grandson's memory. How disappointed he must be up there in heaven, looking down at her, she thought. Lorain quickly and roughly wiped her tears away, shoved the items back in the box, and put the lid on it. She grabbed her purse and dashed out of the room.

"Where you going in such a hurry?" asked Eleanor, who was sitting on the living room couch with her feet propped up, drinking wine.

"I'm going to get my baby," Lorain said, then ran out the door.

Eleanor took a sip of wine, smiled, and said, "That's my baby." She looked up to the heavens. "I knew she'd get it right eventually."

Chapter 27

Lorain pulled up in front of Unique's apartment, got out of the car, and rushed to her door and began knocking. She knew that it was late and that she hadn't called before coming over. There was a chance Unique might not even answer the door. She knocked again. There was still no answer. She turned around and looked into the parking lot. Unique's car was nowhere in sight. It wasn't that she simply wasn't answering the door. She wasn't home.

"No," Lorain said, disappointed. She'd told herself that she wasn't sleeping one more night until she fixed things with her oldest daughter. She couldn't see how continuing to run, hide, and lie was ever going to make things right. Maybe Lorain couldn't have everything she wanted, but she could have everything she'd ever prayed for, which was a great husband and a wonderful relationship with her children. Hopefully, after setting things straight, admitting her faults, and quitting them with both Nicholas and Unique, she could get what she'd prayed for.

Lorain raced back to her car. She'd set out on a mission to talk with Unique before she rested her head, and that was exactly what she was going to do. And she knew exactly where she might find her daughter.

Lorain knocked on the door and waited impatiently. It was close to midnight, but she didn't care. Whether it was twelve noon or twelve midnight, she was 100 percent certain she'd get the same not so warm welcome.

It was pitch black outside, but suddenly the porch light came on and the front door flung open. All Lorain heard was, "If it isn't Mama number two. What the devil are you doing here?"

"Funny you should ask that," Lorain said, "considering I came to see the devil . . . and here she stands."

"Wait a minute. You're at my house now—"

"The house my daughter bought you."

"Your daughter? You keep believing that because you gave birth to her, you deserve the right to call her your daughter. But need I repeatedly remind you who raised her?"

"Look, Korica," Lorain said, seething, forcing the words through her teeth. "I couldn't care less about you. I actually came to see if by chance Unique was here."

"She's not, so you can exit stage left. But don't worry. I'll tell her that her wannabe mother stopped by." Korica went to close the door, but Lorain pushed it back open.

"You have gone too far, and I will not sit back and watch you destroy my family. You have caused strife between me and my husband, me and my daughter, and it stops now."

Korica stepped out of the house and got nose to nose with Lorain. "Anything you got going on with your husband is your own doing. Same with Unique."

"Don't you dare try to pretend your hands are clean in all of this. My husband told me about the little talk you had with him at Unique's event when she first got out of jail."

Korica thought for a minute, recollecting the conversation to which Lorain was referring. She wagged her hand upon recalling it. "That little convo. Please. It was the truth, so don't be mad at me. Don't you want your husband to know the truth? What kind of relationship starts off on a lie?"

"You mean like your relationship with Unique? All lies and deceit."

"Here we go." Korica rolled her eyes.

"It was about money then, and it's about money now. What? Are you afraid Unique is going to want to spend all her money on me and won't be able to buy you anything else? News flash, I got my own."

"No, you got lucky and married money with your broke self."

"Oh, I've never been broke. But guess what?" Lorain pointed a finger in Korica's face. "You still ended up broke and broken. Anybody who acts like you has to be hurt and broken, because you know what they say. Hurt people hurt people. But you keep it up, and while you're trying to ruin my relationship with Unique, you're going to ruin your own. Surely, you've heard the saying 'What goes around comes around.' So be careful that the hole you think you're digging for me isn't your own grave."

"Go on somewhere with all that rah-rah," Korica said, putting her hand up in Lorain's face.

Lorain steered her hand around Korica's and stuck it in Korica's face. "Mark my words. And God forbid you ruin your relationship with Unique. Lord only knows how you're going to keep up with the taxes on this house when all you've ever known is Section Eight housing."

Korica hit Lorain's hand out of her face. "Don't you ever talk down to me like that, ever! I deserve this right here." Korica pointed behind her at her house. "You have no idea what I sacrificed to take care of the daughter you threw away. I earned this here."

"Earned?" Lorain couldn't believe Korica had let that word come out of her mouth.

"You heard me. And what have you done to earn anything? All you did was meet up with Unique again by chance after I had already reared her. You weren't even a decent enough human being to try to find out what happened to the baby you threw in the garbage. Humph. Sounds to me like that makes you the trash."

Lorain shrugged her shoulders. "You can stop trying to say that with such venom. It doesn't hurt anymore. I've repented and atoned."

Korica threw her hands up. "God, you Christians kill me with that nonsense! You think that because you say ten Hail Marys, do three laps around the church sanctuary, and throw up in a bucket while someone slings a prayer cloth over you, the things you've done in your life will have no consequences. Can't you see that you're still paying for everything you've done?"

Lorain took in Korica's words. Did they have some validity? Sure. Lorain had repented and done her best to atone, but then she'd tried to run off like a coward before she ever really had to face the music. God had given her a second chance to connect with the baby girl whose childhood she'd missed out on, and then what had she done? Let some hood rat bully her into giving up Unique all over again, and for what?

"Why, Korica?" Lorain asked her, exhausted and tired of fighting with her. "I did what you asked. You told me I could have the girls as long as I gave you Unique. But then money comes into the picture, and you renege? Is that all you're going to do the rest of your life? Manipulate people, pretend that you love and want them whenever there's a financial gain for you?"

"Don't you dare act like you know me, my story, and why I do what I do, Mrs. . . ." She looked Lorain up and down. "Mrs. Doctor's Wife. I bet you never went a day in your charming little holy life without."

"Now, I ain't been saved all my life," Lorain replied.

"That's apparent," Korica shot back. "But have you ever lived in the projects? Ever been on food stamps? Welfare? Medicaid? Ever had the eye doctor bring out a box of ten pairs of ugly glasses to select from because that's all Medicaid would pay for? Ever worn the same pair of jeans every week with a different shirt and hoped no one noticed?"

The more Korica spoke, the more emotional she got. "Ever had to take cold baths in the dead of winter because there was no gas? Ever had to cook all yo' meals in Crock-Pots and on hot plates? Use a cooler instead of the fridge because the electric bill never got paid, so you pretending with your kids y'all camping indoors, trying to make it fun? You got the little ones who don't know no better and the older ones just playing along to keep from seeing the shame in my eyes." Korica swallowed her tears and continued. "You ever have to sleep with your mama's boyfriend while she watched so he'd pay the rent so you and your brothers and sisters wouldn't get thrown out in the streets?"

Lorain had no words for the scenarios Korica was throwing at her.

"Witch, you have no idea what you'll do for money unless you've been in one of those predicaments. Don't mean I'm a bad person. Just means I'm sc . . ." Korica halted her words. She couldn't say what she really wanted to say. No, she was way too strong for that. So Lorain finished her sentence for her.

"Scared."

A tear slid down Korica's face as Lorain said the word.

"I get it. I get it, Korica," Lorain assured her passionately. "No, I might not be scared of doing without, but I am scared of another thing—the truth. Girl, my truth is so raggedy and messed up, I don't think it could ever get repaired and be made to look decent."

Korica let out a harrumph. "Is that so? I thought y'all's God could fix anything."

"Why do you say that?" Lorain asked in a perturbed tone. "Why are you always saying y'all's God? Don't you know that He's your God too?"

"Huh. Yeah, right." Korica folded her arms and rolled her eyes. "Let me guess. God loves me. God will give me my heart's desires. God will never leave or forsake me. God will provide for me. Well, where in the devil's hell was God when my daddy left us for dead? When all my mother was doing was telling us kids how much she hated us? When men were using me and abusing me? Staying with me long enough till I could give 'em a baby? When all I wanted was a regular house to live in and not some drug-infested, prostitute-, pimp- and gang-infested project? When I was being molested? Raped? When my stomach cramped at the end of the month, when my stamps ran out, and I could make sure only that my kids ate? I couldn't risk eating 'cause then one of them might not have get enough.

"Where was God when I had to use paper towels for pads when it was that time of the month because it was either a pack of diapers for my baby or a pack of maxi pads for me? God wasn't loving me then. Providing for me. Forget about giving me my heart's desires. What about my stomach's? What about the basic necessities of life? I sure felt forsaken, unless God was sitting right there in the room, like some big ole pervert, while them dirty old men was running up inside of me?"

"Enough!" Lorain said. "Stop it!" She couldn't take any more. She had watched Korica speak with such pain, hurt, and agony. It was almost as if she was standing there, watching herself. She, too, had once felt that broken. But God? When and why had Lorain strayed so far away from God? When had she forgotten about

His mercy and amazing grace? Why had she turned to the father of lies, worshipping him by continuing to live lies? She should have been a reflection of God's glory to women like Korica, but instead, a woman like Korica was reminding her of this fact. Before Lorain knew it, tears were streaming down her own face.

Korica tilted her head from side to side, looking at Lorain. "Are those tears for yourself?"

Lorain wiped her tears away, shaking her head. "From hearing your story," Lorain admitted. "I didn't know—"

"Don't you dare cry for me!" Korica snapped. "You save those tears for your own darn self." Korica turned her back to Lorain. "Like I need your pity."

"You're right. You don't need my pity, but, sista, something we both need is God's grace and mercy. And He's not just my God, in spite of what you might think. He's your God too, Korica. I know you've struggled, I know you had it hard, and the fact that my selfish act resulted in you having one more mouth to feed, which meant one more burden on your already heavy load . . . I'm . . . I'm sorry. And not only am I sorry, but I thank you, my sista. Thank you. You did what I couldn't. You did what I didn't. Thank you. God knew you were the chosen one to teach Unique how to be a fighter, how to make it. It's because of you that my baby girl survived jail and the death of not one, but three of her babies. And then she was strong enough to let the other two go." Tears were now streaming down both Korica's and Lorain's faces.

Slowly and hesitantly, Lorain placed her hand on Korica's shoulder. Korica looked down at Lorain's hand and then over her shoulder at Lorain's face.

"Thank you for raising the baby I threw away and left for dead," Lorain said. "Thank you for being the strong black woman that you are. Thank you for holding me accountable with my child, and with my husband, for that matter. Although it felt like a thorn in my side, you were pushing me, testing me, and I failed miserably. Now here you are, back again, and I'm still failing." Lorain removed her hand from Korica's shoulder. Korica still didn't turn her body completely around to face Lorain. "Well, you know what? No more. Not this time. Never again will I sit around on pins and needles, waiting for someone else to pull the rug out from under me, revealing all the mess I've been sweeping up under it. I will not be a puppet to the lies and a prisoner of my truths." Tears fell like a stream from Lorain's eyes. "Glory!" she shouted.

Korica turned around and looked at her.

"Hallelujah! In the name of Jesus, I repent for the lies, secrets, and wrongdoings. And, God, I come to you not because I've been revealed and caught, but because I owe you that. You've given me too much and done too much for me. And I pay you back by grieving you." Lorain stomped her foot and shook her head. "Please forgive me, God. Wash me, God. Give me a clean heart and a clean mind. I know the world likes to hold our past against us, but, God, you are a God of second chances, third, fourth, and fifth ones. You are a God of fresh starts. And I thank you. God, I thank you."

With each word Lorain spoke, she felt as if chains were falling off. She felt like she could float. A huge weight was being lifted as God received her prayer. "Yes, God!" she shouted as her feet, with a mind of their own, began to move. And she jumped and she leaped right there on Korica's porch.

"Oh, my goodness! Is this that Holy Ghost stuff they be talking about?" Korica said, not knowing what to do with the woman who was happy in the spirit right there on her porch. She attempted to grab hold of Lorain, but Lorain's arms were just a-flailing as she cried out to God.

Korica was in a panic as she watched Lorain flop around, speak in tongues, her head bobbing up and down and her arms waving at the ground while her feet moved faster than James Brown's at a concert. When all her attempts to grab hold of Lorain failed, she did the only thing she could think of. She cupped her hands around her mouth and yelled out, "Somebody call nine-one-one!"

Chapter 28

"Are you sure you're okay to drive, ma'am?" the EMT said to Lorain as she sat in her car and talked to him through the rolled-down window. The gentleman, who was of medium height and had brown skin, was genuinely concerned.

"Yes, I promise you all is well," Lorain assured him. "I'm sorry you all wasted your time coming out, but I assure you I'm one hundred percent healthy."

Not one, but two of Korica's neighbors had actually called 911. And it hadn't made things look any better when the ambulance pulled up to find Lorain laid out in the spirit on Korica's porch. The heavy scent of ammonia entering Lorain's nostrils had brought her out of her spiritual coma. This wasn't the first time Lorain had been laid out in the spirit, but it was the most powerful time. When she'd come to, she was dizzy and a tad incoherent. She figured God must have needed to put her under a little bit longer than usual . . . taking her a little bit deeper in Him. Her stomach had felt queasy, but she was sure that had everything to do with that horrific smell.

"In all honesty," Lorain said to the EMT, "I think she's the one you need to check on." Lorain nodded toward Korica, who sat on her porch, still spooked by the entire incident.

The EMT looked back up at Korica. "Yeah, looks like she's seen a ghost." He chuckled.

"She did." Lorain then said under her breath, "The Holy Ghost."

"I'll go check on her. You take care, miss."

"Thank you," Lorain said as he walked away. She rolled her window up and then started her car. She looked over at the passenger seat, at her cell phone. She picked it up and saw that she had back-to-back missed calls from Eleanor. She was about to call her to let her know she was okay when she saw that Eleanor had texted her as well. The one thing Lorain knew about her mother was that she never sent text messages. She didn't read 'em, and she didn't send 'em. So something had to be up.

Lorain opened the text and read it. She threw the phone back down on the passenger seat, backed out of the driveway and drove back to her mother's place as quickly as she could. She didn't care how many traffic laws she broke. She was about to lose her daughter for good.

"You can't pick up and move to Atlanta," Lorain said to Unique as she, Unique, and Eleanor sat in Eleanor's living room.

When Lorain had read the text that her mother had sent her, her heart had nearly stopped. The text read,

Unique is here at the house, on way to airport. Moving to Atlanta.

She had hoped it was all a misunderstanding. But here Unique sat, confirming that she had an early morning flight she planned on catching after making her rounds of good-byes. She had a one-way ticket to Atlanta and did not foresee that she'd ever be back.

"But what about Terrance?" Lorain asked in a panic. "Is that where he's making you move?"

"Mom, Terrance isn't making me do anything, because there is no me and Terrance," Unique told her.

"What?" Lorain was shocked to hear that. But if she'd kept in touch with her daughter more, maybe she'd have known that. "What happened?"

"It's a long story, but in short, he walked in on me and one of my babies' daddies while we were mourning the death of our son. It didn't look good, if you know what I mean." Unique didn't have to go into details. It was clear to both Lorain and Eleanor that Terrance must have walked in on something he couldn't deal with. Unique saw the look in Lorain's and Eleanor's eyes and wanted to clear something up. "I didn't cheat on him or anything like that. Yes, Eugene and I shared a kiss, but—"

"Eugene?" Lorain interrupted. "Your oldest son's father. The girls' . . ."

Unique nodded, putting her head down in shame. "Yeah, him. I don't know what happened. I got caught up. As always, he was saying all the right things—"

"I know what happened," Lorain said. "It's a setup." She looked at Unique. "We've been played."

Lorain went on to share with Unique all her dealings with Eugene. In the midst of doing so, she also shared with Unique the feelings she'd had toward her with regard to the girls. All of this had played a part in her getting caught up.

"I feel so awful, Unique," Lorain cried. "I'm so sorry, baby girl. I blew my second chance with you. I pushed you away . . . and now all the way to Atlanta."

"Mom, please don't think that," Unique said, hugging Lorain. "I think so much has happened in our lives, past and present, that we've only been doing what we grew up learning how to do—survive by any means necessary.

But as Christian women, we should have had enough faith in God to know that the battle was not ours. I love you. And I don't love you any less right now. I know at first, when I found out you were my biological mother, I said some things that made you feel like crap, but that was the hurt, abandoned little girl in me talking."

"I know all about that," Lorain told her.

"But when the godly woman in me said she forgave you, I meant it. All I care about is our now. And let's not let life get in the way of our now ever again. Okay?"

Lorain agreed. "Okay, baby."

The two women embraced as Eleanor began to sniffle. With her sniffling seeming to purposely get louder and louder, both Unique and Lorain finally turned their attention to Eleanor and pulled her in for a hug.

The three generations of women hugged, kissed, apologized, and forgave for the next few minutes.

Unique was the first to remove herself from the embrace and stand. "Now that that's all said and done, I need to—"

"You can't leave, Unique," Lorain stood up and declared. "What about me? What about your daughters?" A hush fell over the room. Lorain couldn't believe it herself that those words had fallen from her mouth.

Unique took Lorain by the hands. "Heaven and Victoria are your daughters, my sisters, and that's the way it is always going to be . . . forever." Unique said it in such a way that it removed all doubt from Lorain's mind that Unique would ever try to take the girls from her. But then, of course, there was still one other person who possibly could.

"Eugene," Lorain said under her breath. Fear filled her eyes.

That quickly, Unique, too, had forgotten about Eugene's devious self.

"I suppose he is a ticking time bomb we need to figure out how to diffuse," Unique said.

"Come on!" Lorain said, grabbing her purse. "I know where to find him! But I'm going to have to make a phone call first." Lorain grabbed her cell phone and began to dial.

"Who are you calling?" Unique asked.

"Someone who I should have called in the first place!"

Chapter 29

"Oh, I see both you wenches showed up," Eugene said after opening his hotel room door. He rubbed sleep out of his eyes. It was six o'clock in the morning. The sun was barely lighting the sky. "I figured it was only a matter of time before the left hand told the right hand what was up." He looked at Unique. "That's exactly why I stopped foolin' with yo' moms and did my own thing."

"Eugene Brown, you should be ashamed of yourself," Unique scolded. "How you gon' come to my house and share all those things you said to me about our son and then blackmail his grandmama? I'm not gonna believe you are that kind of monster."

He shrugged. "You wasn't trying to fool with me. You dropped me off at my mom's crib that night like I wasn't nothing. And you ain't even tried to holla at ya boy since." He snickered. "And I had given you my best performance yet. A brotha even cried." He said it as if he was so proud of himself for having faked his emotions so well.

"But what about everything you said? Was that all an act?" Unique couldn't believe it. "The time we spent at our son's grave site . . ."

Eugene sucked his teeth. "Girl, please," he told Unique. "I didn't mean none of that mess. You know how I do. I say what I need to say to get you right where I want you. I thought I'd be able to sweet-talk my way out of my mama's house and into yours. The whole thing

Miss Korica had lined up looked like it was going to be a bust. I had to look out for self."

"What do you mean, what my mother had lined up?" Unique's blood was starting to boil. Had her instincts been right all along that evening at her house when Terrance showed up while Eugene was there? Had Korica been behind the whole thing, setting it up for Terrance to catch her with Eugene?

"Man, I ain't tryin'a talk about Miss Korica. I'm tryin'a talk Benjamins."

Unique grabbed Eugene by his shirt. "You better get to talking right now."

"Unique, please, let him go," Lorain told her. "Come on, Unique."

Unique looked over at Lorain. Lorain was able to calm her daughter with her eyes. She released Eugene's shirt. "Talk," she insisted.

Figuring he wasn't going to get what he wanted unless he gave them what they wanted, he got to talking. "Yo' moms was supposed to get you to forgive me. You and I were gon' hook up, get the twins and the money that came along with the twins. For me, it was all about the money. I think your moms had other intentions." He looked at Lorain. "I love money. . . . Miss Korica knows that about me. But, see, Miss Korica hated you more than I loved money. She was losing focus. She wanted to live a comfortable life with her happy little family—Unique and the twins. I was trying to get paid, and at first, I thought that was all Miss Korica wanted too. Stuff was about to get too messy. Like I said, I had to look out for self."

"So all this started with you wanting me to forgive you?" Unique asked.

Eugene shrugged. "I mean, I ain't gon' lie. That part was true, the whole thing about me wanting you to forgive me. I was being one hunnid. I told you that in all the letters I sent you."

"What letters?" Unique questioned.

Eugene had mentioned the letters before, but Korica had talked over him and Unique had been too angry at the time for his words to register.

"All those letters I sent to you at your sister's house. Your mom gave 'em back to me. She said you hated me so much that you didn't even open them. But she said she would talk to you and get you to soften your heart or some mess like that."

"Eugene, I never got any letters from you."

Eugene twisted his lips like he didn't believe her. "Your sister even told me she gave them to your mom to give to you."

"When did you talk to my sister?"

"I called her house a couple times, looking for you," Eugene answered. "She finally accepted one of my collect calls and told me you wasn't staying there no more." Eugene was tired of talking about something that was nothing to him; he was ready to talk about something far more important in his book.

He went on. "Long story short, your moms was trying to play me stupid, use me as a pawn in whatever game she's trying to run. I ain't falling for the okey doke. I couldn't trust your moms after that incident with her sending ole boy to your house, knowing I was there. I had just talked to her the day before, letting her know I was meeting up with you, so she knew good and well what she was doing. At that point, I didn't know who was trying to play me and who was on my team. So, as you can see, I went free agent."

Unique shook her head in disbelief. She couldn't breathe. It felt as if her lungs had been punctured or were filling up with fluid. She stood there, speechless.

"Anyway," Eugene said to Unique, "you can take that up with Miss Korica." He looked at Lorain. "All I want to know is if you got the rest of my money. I'm tired of dealing with you hood chicks turned rich chicks, now that y'all think y'all all that."

"No, I'm taking it up with you," Unique said with rage in her eyes.

"Like I said, it was all Miss Korica's doing," Eugene told Unique. "She started all this. She was waiting for me the day I got out of jail. She told me about the twins and about how you got all that money in that settlement against the state for jailing you, making you miss the boys' funeral, and everything. She said that most of it was sitting in a trust for the girls. Said if we got back together, I'd have access to the money, blah, blah, blah. I ain't even know how much it was, but, shoot, looking at that house you bought your mom, I could clearly see that you had kept some for yourself. Figured I'd kill two birds with one stone. Hook up with you and get whatever you had, plus whatever was for the girls."

Unique stood paralyzed. Had the woman she'd felt indebted to since she was a little girl turned on her? All along, had she been no better than those foster parents, who had wanted only the check that was attached to Unique and not Unique herself? And what about Korica's talk about wanting a relationship with the twins? Was it really all about money? These were all questions Unique allowed to swarm around her head, knowing if she voiced them aloud, neither her baby daddy nor her mom could provide the answers. Then again, no answer would make enough sense to soothe the pain Unique's heart was suffering right now.

Lorain wasn't the least bit shocked by what Eugene had said. Lorain had always surmised that Korica would do about anything to get what she wanted, even if it meant risking her relationship with Unique. After all, Lorain had pretty much done the same. *Takes one to know one,* she thought. So she didn't even bother addressing Korica's actions, knowing she'd be nothing short of the pot calling the kettle black.

"And what about the girls, Eugene?" Lorain asked. "Would you have even wanted them?"

He was silent at first. "Unique is a good mother. She would have looked out for them while I did my thang," he finally said.

"Oh, so just how it was with Junior," Unique said. "You would have left me to raise them alone."

Eugene steered around that issue. "None of that matters. Why are we even talking about it? Heck, you got paid. I should have gotten paid too. I just want what's coming to me."

"Oh, you're gonna get what's coming to you, all right," Unique said.

"Yep, the same way you did. I wanna be ballin' out of control too."

"That's where you're wrong," Unique said. "I didn't keep a dime of that money for myself. If I had, I sure as heck wouldn't be living in an apartment."

"You don't owe him an explanation," Lorain told Unique.

"I know I don't, but I'm going to give his sorry a . . . his sorry behind one, anyway. I know I shouldn't care what this lowlife thinks of me, but a part of me does. So I want him to know I'm not cut from the same cloth as my mother. I've never been out for myself or wanted to benefit financially from anyone, especially the twins."

Unique went on to explain that the criminal defense attorney who had helped free her from jail had referred her to a civil attorney. That attorney had helped Unique file a case against the state of Ohio for sitting on evidence, causing wrongful imprisonment, and making her miss her sons' funeral. It was a nice amount of money, and it could have easily brought an end to Unique's days of pushing cosmetics and mini sandwiches. But that money wasn't for her to live off of. She opted to repay the people who had made her life better in other ways. Korica was first on her list. Unique couldn't describe how it felt to be able to buy her a house and show her how much she appreciated what she'd done for her over the years.

Lorain had told Unique about a set of Louis Vuitton luggage she'd seen in one of the shops at a hotel she was staying at in Vegas. Nicholas had already paid so much to send her and Eleanor on the trip that she couldn't see herself asking him for that obscene amount of money to purchase the luggage, so Unique got it for her.

Unique didn't even buy herself a car, despite the fact that at the time she got the money, she hadn't yet earned her Cadillac. Unique upgraded the boys' headstones, and the money that was left, she put into a trust fund for the twins. The money could be withdrawn only by the girls' legal guardian. Not even Unique had access to it after she signed it over. Lorain had even had the decency not to touch the girls' money.

"Blah, blah, blah," Eugene said. "That all sounds nice, but it's too confusing for me to try to even come close to figuring out. Sounds like either way it goes, there wasn't nothing really in it for me. I mean, hearing you say all that, I could probably get custody of the girls and come out better financially." He looked at Unique. "It won't be hard convincing the judge that you don't want 'em. I mean, heck, you gave 'em away. But I ain't got time to be going to court and going through no hearing and stuff. I'm trying to get paid now!"

He looked at Lorain. "So pay me the other part of the twenty-five Gs, and you won't have to worry about me coming back, trying to get the girls, get more money or anything. I'm 'bout to hook up with these cats from New York and flip that twenty-five, so that I'll be sitting sweet." He rubbed his hands together.

Lorain and Unique looked at each other. Unique was done with this clown. She didn't want to hear anything else he had to say. She nodded at Lorain, her signal to proceed.

Hesitantly, Lorain pulled a manila envelope out of her purse. She handed it to Eugene.

He opened the envelope and looked through it. "You better not have played me this time."

"Eugene," Unique said, "you played yourself."

Just then two detectives walked up behind Unique.

"Mr. Eugene Brown," one of the detectives said, "you are under arrest for extortion."

The other detective pulled out a pair of handcuffs.

Lorain and Unique backed out of the way right on time, as two squad cars pulled up. Several police officers swarmed the hotel, while the detectives took Eugene down and handcuffed him.

"You dirty witches," he shouted at Unique and Lorain, who stood off to the side and embraced.

"We did it," Unique said in a relieved and heartfelt tone as she hugged Lorain.

"It's over," Lorain said, and so much was over, indeed. All the lies, betrayal, and deceit, and, of course, her dealings with Eugene.

The women helped one another remove the wiretaps that had been planted on them by the police. The police read Eugene his rights.

"You okay?" Lorain said as she watched Unique look at Eugene as he was being arrested.

"Yeah. I'm glad all of this is over with."

"What about Korica?"

"You know, I can't even talk about her right now, let alone to her."

"But you need to. Trust me, Unique, everybody has a reason for why they do the things they do. We all have a story. We all have pain and fears that drive us to do things we ordinarily wouldn't do if we truly trusted in the Lord to do what He is supposed to do. But no, we always get impatient, getting in God's way and our own. So go talk to her. Sometimes we have to get out of our own emotions and hear people out."

Unique snapped her head back and looked at Lorain, her eyes bulging. "Wow. I can't believe it. Sounds like you're on her side."

"Honey, I'm on God's side."

Unique smiled. "You're right. If I've learned anything at all from all I've been through, it's that life is too short."

"Amen to that!" Lorain agreed. "So are you going to talk to her?"

"I'll think about it. I don't know if I can stand to see her right now. I might lose my Christianity," Unique joked. "I wanted to say good-bye to her, but I might have to give her a call from Atlanta."

Lorain's face dropped. "What? You're still going to Atlanta?"

"I missed my flight, but I'll catch another one. I have to go and get away from Ohio, period. There is so much I need to do." She looked around. "And there's not enough space here for me to do it."

Now that their relationship was mended, Lorain wanted nothing more than to connect with Unique. How would that be possible if Unique was all the way in Atlanta? "But—"

"Please don't try to talk me out of it," Unique said, cutting Lorain off before she tried to talk her into staying. "I really feel in my spirit this is what I need. When I was away in West Virginia, it felt good. I was able to clear my mind, and I was really able to reflect on some things. Then I got into a relationship with Terrance and . . . I don't know." Unique shrugged. "I want to go back to that place where it's just me, my thoughts, and, of course, God."

Lorain opened her mouth to continue with her plea, anyway. On second thought, though, she decided to relent and honor her daughter's wishes. "I'm going to miss you," Lorain said. She tried to hold in her tears, but she couldn't, and she cried a river. "The girls are going to miss you too." Lorain added, sniffing. "Speaking of the girls, that day you put the girls on the bus, you made them excited about the lunch I'd packed them. What did you say to them?"

"It's simple," Unique said. "I told them to simply pretend that it was something that it wasn't. I told them that when they bit into the cheese sandwich, to pretend that it was a fat, juicy burger dripping with ketchup and mustard. I told them that when they ate the Wheat Thins and cucumbers, to pretend like they were their favorite animal at the zoo and that was their favorite treat to be fed."

"Pretend, huh?" Lorain said. "That was easy enough."

"Of course. After all, I'm sure that when it comes to pretending, they get it, honest."

What Unique meant to be a joke only made Lorain cry. "I'm going to miss you," she repeated.

"Don't cry. It's just an hour-and-forty-five-minute flight away," Unique told her. "That's quicker than the three-hour drive to West Virginia." Unique grew sad at the mere thought of West Virginia and Terrance.

Lorain could read the expression on her face. "Do you plan on talking to him and telling him good-bye?"

Unique shook her head no. "But maybe I'll call him once I get settled over there in Atlanta."

"I'm so sorry, baby," Lorain said, apologizing to Unique, running her hand down her cheek. "I keep messing up all my chances to be in your life, and now you're leaving again." Lorain looked up. "Please, God, I'm sorry. Don't take her from me."

"Please, I love you." Unique threw her arms around Lorain. "In body we may be miles apart, but our hearts are connected. Honestly, I can't let you take all the blame. I kind of distanced myself from you too, because of the girls. It's all still so hard for me."

The two women sniffled and wiped their tears.

Lorain felt a hand on her shoulder. She looked back and saw Nicholas standing there. She turned around and embraced him. "Baby, thank you," Lorain said. "I should have told you everything that was going on before it all got so jacked up."

"Shhhh," Nicholas said, rubbing his hand down Lorain's back. "It's all over with now. That wankster is going where he belongs, back to jail."

"I'm so glad that the third time I called you, you didn't hang up on me and you stayed on the phone long enough for me to tell you everything that had been going on," Lorain said. Lorain had called Nicholas and had told him how Eugene had been blackmailing her. He'd insisted on calling the police, who organize a sting to trap Eugene.

"Well, I have a confession to make," Nicholas said. "I stayed on the phone and listened to you talk only because by the time you called me the third time, your mother had made her way over to the house. She told me that if I didn't stay on that phone and hear what her baby had to say, not only would I never again get any of her famous neck bones, but she'd also break my neck bone."

They all burst out laughing.

"What's so funny?"

They all looked up to see Eleanor walking toward them. She had driven to the scene with Nicholas and had been waiting in the car, in keeping with his instructions, while everything went down.

"*You* are what's so funny," Lorain said. "And I love you." Lorain gave Eleanor a huge, wet kiss on the cheek.

Eleanor wiped it off. "It ain't kisses from you I want." She turned to see the police throw Eugene in the back of the police car. "I wants me some thug passion. That boy is hot!"

"Grans!" Unique said.

"What? You don't want him no more," Eleanor said. "And she never wanted him." She pointed at Lorain. "Hey, might as well keep it in the family."

They all laughed and embraced.

Lorain had the hugest smile on her face. It felt good to be laughing instead of crying.

Chapter 30

"You ready, baby?" Eleanor asked Lorain as she entered the New Day church dressing room that the dance ministry used to change clothes in. Whenever the church had weddings or baptisms, this room was designated the dressing room. It was a nice-size dressing room, as it allowed the eight members of the liturgical dance ministry to move freely about and practice steps before going to minister in dance in the sanctuary. Everyone had always said the full-length mirror made the person looking into it appear even more beautiful. Pastor Margie had said this was God's way of showing His children how beautiful they were in His eyes.

Lorain looked at herself in the mirror, admiring the mermaid-cut dress she'd picked out that day in the bridal shop. She'd gotten it in off-white so she didn't have to endure her mother's comments. "I'm absolutely ready." She smiled. She was truly happy to be renewing her vows with Nicholas today. Since New Day was where Lorain had met the Lord, she wanted it to be the place where her love was renewed with her earthly Lord. She was truly excited about today. Try as she might, though, to keep that smile on her face, it faded away.

"It's okay, baby." Eleanor walked over to Lorain and placed her hand on her shoulder.

"I wish she was here. I miss her so much. The two months she's been gone feel like two years. I took our time for granted, so it serves me right that the time I really want her here—need her here—she's not."

Although for the past couple months Lorain had talked to Unique every day and the two were becoming close again, Unique felt it was too soon to be heading back to Malvonia for the ceremony. She was getting settled and situated down in Atlanta. Even though she wasn't attending Lorain and Nicholas's wedding, she'd sent a gift, which had arrived a couple days ago. Still, Lorain would have much rather had her maid of honor there. She was grateful, though, that Heaven and Victoria were there to be her junior bridesmaids.

"I miss her too, but it's going to be all right. The big day of the surprise wedding is finally here. Of course, it ended up not being a surprise," Eleanor reminded her daughter.

When Nicholas calculated the amount of money that Lorain had taken from their account and that to try to pay off Eugene, the numbers didn't added up. There were still some unaccounted-for missing funds, and this sent up a red flag. Lorain was done with the lies, so she told Nicholas the truth about the surprise wedding she'd been planning.

There was a knock on the door.

"Must be show time," Eleanor said, walking over to answer the door. When she opened the door, she thought she would just about faint.

"You did say the wedding colors were cream and fuchsia, didn't you?" Unique spread her hands down the long, formal fuchsia gown she was wearing. "I hope this works. It's all David's Bridal had on the rack that fit me at the last minute."

"My baby!" Lorain put her hands to her face as her eyes filled with tears.

"No, no, don't cry. I'd have to fix your face, and my Mary Kay stuff is all the way out in the car."

Lorain spread her arms wide. "Come here, you."

Unique walked over and hugged her mother.

"I thought you weren't coming?" Lorain said, holding on to Unique tightly. "You said this town reminds you so much of death that you felt so suffocated that it might kill you."

Unique pulled back. "Yeah, well, while I was sitting in this church around the corner from me during Bible study the other day, as a result of the lesson, I realized something about myself. I learned that everything that kills me makes me feel more alive in Christ. So I'm gonna be okay."

"I know you are. You're my daughter." Lorain looked at Eleanor. "And I'm the daughter of her."

"That's right," Eleanor said. "And we don't die. . . ."

All at once the ladies yelled out, "We multiply."

As they laughed, there was a tap on the open door. It was Paige, who told them she'd just finished singing, so it was time for them to take their places. The women gladly exited the dressing room. Five minutes later they were all standing at the altar, and Pastor Margie prepared to join Lorain and Nicholas in holy matrimony . . . again.

The church was nicely and modestly decorated with cream flowers with fuchsia accents. Surprisingly, Lorain had gone much more over the top when decorating her home for the doctors' wives' meetings than she had when decorating the church for her wedding. For the first time in a while Lorain had realized that it didn't matter how much money was spent to dress something up and make it look pretty or make it to appear as though it was something that it wasn't.

Eleanor was right: people would see through to the real, anyway. Once all the bells and whistles were removed, it was going to be what it was going to be. Besides, she didn't want something that would take attention away from the day's true meaning, which was she and Nicholas confessing their true love for one another. She didn't want to try to impress man; she wanted to be blessed by God. Money couldn't buy love or a blessing from God, so she might as well keep it in the bank.

The vows were read, and rings were exchanged. The couple had opted to exchange the rings they already had. Of course, Lorain had pawned hers in an effort to raise money to pay Eugene off, but they'd gotten it out the shop. Finally, Pastor Margie pronounced them "still husband and wife."

"Cerise, I'm so glad that you could make it," Lorain said to the dance mom.

After the ceremony, pictures were taken while all the guests congregated in the church welcome center, where the wedding reception was taking place. Before long Lorain and Nicholas made their grand entrance. The room had a dozen round tables that sat ten. The bridal party's head table was the only oblong table in the room. It was covered with a cream-colored tablecloth, and at the center were four fuchsia-colored candlesticks resting in a crystal candleholder. Each round table was dressed in fuchsia-colored linens. A satin and sheer fuchsia bow decorated each chair. A crystal vase with a single cream rose was the only decoration on the round tables. Lorain thought she'd never admit it, but less was more. Less dramatics and more living life to the fullest.

"I'm glad you invited me after . . . you know."

When Lorain and Nicholas were going over the bank accounts and credit card statements, trying to get everything back in order again, Lorain had spotted a payment to Cerise's PI company. Nicholas had to share with her that Cerise was actually the one who'd sent him the pictures of her and Eugene. She was the PI he'd hired.

"Girl, that was just business. No harm, no foul," Lorain told her. Cerise's findings hadn't broken up their marriage. They'd just broken down that barrier that had been prohibiting them from communicating properly. Ultimately, the results of Cerise's investigation had forced Lorain to be honest about a lot of things with a lot of people.

"So you're not mad?" Cerise asked. "This isn't some setup where before the night is over, you're going to spill red wine all over my dress?"

The two laughed.

"No, not at all," Lorain assured her.

Cerise was relieved. "Thanks for forgiving me."

Lorain took Cerise's hands in hers. "There was never anything for me to forgive."

Cerise frowned. "Wish I'd known that before I spent a grand on the guilt crystal punch set I bought you guys as a wedding present."

Once again the two laughed.

"I hate to interrupt," Nicholas said after he approached the women and put his hand around his wife's waist. "But it's time to throw the bouquet."

Nicholas led Lorain over to the dance floor. Dante "Quick the DJ" Lee announced what was about to happen and instructed all the single ladies to take to the dance floor. He played Beyoncé's song "Single Ladies" to get them pumped up and moving.

Once the women had swarmed the dance floor, Lorain turned her back to them. The DJ did the countdown, calling, "Five, four, three, two . . . one," and Lorain threw the bouquet over her shoulders and let it fly. When she turned around, she couldn't believe the sight before her. Those women, dressed to the nines, were piled on top of each other on the floor. The other guests were laughing so hard that tears were falling from some of their eyes.

Once the dust settled, the women began to stand up, and suddenly a hand holding the bouquet shot straight up in the air and could be seen through the crowd.

"You go, girl!" Lorain said, laughing. She'd always wanted to tackle Korica down to the ground, and she'd missed out once more. *Oh well,* she thought. That desire was no longer in her, anyway.

"I am going to go," Korica said, brushing the dirt off of her dress, "right over there to my date, especially now that he knows what my intentions are." Korica rolled her eyes and did a sassy strut over to her date.

Lorain recognized Korica's date as the EMT from the day she fell out in the spirit at Korica's house. "I see you went back and checked on her, all right," Lorain said to the EMT upon approaching the couple.

Korica had her arm linked with his, as if she dared any single broad up in that church to even look at her man. "He sure did."

"Well, I'm glad to see things worked out," Lorain said.

"Me too. If you hadn't hurt yourself and fallen out while dancing, child, I would have never met him." Korica looked at her date, starry-eyed. "That Holy Ghost dance worked a miracle for me. I know that much."

Lorain laughed. "Well, you two have fun. I'm going to go greet some of the other guests." Lorain started to walk away.

"Lorain." Korica put her hand on Lorain's shoulder. Lorain turned to see what Korica wanted. "You're welcome."

It had already been such an emotional day for Lorain. She had been convinced that in order for this moment to take place, for her to stand there with Korica, hell would have to freeze over first. Only God could be in the midst of this. Thinking about how far the two women had come and how great God was brought tears to Lorain's eyes. Before a tear could fall, the DJ chimed in to save the day. He put on a popular song that got everybody riled up.

"Uh-oh," Korica said, snapping her fingers. "I might not know how to do the Holy Ghost Dance, but, baby, you sho' can come watch me wobble." Korica strutted off to the dance floor, dragging her date with her.

Lorain watched as Korica started teaching her date the dance. Most of the wedding attendees joined them on the dance floor, including Unique. Lorain let out a sigh of relief when she saw that Unique was out there dancing with Korica. God had allowed Lorain and Unique to reconcile their relationship, and He had allowed Unique and Korica to do the same with theirs. It was proof that what God did for one, He did for the other. He was no respecter of man. He blessed both the just and the unjust . . . even the unjust who thought they were just.

"Never thought I'd lived to see this. Thought for sure y'all would all kill me first with all y'all's drama."

Lorain turned around to see her mother standing there. She smiled and put her arm around Eleanor's shoulder. She then looked back toward the dance floor. "I can't believe it myself. My daughter and the woman who raised her."

"Sounds like the name of a Lifetime movie to me."

"I agree," Lorain said. She looked up to see Nicholas standing by the cake, trying to flag her down. "I guess it's time to cut the cake."

Eleanor followed Lorain's eyes over to the cake table. "I'm about to say something I thought I'd never say unless I could go ice-skating in hell."

"What's that?" Lorain asked.

"This whole surprise wedding thing . . . You were right. Look at that husband of yours over there. You'd think he was at Disneyland. He knows the whole agenda of what's supposed to go down at a wedding better than you do."

Eleanor was right. Nicholas had signaled Lorain when it was time for their first dance, had informed her when it was time to toast and to throw the bouquet, and now he was alerting her that it was time to cut the cake. "I know my man, Mama." Lorain stared at Nicholas with both love and lust in her eyes.

"I still say it would have been cheaper just to give him some—"

"Mommy, I think Nick is signaling you," Unique said after coming off the dance floor.

"He is. It's time to cut the cake. Come on, everybody." Lorain led the way.

Lorain and Nicholas cut the cake as the photographer, Ryan, with his H2J photography, snapped photos. They were thankful that Paige had recommended him. They had a splendid time smashing cake in each other's face. Lorain felt so happy to be giving her husband the wedding he'd always wanted. It sounded funny, Lorain saying that, because it was usually the man who said that about the woman. Lorain didn't care, though. She would have married him again and again and again.

"Lorain, darling, you look beautiful. What a beautiful wedding," Lance said to Lorain in his Italian accent. He kissed Lorain on both cheeks.

"Thank you, Lance." Lorain looked at Tabby. "Thanks for coming." Lorain's words were kind of dry. She hadn't really dealt with Tabby since their make-up lunch, but with the way it had ended, Lorain wasn't sure whether they'd really made up or not.

"Of course," Tabby said. She then looked at her husband. "Lance, honey, I think I'll have that piece of cake now."

He smiled and walked off, leaving the two women alone. Before doing so, he said to Lorain, "Congratulations to the two of you. Beautiful couple, just like my Tabby and me."

Lorain smiled as Lance walked away. "Wonderful husband you've got there," Lorain told Tabby. She wasn't just making conversation. Lance was over the top nice. He seemed to love everybody. He was always shaking hands, kissing cheeks, and patting backs, and he always had a huge, genuine smile on his face. As nice and as laid-back as Lance seemed to be, Lorain had no idea how he'd ended up with a stuck-up black chick like Tabby.

"Thank you," Tabby said.

"You look nice." Lorain was trying to keep the conversation going to avoid an awkward silence. But Tabby really was wearing the heck out of that MAC makeup. A dark-skinned black woman, Tabby had complained that finding the right shades for her complexion had been challenging, until she discovered MAC.

Tabby returned the compliment. "Thank you. So do you."

After five seconds of awkward silence, Lorain couldn't take it anymore. She had to keep the party moving. "All right, then. Well, it was nice . . ." Lorain started to walk away.

"Lorain, wait." Tabby reached out and grabbed Lorain's hand. "I know."

Lorain looked confused. What did Tabby know?

"I know about the twins. Your girls."

"Okay, yes, everybody knows about them. They were my junior bridesmaids." The girls were adorable in their cream dresses, with fuchsia silk bows tied around their waists. They wore identical curly ponytails that sat on top of their head and were tied with a ribbon that matched the bow around their waist.

"No, I mean, I know who they really are. Who you are to them."

Lorain almost lost her breath. Tabby quickly put her hands on Lorain's shoulders to calm her.

"Wait, Lorain. Before you blow a gasket, I want to tell you something."

"How did you find out? Did you go snooping on the Internet again?" Lorain tried to remain calm, but she would mop the floor with Tabby if she made a scene and tried to put the information on blast. Lorain absolutely did not want her girls finding out the truth this way. At this point in life, Lorain couldn't have cared less what the rest of the world said about her, but she was not going to let her daughters be hurt. That look in her eyes, the one Ivy had called her on that day in the bathroom, let Tabby know it would be an act of suicide for her to open her mouth about it.

"I didn't go on the Internet, trying to dig up information on you. Actually, you told me. Well, you didn't *tell* me. You were telling your mother. I was in a bridal boutique one day and overheard a conversation you were having with your mother."

"You didn't speak up so I could acknowledge you? You were off in the racks, eavesdropping? Pardon me, but the last time I checked, that was called snooping. No, you weren't doing it on the Internet, but you were still snooping all the same."

"I guess you're right." Tabby put her head down.

"That's what you were alluding to at our lunch," Lorain said.

"I was going to mention it, but then I thought you might think I was blowing the steam in the mill of rumors . . . or whatever it was you were accusing me of."

Lorain shook her head. Not even on her wedding day could she be free of drama. She'd planned on en-

joying her wedding day and spending the night enjoying her husband, without any dark cloud trying to rain
on her parade. If Tabby wanted to bring the rain, then
Lorain could certainly bring the thunder. "So, I'm not
going to play games with you, Tabby. Let's do this. What
do you want?"

"Nothing, Lorain. I wanted you to know that your secret is safe with me. I promise. You and Nick are good
people." Tabby looked over at Nicholas, who was on the
dance floor, dancing with the twins. "And your girls are
the loveliest and the sweetest. I would never do or say
anything that could jeopardize your family and how you
are raising your girls."

"Good." Lorain exhaled and smiled. "I'm so glad to
hear that." She took Tabby's hands in hers. "Because
if you ever thought twice about doing it, your whole
life would change. I'm sure if I did a little snooping of
my own, I'd have something to take to the authorities
regarding the writing of illegal prescriptions. Surely,
the medical board would take your husband's license,
and he'd lose his U.S. citizenship. You'd no longer be a
doctor's wife, but the wifey of a felon you holdin' down
while he serves his time. Which is something I'm sure
since the day you moved out of the hood, you swore you
would never be."

Lorain snapped her fingers. "In the blink of an eye,
you'd be exactly who you've been trying so hard for
years not to be . . . the hood rat that you really are up
underneath that makeup and couture." Lorain spoke
with a smile on her face the entire time. Anyone on the
outside looking in would think they were witnessing two
best friends catching up.

Tabby's hands were sweaty, and Lorain could feel
them trembling. Tabby's eyes almost watered at the
thought of how easily her dream life could turn into a
nightmare.

"It would be a shame," Tabby said nervously, forcing the words out. "So good thing I don't have to worry about that. Like I said, my lips are sealed." Tabby pulled her hands out of Lorain's. She used her index finger and thumb to pretend to zip her lips closed.

Lorain kissed her on each cheek. "Thank you so much for coming. I'll see you at next month's meeting." Lorain walked away, making a mental note to thank Ivy for her advice. This time she'd pounced on the hunter before she could ever become the prey.

"Lorain, girlfriend, girlfriend!"

Lorain turned around to see a tipsy Carrie stumbling her way with a half-filled glass of wine in her hand. "This wedding is off the chain. And I was looking through your gifts . . ." She paused to take a sip of wine.

"As only you would," Lorain said with a chuckle.

"And you got some good stuff. Heck, I'm renewing my vows next year if it means I'ma get hooked up like this." She play hit Lorain on the arm amid her drunken laughter.

"There you are. You got away from me." Just in time, Carrie's husband walked up and grabbed ahold of her before she could topple over in her tipsiness.

"Hey, baby," Carrie said, slurring.

"Hey." He looked at Lorain. "Congratulations. You make a beautiful bride."

All of sudden Carrie copped an attitude. "Oh, so now you like black women?" Carrie said to her husband, whose cheeks turned red. His blue eyes nearly burned a hole through Carrie for causing him such embarrassment. "No, honey. That's just what you tell brides."

"Oh, so on our wedding day, when you told me I made a beautiful bride while we were having our first dance, you were just saying that?" Her eyes filled with tears. "You didn't mean it?" She shook her head as the alcohol began to amplify her emotions. Her long blond hair, which she wore hairpieces in, swung from left to right.

"No, honey, I meant it," he said, trying to reassure her and balance her at the same time.

"I had my hair pinned up like you liked it," Carrie cried. "I had even gone to the tanning salon for a whole month." She looked at Lorain with disdain. "But had I known you liked black chicks, that this white girl from the trailer park wasn't good enough for you . . ." Carrie's words trailed off as she began gagging.

"Come on, honey. I better get you out of here." He took hold of his wife and carried her away, calling to Lorain over his shoulder, "Thanks again for the invite. Tell Nick I'll see him on the golf course next week."

Lorain nodded and shook her head. Those doctors' wives were a trip.

When Lorain turned around, she almost ran smack into Unique. "Oh, baby, I'm sorry."

"It's okay," Unique said.

"You having fun?"

"Yeah, but I'm getting ready to go. I've already told everyone else good-bye."

"Awww, I wish you could stay longer."

"Until when? Until after your honeymoon?" She chuckled. "I'm sure you don't want me sticking around during your wedding night." Unique winked three times. "That's baby-making time. Give me and my sisters a little brother or sister."

"Too late for baby making," Lorain said.

"Please, it's never too late. Didn't Halle Berry have one at, like, forty-seven or forty-eight?"

"No, I mean it's too late to make one because one has already been made."

It took a couple seconds for Unique to get what her mother was trying to say. "Wait a minute! Are you trying to say that . . ."

Lorain stood there, nodding her head, a smile lighting up her face. "I thought the stress of life was making me sick." She put her hands on her stomach. "And here it was a life was making me sick."

"Congratulations. I know Gran is beside herself."

"Shhh." Lorain put her index finger to her lips and looked over her shoulder to make sure no one was within earshot. She then looked back at Unique. "I haven't told her yet. But that's one of the reasons why I opted for the cream dress instead of the white one. I would never hear the end of her mouth."

"You got that right."

The two women laughed, and Lorain shared her due date with Unique.

"Well, I better get out of here," Unique said.

"I'm glad you came. It was a great surprise. Thank you." Lorain hugged Unique. "Let me walk you out." She squeezed her. "Get in all the time I can with you."

Lorain walked Unique outside the church doors. "Thanks again for coming, baby. I love you."

"I love you too. And congratulations, Mommy."

Lorain's mouth spread into a smile. "You said it. You called me Mommy."

"Yes, I called you Mommy. That's who you are, aren't you?" Unique said.

"You have no idea how long I've been waiting to hear you say that word to me, daughter. This is the best wedding gift I could have ever received. I love you."

"I love you too," Unique said. "Now, you better get back inside and go dance with that husband of yours."

"Yeah, I better. Besides, I think I probably need to leave the two of you alone to talk."

Unique had a confused look on her face. Lorain nodded, indicating that Unique should look behind her. Unique turned to see a car pulling into the church parking lot.

"Terrance," Unique said, then quickly turned to look at Lorain. "You didn't."

"Guilty as charged." Lorain shrugged. "I called him up and told him to come, because something told me you'd be here." Lorain winked. "Mother's intuition."

Unique shook her head and cracked a smile.

Lorain kissed her on the cheek. "Guess I'm more like Korica than either of us wants to admit."

"You got that right," Unique said as Terrance got out of the car and started walking toward the church.

"Talk to him, honey. That's all," was the advice mother gave daughter.

"I will," Unique said. "I just pray that all goes well, that Terrance and I can at least still be friends."

"Then I say before he gets up here, close your eyes and take five seconds to pray. Because you know what I learned?"

"What is that?" Unique said curiously.

"Sometimes you get exactly what you pray for." Lorain kissed her daughter on the cheek and then went back into the church, glad that through hell and high water, each and every one of her prayers had indeed been answered.

Readers' Guide Questions

1. Can you put yourself in Lorain's shoes and sympathize with the way she felt she needed to interact with Unique in order not to jeopardize losing the girls?

2. Do you feel Lorain was too gullible when it came to Korica's and Eugene's threats? Should she have allowed their words to dictate her actions?

3. Did you at any time think Unique was going to hook back up with Eugene? How did you feel about him after finding out that the conversation and the breakthrough that he had with Unique was all an act? Do you believe it was all really an act, or do you think that maybe he was trying to play hard?

4. Can you understand why Korica felt so threatened by Lorain?

5. Do you feel Unique was indebted to Korica for taking her in and raising her? Do you feel children are indebted to their parents, period?

6. If you read *I Can Do Better All By Myself,* then you know that Nicholas proposed to Lorain a couple times and that she declined. The day Lorain finally decided to accept his proposal, she was distracted by the news that her grandkids had died. When Lorain eventually got around to telling Nicholas she wanted to marry him, it was only after Korica planted a seed of fear in her about being looked at as a single woman who was unable to raise twins without a husband. Given everything that transpired before they tied the knot, do you think Lorain

and Nicholas's marriage was any less genuine? Do you feel Lorain only used Nicholas and didn't love him?

7. Korica always seemed to be out for herself. When she opened up to Lorain about her struggles in life, did you feel any sympathy toward her at all?

8. Did the fact that Eleanor was always in her daughter's business annoy you, or did you feel her often humorous input allowed for a different understanding of events and actions?

9. Do you know anyone who allows the hurt and pain of the past to dictate their current life? Do you do this?

10. Could you feel the anguish and torment Lorain was putting herself through, or did you think she was no better than Korica?

11. Do you think that Unique really wanted to go to Atlanta and start new ventures of her own, or do you think she was still running from her true feelings about the death of her sons and the birth of her daughters? Can you imagine how those events could possibly affect her?

12. What race did you assume Tabby and Carrie were? Did this lead to stereotyping on your part?

13. Have you read books belonging to the "New Day Divas" Series and the "Still Divas Series," or did you start off with the "Always Divas" Series? Did this book make you want to go back and read all the others in the series?

About The Author

Joylynn M. Ross is now writing as BLESSED-selling author E.N. Joy (Everybody Needs Joy)

BLESSEDselling author E.N. Joy is the writer behind the five-book series "New Day Divas," the three-book series "Still Divas," the three-book series "Always Divas," and the forthcoming three-book series "Forever Divas," all of which have been coined "Soap Operas in print." She is an *Essence* magazine bestselling author and has written secular books under the names Joylynn M. Jossel and JOY.

After thirteen years as a paralegal in the insurance industry, E.N. Joy finally divorced her career and married her mistress and her passion: writing. In 2000 she formed her own publishing company, where she self-published her books until landing a book deal with a major publisher. Her company has published *New York Times* and *Essence* magazine bestselling authors in the "Sinner Series." In 2004 E.N. Joy branched out into the business of literary consulting, providing one-on-one consultations and literary services, such as ghostwriting, editing, professional read throughs, and write behinds. Her clients include first-time authors, *Essence* magazine bestselling authors, *New York Times* bestselling authors, and entertainers. This award-winning author has also been sharing her literary expertise on conference panels in her hometown of Columbus, Ohio, as well as in cities across the country.

Not forsaking her love of poetry, E.N. Joy's latest poetic project is an ebook of poetry entitled *Flower in My Hair*. "But my spirit has moved in another direction," she says. Needless to say, she no longer pens street lit. (Two of her street lit titles, *If I Ruled the World* and *Dollar Bill,* made the *Essence* magazine best sellers' list. *Dollar Bill* was mentioned in *Newsweek* and has been translated into Japanese.) She no longer writes erotica or adult contemporary fiction, either. *An All Night Man,* a collection of novellas to which she and three other authors, including *New York Times* bestselling author Brenda Jackson, contributed, earned the Borders Bestselling African American Romance Award.

You can find this author's children's book, entitled *The Secret Olivia Told Me* and written under the name N. Joy, in bookstores now. *The Secret Olivia Told Me* received a Coretta Scott King Honor from the American Library Association. The book was also acquired by Scholastic Books and has sold over one hundred thousand copies. E.N. Joy has also penned a middle grade ebook, entitled *Operation Get Rid of Mom's New Boyfriend,* and a children's fairy-tale eBook, entitled *Sabella and the Castle Belonging to the Troll.* Elementary and middle school children have fallen in love with reading and creative writing as a result of the readings and workshops E.N. Joy gives in schools nationwide.

E.N. Joy is the acquisitions editor for Urban Christian, an imprint of Urban Books, the titles of which are distributed by Kensington Publishing Corporation. In addition, she is the artistic developer for a young girls group called DJHK Gurls. She pens original songs, drama skits, and monologues for the group that deal with issues that affect today's youth, such as bullying.

You can visit BLESSEDselling author E.N. Joy at: www.enjoywrites.com, or e-mail her at: enjoywrites@aol.com.

UC HIS GLORY BOOK CLUB!
www.uchisglorybookclub.net

UC His Glory Book Club is the spirit-inspired brain-child of Joylynn Ross, an author and the acquisitions editor at Urban Christian, and Kendra Norman-Bellamy, an author for Urban Christian. It is an online book club that hosts authors of Urban Christian. We welcome as members all men and women who have a passion for reading Christian-based fiction.

UC His Glory Book Club pledges its commitment to providing support, positive feedback, encouragement, and a forum whereby members can openly discuss and review the literary works of Urban Christian authors.

There is no membership fee associated with UC His Glory Book Club; however, we do ask that you support the authors by purchasing their works, encouraging them, providing book reviews, and, of course, offering your prayers. We also ask that you respect our beliefs and follow the guidelines of the book club. We hope to receive your valuable input, opinions, and reviews that build up, rather than tear down, our authors.

WHAT WE BELIEVE:

—We believe that Jesus is the Christ, Son of the Living God.

—We believe that the Bible is the true, living Word of God.

—We believe that all Urban Christian authors should use their God-given writing abilities to honor God and to share the message of the written word that God has given to each of them uniquely.

Urban Christian His Glory Book Club

—We believe in supporting Urban Christian authors in their literary endeavors by reading their titles, purchasing them, and sharing them with our online community.

—We believe that everything we do in our literary arena should be done in a manner that will lead to God being glorified and honored.

We look forward to online fellowship with you. Please visit us often at www.uchisglorybookclub.net.

Many Blessings to You!
Shelia E. Lipsey,
President, UC His Glory Book Club

When All Is Said and Prayed
(Paige and Tamarra's Story)
Book One of the "Forever Divas" Series
Fall 2015

Keep up with the divas by liking the New Day Divas Fan Page on Facebook.

ORDER FORM
URBAN BOOKS, LLC
97 N. 18th Street
Wyandanch, NY 11798

Name (please print):_____

Address: _____

City/State: _____

Zip: _____

QTY	TITLES	PRICE

Shipping and handling-add $3.50 for 1st book, then $1.75 for each additional book.
Please send a check payable to:
Urban Books, LLC
Please allow 4-6 weeks for delivery